COMPLICATED CHOICES

RISA NYMAN

IMMORTAL WORKS
SALT LAKE CITY

Immortal Works LLC
1505 Glenrose Drive
Salt Lake City, Utah 84104
Tel: (385) 202-0116

Cover Art by Ashley Literski
http://strangedevotion.wixsite.com/strangedesigns

ISBN 978-1-953491-58-9 (Paperback)
ASIN B0C9CDWW5Z (Kindle)

*This book is dedicated to those who were there at the beginning of my
journey:
my parents, Mildred a"h and Edward z"l Sharzer
and my dear brother, Leonard Sharzer*

CHAPTER
1

This wasn't the summer I was supposed to have.

Dealing with streams of baby barf and explosive poop can't compete with the adventures all my friends got to have before our last year of high school. This is a heavy price to pay for a mistake that's not my fault.

I push Harry's stroller into Cold Spring Park on this final outing before the end of summer break and before he becomes the responsibility of day care. My sentence in baby prison is almost over, and I'm about to inhale the sweet smell of freedom. I follow our usual route, which winds behind a cluster of oaks and maples and is far enough away from the main path to limit the chances people will bother us.

Once Harry scarfs down his bottle and conks out, I resume watching the movie *Titanic* on my phone for the hundredth time. I'm at the scene where the ship goes vertical and knifes into the water. This shatters me because I hope that one time the ending will change, and Jack will survive his night in the frozen ocean; but that never happens.

A staccato tapping next to my bench interrupts the part where Rose swims in the frigid water to grab the whistle and signal the rescue boat. I readjust my Red Sox cap to shield my eyes from the sun and see a lady with crinkled skin and an oversized floppy hat, using her cane to provide the beat that draws my attention.

She peers under the hood of the stroller with a sense of entitlement, as if it's her God-given right to stick her face into Harry's. And if she remains true to type, she will soon offer some unsolicited advice about what I'm doing wrong with the kid.

Bingo! She breaks a record. It only takes her a second before she removes the baby's blanket and tosses it on the bench beside me. "He's way too covered for such a hot day."

Some beach balls she has! I chew the inside of my cheek to activate my long-suffering, inner editor who prevents me from spouting off and risking the possibility this old hag finds a reason to report me to some agency for baby neglect. We don't need people snooping in our business.

Probably annoyed at not having his blanket, the poor little dude wakes up from his milk coma. With her face inches from the baby, she makes an irritating noise at him like a cricket on drugs. "Chichi. Chichi." At almost four months old, Harry demonstrates he has no standards and smiles at her weird sound because he's an attention hound.

"My, my, the baby is the spitting image of you," the lady announces with the pride of an ancient explorer discovering a new continent.

What I want to reply is: *Lady, if there's any spitting to be done, I'll be doing it, and it won't be directed at any image.* But again, my inner editor warns me against an over-the-top response.

After Mom and Dad divorced when I was in ninth grade, I put my editor on hiatus, because Dad took his teasing and vast array of nicknames for me with him to Wisconsin. Then baby Harry arrived, and I had to bring my inner editor out of hibernation to deal with all the people who assume they know me and my life.

This lady is no different. She doesn't take my silence as a hint to move the hell on and continues talking. "You're so blessed to have such a beautiful baby boy."

My lips clamp shut as my editor starts to engage, but this time I'm determined not to let the comment slide, and I start to reply, "He isn't—"

The dried-up person hovering in front of me cuts me off, unable to restrain herself from expressing her judgments about me. "Must be difficult at your age. I wish you well, dearie."

Then she scampers off as fast as those old legs will go, which is pretty slow, probably eager to share her juicy story with her gossip group. I can guess her opening line: "I met a troubled teenager and her baby in the park..."

School can't begin soon enough. I check the time, and we leave the park for our appointment at Sunny Acres, which is a name more suited for an old-age home than a day care. But the place is close to home and school, and I suspect it will be my job to get the kid there and back.

Harry and I arrive right on time. I press the intercom and survey their yard full of brightly colored plastic cars waiting for some kids to take them for a test-drive. It winds me up that Harry might have his own set of wheels before me.

A voice from the speaker by the entrance asks for my name. Once offered and accepted, a long loud buzz unlocks the door, and I push Harry's stroller inside. As I unbuckle the baby, I give him one last warning. "You'd better make a good impression. I'm going back to school tomorrow. I'm done with the constant babysitting."

Harry replies with his standard gummy grin, his go-to expression for anyone who notices him.

A grandmother-type opens the door. "Welcome. I've been expecting you. I'm Mrs. Sample." Her lips curve into a broad smile, and her eyes dance with delight at seeing us. Her body has no sharp lines.

Sample is an odd name. I stifle the urge to ask if her first name is Free. This day care costs a fortune. The sight of the humongous check Mom gave me this morning payable to Sunny Acres stunned me. You could go to college with that kind of dough.

When I first saw the amount, I asked Mom, "How much exactly are you paying for day care?" I was sure she wrote that check while in one of her head fogs and added a few too many zeros after the two.

"If you pay the year in advance," she explained, "you save $5,000, and we could use the extra money."

"You can't save the $5,000 unless you actually have that cash stashed somewhere. Do you?" She hasn't worked since Harry was born, and I have no idea how we're living.

"It's fine. I have a special account," she said and scrunched the edge of her blanket under her chin before she turned toward the wall. Clearly a brush-off, preventing any more talk of money. Since the pregnancy and birth, this has been her typical reaction to difficult subjects. She retreats into whatever turmoil consumes her mind, caused by this unplanned pregnancy.

Her unplanned pregnancy, not mine.

I couldn't resist taking a selfie with that check because I'll never see a number that large with a dollar sign in front of it again, but this photo will not go on Insta. My friends might think we became instant millionaires.

"Let me show you around," Mrs. Sample says. "You will see what a caring and idyllic place this is." She pats Harry's head, eyeballing her prospective student. Are they called students in day care? I'm a work-in-progress learning about babies, and I still resent even having to know all this stuff. My future plans don't include anything to do with babies for years.

"You two look so much alike. I bet everyone tells you that." And you've won the grand prize, Mrs. Sample! Everyone does tell me that. All summer I've been assaulted by innuendos, side-eye glances, and tsk-tsks wherever Harry and I go. I rage when I imagine how much energy they give to constructing their stupid assumptions.

Mrs. Sample takes me through a few rooms filled with babies, cribs, and an impressive pile of diapers. In one room, a guy with a massive untrimmed beard that accentuates his pointy nose is playing guitar and singing for a group of babies older than Harry. Two women supply some kids in highchairs with handfuls of Cheerios. This place is pretty cushy. Nothing but the best for this baby sponge.

"Would you like to leave him here while we go to my office? I want to review the forms to make sure we have all the information we need and that your mother signed everything," Mrs. Sample says.

It's probably a good idea to get him used to this place, so I hand

Harry to one of the teachers, or aides, or whatever these people are called, and follow Mrs. Sample's plushy rear-end into her office.

She sits in front of her computer and reviews each of the papers I brought, occasionally asking me something about Harry. Of course, I have all the answers about the kid because I do everything for him. She must be blown away by such a well-informed sib, but this is one exam I'm not proud to ace.

Being saddled with this brother, I mean half-brother, at seventeen was a shock. I had stopped pestering my parents for a sibling by the time I was eight and figured out I was better off with the status of being the only and supreme. A baby would've crowded me out of my lofty position. And now I'm convinced that theory was correct.

I'll have nothing in common with Harry except our mother. He won't relate to my songs or TV shows. Hell, Googling will probably be history, and we'll all be wearing our AI by the time he's in middle school.

Mrs. Sample finishes entering information into her computer and studies the check, but unlike me, she doesn't flinch at all those zeros. I could be tooling around Newton in a cute white VW with that money if Harry didn't show up.

"All the paperwork is fine. It was nice to meet your mother, even if it had to be on Zoom. I hope she's feeling better. We'll see Harry tomorrow." Boy, did I do a lot of prep to get Mom ready for that call and make sure she didn't have a meltdown in front of Mrs. Sample. Mom came through that time.

I retrieve Harry from the backroom. No tear-stained cheeks, no gag-worthy odor, and still in dry clothes. Without me for the first time, and he toughed it out.

Mrs. Sample shows us to the door. Her round face exudes friendliness and warmth, which must come from cooing to babies all day long.

"So, bro," I ask, as I settle him into his stroller, "meet any cute girls today?" He seems to nod his head and smile. My mind is playing tricks, but Sunny Acres is pretty zen. Harry's one lucky, dopey dude.

WHEN I ROUND the corner onto Ivanhoe Street, I spot Mads sitting on the bottom step of our walkway, so I give the stroller the gas, so to speak, the rest of the way.

"I'm back!" Mads shouts, jumping to her feet as her sun-streaked blonde ponytail bounces behind her. We hug, and immediately I notice the intense contrast in the color of our arms. I'm paper-white next to her rocking tan. I bet she lived in her bikini all summer.

"Aww, let me see the baby," she says. "When I left, he was the size of a bean, a long string bean with a big head on top. He is def cute."

"Aren't all babies cute?"

"This one sure is. With those wisps of brown hair, he's even more like you. Do I detect the beginning of a dimple right there, like yours?" She points to his left cheek.

"No, those lines are baby wrinkles." But I know she's right. Everyone is right. He resembles me more than Mom. I imagine someone in the vast universe is having a good laugh, making me constantly explain he isn't my baby.

"I never heard about baby wrinkles, but what the hell do I know? I do know it's shopping time, Claire Bear!" Mads exclaims.

"Finally! The summer seemed endless, and I thought this day would never come. But I don't want to have to bring Harry with me."

"Isn't your mom any better? Can't she take care of him?"

Mads knows all the gruesome details of Mom's slippery slide into despair since she got pregnant by some rando. Mom never dated or cruised dating websites after the divorce. She worked, went out with friends, and the two of us filled the empty space that Dad left. She said she didn't need a man in her life, which was fine with me, because I hella didn't need a stepfather. But the pregnancy announcement hit me with the force of an asteroid.

"A little better." I lie to Mads because I don't want to drag myself down today.

Inside the house, Mom's stretched out on the living room recliner, her second favorite place after her bed. She's probably zoned out after thrashing over everything that has gone wrong in her life.

With a light touch, I poke at her shoulder. She opens the two cavernous holes that hold her eyes. I'm sure Mads will notice how thin she is, nothing like her former self. Before she got pregnant, her hair was in place, she wore perfect makeup and didn't spend every day in sweatpants. This is an impostor who's refusing to release my real mother.

"Hi, Mrs. Jackson," Mads says.

"Nice to see you, Madison. Did you like being a camp counselor?"

A perfectly normal question, but it tears at my guts. Mads's summer was supposed to be my summer too. Last year, when we were juniors, we made plans to be camp counselors together, but then there was Harry. I swear that baby was born with a tiny dagger in his fat little hand aimed at my life.

"Yes, it was so fun," Mads replies to Mom.

"Mom," I say and plunk Harry down on her lap, without checking if she's ready for him. Why should I have to ask that? She should want him, but one never knows where her head is at. "Mads and I want to go to the mall to shop for new outfits for the first day of school."

"Of course," Mom says.

"And I don't want to bring Harry."

Her lips strain to form an uneasy smile, which is the best she can muster these days. "Leave him here with me."

That's the right answer, and I wish I could trust that, but experience makes my gut uneasy as if I ate a plateful of bad sushi. This wouldn't be the first time she assured me she could handle him, and it turned out to be an epic failure.

"If you're too tired, you should tell me." I give her another chance to back out. I wish Mads didn't have to witness this awkward dance Mom and I have to do as I weigh her state of mind.

"I'm sure," Mom says. "You deserve a day off. Take my credit card."

"Okay." I asked twice. That's enough. I grab Mads's hand, stop by Mom's purse for her credit card, and as we hurry out the door, I call back, "Bye."

Mads drives and once we're off, I ask, "So, did you finally lock down a boyfriend on the last day of camp?" Scoring boyfriends was one of our summer goals along with starting our college bank accounts for spending money.

"I wish," she says. "And if I don't get a drink of some tall handsome dude soon, I might die from dehydration. And what about you, Claire Bear? How's your love life? Whenever we FaceTimed, you dodged the subject, so I began to suspect you were hiding someone from me."

"Yeah, like that could happen in my situation. Any guy who isn't unconscious would run from me as if I'm spreading the plague. Every boy's dream is to date a girl pushing a baby stroller. No boyfriends until college. I can't handle a relationship now. My plate overflow-eth."

"College men can be tasty." Mads smacks her lips, and a spot of drool emerges. My instinct after spending hours with the king of drool is to wipe her mouth, but I resist and laugh at myself about how crazy I'm getting.

"So, are you now officially bonded with the baby?" she says.

"If you call simultaneous barfing a form of bonding, the answer is yes."

"Ew...that's foul."

"Yup, he hurled, and it triggered me. And one day he had the worst diarrhea, and I—"

"La, la, la," Mads says, covering her ear closest to me. "Don't need the deets. You know, your mom wouldn't be the only unmarried woman to get pregnant by mistake. If she doesn't get help, you may become a high school dropout to work as a full-time babysitter."

"That's lunacy. I'm the least likely dropout candidate in the world." Mads knows my record is stellar—APs, National Honor Society, first prize in the science fair in tenth grade, and a power player in student government. My motivation is on steroids, and I have plans, big plans: Ivy League, law school, and public office where a person can make real change.

"Stop procrastinating and get her to an actual doctor who will fix her head."

"I'm going to try."

"Trying is a weasel word. Just make her do it."

Yeah, right. As if it's so simple. Pushing too hard might cause Mom to spiral further, because she can't cope with her new normal that she named Harry. I'd be the one left to pick up the pieces and reassemble my mother.

Mads parks. We hook arms and head for Taylor Imports, our starting point. We haven't deviated from this routine for finding the perfect first-day-of-school outfits since seventh grade.

Mads gets to business right away, riffling through the racks, and I do the same but at a slower speed, unsure of myself in the fashion arena. In a short time, we each have armfuls of items and head for the dressing room. As usual, we model the clothes to get a thumbs up or down or sometimes only a good laugh. Mads's opinion about fashion is way superior to mine, so her approval is more valuable.

When Mads pulls back the dressing room curtain and walks out in a teal crop top, I'm immediately drawn to a shining object on her belly. "I can't believe you pierced your belly button, and you didn't tell me when we talked."

"Oh, that. I was saving it to surprise you. I got it right after my birthday to celebrate being eighteen. A bunch of us had a day off and went into town to do some piercing. One kid got a tattoo and dared the rest of us to do it too, but I settled for the belly jewelry instead. It's so cool."

"Did you show it to your mom?" Her mother is so conservative, which I think is part of the job requirement to be Newton North

High School's vice principal. Mrs. Sunday excels in tamping down all the new ways students find to "express" themselves.

"Not yet. Keeping it out of sight for now. You should get your belly button pierced. It's great with crop tops and bikinis. Oh, wait, I forgot you're not eighteen yet. You'd need permission."

"If I had your bod, I might do it. Every part of you is perfect. I'm too skinny like a piece of spaghetti, remember?"

"That's so old. Your dad can't call you spaghetti anymore since your boobs came in. You're definitely more tortellini."

I smile and redden. "But mine are humble around your magnificence, Maddikins."

I expect a sharp reply, but instead she scolds me. "You cannot buy that top. That orange makes you look like a bowl of mac 'n' cheese."

After almost an hour, we neaten up our cyclone-strewn dressing rooms and exit with a new outfit for the first day of senior year. Mads buys light-washed jeans with knee holes and an ombré pink top with a V-neck low enough to challenge the dress code. I opt for some black leggings and a fuzzy blue tunic.

When I put the credit card in the machine, the offensive word "Declined" flashes back at me. It can't be right, but I bet that's everyone's reaction in this circumstance.

"I must have put the card in wrong," I say as the heat rushes to my face. I rub on the magnetic strip, blow on the chip, and try again.

"Hmmm...don't know what the prob is," I say, talking to Mads, but she's busy trying on hair clips and not paying attention to me, or maybe she moved away to leave me with my embarrassment.

This makes no sense. Mom can find twenty grand for Harry's posh day care, but $53 for my outfit is a budget-buster.

CHAPTER
2

In pre-Harry days, I'd call Mom and ask her what to do, but now I'm flying solo and just grateful she isn't calling me.

I have enough cash for the clothes, but I'll have to borrow money for lunch or convince my stomach its demands are unreasonable.

Before my parents split, Dad handled the financial stuff and was always lecturing me on the dangers of going into debt. Borrowers have no peace of mind, he claimed, and drummed that into me. When I wanted even the simplest thing, he'd make me prepare a budget and show my research on prices, including taxes, and provide a thorough explanation of why I needed whatever it was.

One thing all those financial drills accomplished was to make me one pain in the ass in student government meetings, insisting every project had to have a written budget. One day, when I run for Congress, good budgeting skills will part of my campaign platform.

"To the food court," Mads orders after my purchase is bagged.

We don't have to discuss where to go because Rosita's, the home of the most exquisite burritos in the world, is part of our ritual mall trip. I stand behind Mads in line, breathing in the aroma of the delicious spices and listening to the crackling, sizzling meat on the grill. My phone beeps, and my brain goes numb. This might be the come-home-now call, but it's a text from Mads, who's standing a foot in front of me.

Hunk twelve o'clock.

I send an emoji of an owl with a question mark.

Duh. The guy in front of me.

I peer over her shoulder and see a tall dude with broad shoulders and the outline of an amazing butt under those clingy shorts.

> Going to make contact.

She gently bumps into him. A typical Mads move. He turns around, and he's dazzling. His deep brown eyes are piercing, but not in a menacing way. Tight curls are piled high on the top of his head which is shaved on the sides. He smiles at Mads, showing off perfect teeth surrounded by dark lips. He's a work of art.

"Sorry," Mads says, returning his wide smile. "Lost my balance for a sec."

What an actress.

"No problem," the hottie replies.

When I'm able to stop staring at his face, I notice he's wearing a Newton North T-shirt with a tiger on his chest. He's one of us, but I don't recognize him from school. I text Mads.

> Ask him if he goes to NNHS. T-shirt.

Her phone hand is by her side, and when it vibrates, she steals a glance to read my message and immediately says to the guy, "Nice T-shirt. We're Tigers too."

The dude lowers his eyes as if to remind himself what he's wearing. "I didn't even notice the tiger," he says. "Do you—"

Before he finishes his question, the lady behind the counter says, "Next!" and that ends the conversation. After he orders, he moves toward the checkout, and Mads turns to me and pretends to fall into a swoon.

We're up next. "Mads, can I borrow some money for lunch?" I ask. "I'll pay you back tomorrow." Sometimes you have no choice and have to break your own rules about going into debt. I'll pass out if I can't get anything to eat, and the rumbling in my stomach will be heard all over the food court.

"Of course, Claire Bear. I think I'm in love." She flutters her eyelids at me.

I order a burrito with everything on it and a diet soda. When we get to the register, the tiger T-shirt guy is waiting for us with his overstuffed wallet open. He pulls out some money from a bunch of bills.

"Allow me," he says. "You're the first two Newton North High School girls I've met, so lunch is on me."

That's a load of cash. I never saw a kid with that much money. The only person I know who flaunts dough is my uncle Pat, who is convinced that being rich means you're smarter than everyone else and are allowed to boss people around, especially my mother.

It's bad enough Mads was going to lend me money but having to accept money from a guy can lead to mistaken expectations. What if he makes demands for payback in a form I can't agree to? But this time, there's nothing I can do about it because I don't have money to pay for my lunch, and it's obvious this hot dude has melted Mads's brain.

The guy takes his change from the lady and points to an empty table nearby, assuming we'll be his eating companions. I guess if you pay for someone's lunch, they owe you that. Mads's eyes are on high beams, and her lower jaw has unfastened. This hunk has hypnotized her. I fear there'll be a heaping side of flirting to go with my burrito.

"I'll pay you back at school," I tell the guy, as soon as I sit down.

He dives into his lunch, as if he's been on a three-day fast, and between bites says, "No worries. That burrito is on me."

I say, "Rule number seven: never accept free food in the mall."

He almost sputters out a mouthful of chewed burrito. "It's a rule?" he asks, raising one eyebrow that seems to mock me.

"Maybe it's rule number two. I forget. I'll bring the money to school. When did you move to Newton?" I ask, waiting for Mads to wake up and get in the game if she wants to reel in this guy. This will be a slam dunk for her, I'm sure. Most living dudes can't resist the gorgeous Madison Sunday.

"Never lived anywhere else," he answers, which surprises me because I've never seen him before. "Just transferred to Newton North for my senior year."

A load of cash and now a suspicious senior year transfer. No one leaves their friends in the last year of high school. This guy may be cute with his neat soul patch and brilliant smile, but he may also be a bad boy. We have to dig into his backstory, and Mads should curb her fantasies until we do.

But after a summer of being on the receiving end of wrong assumptions, who the heck am I to judge someone I know nothing about?

The guy puts some guac on a chip and holds it out to me. I take it from his warm brown hand but notice he doesn't offer one to Mads. He wiggles his eyebrows at me, and his lips curl up into a sly half-grin. What does that mean? And why isn't he directing his attention to the queen of Newton North High School who's sitting so close to him? She's practically in his lap.

I scan Mads's face for a reaction to that eyebrow display and his guac gift, but there's no sign it registered with her. She reaches over and takes a corn chip from his bag. Her crunching must've unlocked her jaw because she speaks at last: "Do you know anyone at the high school?"

"Only the football players. I'm on varsity, and we started practice last week."

He does have an athletic build. The sleeves of his T-shirt are tight on his biceps. Nice.

Mads asks, "So, you must have met Fernando and Charlie?"

Those guys have been our friends since middle school. Nando and I even had a thing in tenth grade until he went off the rails and tried to nail every girl he could in the sophomore class. A perfect example of a sweet boy becoming a jackass.

The guy's eyes indicate no recognition of those names, so Mads offers more information. "Charlie's Asian and he—"

That clicks. "He's a phenom, lightning on the field, and never gets winded. Amazing endurance."

"Yup, and Nando is a hulk with thick, wavy hair. He's a tackler," Mads says.

"Ah, he snaps the ball, the center," he says. "There are lots of new names to remember." He swallows his last bite and starts to clean up his trash.

"And after Nando does his center's job, he tackles," I say, sort of defending the description of Nando's job that Mads just gave.

"Um...yeah." I detect a slight smirk. Perhaps Mads and I have embarrassed ourselves when it comes to football stuff.

As he's leaving, I realize we don't know his name. After presenting me with a chip and a weird eyebrow twirl, I decide it's better for me to hang back in this threesome and let Mads take center stage with him. After all, she has staked her claim. I text her.

Name??????

She peeks at her phone, offers me a slight nod of understanding, and turns full face to the dude, saying, "By the way, I'm Madison and this is Claire." Before he responds, she adds, "Should we call you New Boy?"

He stands, flashes his gleaming eyes and pivots slightly until he's facing me. He does a cute bow as if we're in the king's court during the Middle Ages. "Chad," he says and vanishes into a crowd of shoppers.

What a freaking coincidence. This is the first Chad I met IRL. It's my number one favorite name for a guy. When Mads and I used to make lists of the boys' names we thought we would fall in love with, Chad was always first on my list. Mads had a new favorite name every week, depending on who she liked in our class or who was the throb in the newest boy band.

The name Chad flows through the byways of my brain, sparking a thrill until my phone rings. It's Mom, killing my Chad buzz.

CHAPTER
3

The phone call jacks up my anxiety with wild heart thumps banging against my chest. "Hey, Mom," I say, trying to keep it cazh.

"Sorr... I wish..."

The rest of her sentence isn't clear. "Mom, I don't understand what you're saying. It's garbled." But I do know this means: get home now!

"On my way," I tell her, and my mind focuses in on poor, defenseless Harry and my stupid reveling in shopping and hanging out. I put the phone in my pocket and tell Mads I have to go home.

She understands without asking questions, which I love about her. She's my rock. We speed-walk to the car.

In front of my house, Mads says, "Claire, get your mom help so you can re-enter the real world and stop playing mother to Harry and your mom."

I open the car door, and Mads recites the pledge we invented when we were ten, using a line from an old famous song Mom used to sing: "I've got you, babe."

"Me too, you," I reply using our official response. In those days, we'd swear oaths of allegiance, but we stopped doing that after middle school.

"I'll make her go to the doctor," I promise and hope that's a commitment I'll be able to keep.

"Call me later."

"I will," offering up another promise. Then I add, "It's probably nothing. She gets hyper sometimes with Harry." That part is true, but Mom scares me when she's so agitated.

Inside the house, I expect to hear a howling Harry and a sobbing mother, but it's weirdly quiet—too quiet. I take the stairs two at a time and find them both in Mom's bed. Mom's skin is ashy, and her eyes are wide in panic. Her breathing is quick and shallow. She clutches at her chest as if she has to hold her heart in place, and her lower lip hangs down as she gasps for air like a hooked fish.

First thing I do is move Harry into his crib, so I don't have to deal with him too. I run back into Mom's room in terror. The remnants of my burrito start to make their way into my mouth. I gulp that feeling back. Don't need to be puking now.

She stammers, "Arry...hel...lp." Her eyes plead with me, but I have no idea what I'm supposed to do.

"Mom! What happened?" I shout at her and regret using such a strong tone, which might only make the situation worse. "Should I call 911?" I ask and try to keep my words measured and my volume lower. I reach for her phone, but she shakes her head no. Her legs get twitchy as if she's trying to get up, but she doesn't or can't.

Mom wheezes and finally huffs out, "Gup. Bup."

The heck with whatever the hell she's trying to say. I'm calling 911. I grab her phone from the nightstand and unlock it. As I wait for the screen to light up, she emits a hoarse whisper. "Ba...ag."

"Your handbag? Do you have pills in there?" Maybe her doctor prescribed something for this type of emergency.

She tries to inhale but can't breathe. She's ekes out her words. It takes a hot, scary couple of seconds for her to say, "Ppp...aper bag."

A paper bag. I race to the utility closet and rummage around in our collection of bags to find a small paper one. I dash back and put it in her hand. She squeezes the top of the bag as if she's making it into a ponytail and covers her mouth and nose with it. She breathes into the bag. After a while, her skin pinks up, and her look isn't so terrified. She lowers the bag, and her head slumps backward onto the pillows in utter exhaustion.

Harry decides this is the perfect moment for him to object to being exiled to his crib, but I ignore his whimpers. *Cool it, buddy. You are not the only person here.*

Mom's breathing gradually comes back to normal, and this time when she talks, she sounds much better. "I'm okay," she says. "I must've frightened you. Hyperventilation is scary."

"Is that the same as a panic attack?"

"It can result from a panic attack sometimes. I'm fine now."

I want to ask her if people can die from that, but I'd better leave that question for Googling in case the answer isn't good. Bad thoughts lead my mind down dark alleys and give me a fleeting image of Harry and me at Mom's funeral. I shudder. I can't take any more surprises like today. She has to go to a doctor ASAP. She may be kind of useless with Harry, but we need her no matter what.

Harry's squeals become more urgent. It's not his jam to have to wait for anything. Sunny Acres may have to straighten him out. I go to get him. His face is red, and his eyes are full of tears.

"Hey, man, your mom isn't feeling well. Not everything is about you."

I carry him into Mom's room, still questioning myself about whether I should've called 911 in spite of her objections. That's the heart of my problem. I'm the kid in this relationship and not used to overriding my mother.

"So did something happen to cause that?" I ask as we sit on the bed.

"No, nothing really. I just hung up a call with Uncle Pat."

Her brother has been a certified jerk since Mom got pregnant. He's always telling her how she's ruined her life. It's a mystery to me why she still talks to him. He makes her feel as if she did the worst possible thing by keeping the baby.

"Why did you call him?"

"Um... I had to ask him something."

"Are you going to tell me what?"

"He's helping me with financial stuff," she finally says.

"I don't trust him. Why didn't he ever come here to see Harry? What kind of brother does that?"

"Um...um...he loves me and wants to help. I need him."

"But you let him dump on you, and you never stand up to him and tell him what you want."

"I'm sorry I put you through all this. I'm making a mess of everything." And with those words, her tears roll; my signal to back off. Personally, I don't give a damn what Uncle Pat thinks, but he's not my brother.

"I know having the baby was, is, hard for you. You need to talk to a psychiatrist," I say, finally pushing aside my fears because I can't take another scene like the one I just witnessed. Mads is right. I have to do this no matter what.

"I'm so sorr—" she catches herself because I've told her countless times I've had enough of her apologies and sorrys, which she has been pouring on non-stop since the moment she told me she was pregnant.

"You don't have to be sorry. Stuff happens. You have to get better. I want, no, I demand, you find a real doctor who can help you. A therapist. Those pills your regular doctor gave you sap your energy and do nothing for your mood. They're useless."

"They help me sleep. Okay, I'll go to a new doctor for you."

At least, she feels guilty enough to do it for me, but was that too easy? Am I being played here? My BS meter flips from side to side, gauging whether she'll really come through or she just wants to shut me up. I have to be sure.

"Swear you'll call for an appointment tomorrow."

"Tomorrow. I will. I'm so tired." She doesn't swear to it, but that's the best I'm getting for now. Since the pregnancy, her life is completely upside down. She spends hours in bed during the day and roams the house at night. She has been known to rearrange the kitchen cabinets in the middle of the night, and some mornings I may find the cereal under the sink with the cleaning supplies.

Okay, that's settled. Maybe. I haul Harry to the kitchen and stuff a bottle in his mouth to stop his whimpering. A new doctor will help. Has to help. Soon after Harry was born, I looked up postpartum depression, but she doesn't fit that diagnosis. Her funk began months before the birth. I had been sure when the baby arrived, she'd snap out of it, but it didn't happen. I thought in a couple of months her hormones would recalibrate or whatever it is they're supposed to do after giving birth.

Each day, Mom slips a bit farther away from me. I imagine myself grasping her hand to drag her back into our world, but her hand is oiled, and I can't hold on to her. It's a disturbing vision of the mother who once listened to my every word when I'd lay on her bed after Dad vacated his spot. She and I jabbered about my teenage angst when Nando dumped me and became the sophomore class dope. I'd share all my plans to change the world in ways I was sure no one else had ever thought of. Mom would listen to my stream of consciousness with infinite patience.

Where is that mother now?

ONCE HARRY IS ASLEEP, I clean the kitchen, take out the trash, and do a load of laundry. Mom's contribution to housework could fit into a teacup, a very tiny teacup. Harry changes outfits more times a day than most teenage girls. If we had a working credit card, I'd buy him more clothes to make my life easier.

I shut the lights and go upstairs, first cracking open Harry's door a little in case he cries; dealing with him during the night is also my job. At least in recent weeks, he has taken pity on his sister and mostly sleeps through the night, unlike those days when he first came home from the hospital. I was one of the living dead. Taking care of a new baby is crazy time.

Tonight, I check in on Mom to make sure her breathing is rhythmic and normal. I leave her door open a smidgen too. My phone pings as I'm finishing brushing my teeth. There's an incoming text from Unknown. This rarely happens to me. All my friends are in my contacts list. I usually delete unknowns because internet trolls lurk everywhere, and texting with an unknown is super sketch. There are some wicked bad players on the Internet. I don't read the text, but I don't delete it either.

Once I tuck myself into bed, I FaceTime Mads. "Sorry I didn't call sooner. I know you think he's adorable, but Harry lives to control my every minute. I get no reprieve until he conks out."

"Why did your mother want you home?"

"She had a sort of panic attack after she spoke to her brother. Since Harry arrived, my uncle has made my mother's life a misery. He tells her she's an irresponsible fool, and she crumbles. I don't want her to talk to him, but I can't control that."

"Is she okay now?"

"Yup, and drumroll, please. She agreed to make an appointment with a therapist."

"Well, aren't you the little gloater? Seriously, babe, proud of you. You have to stop being her enabler."

Enabler? Is that what I am? She makes Mom sound like a drug addict, but Mads knows better than anyone what I've had to do to keep things afloat, so maybe she has a point. From even before Harry was born, I might've let Mom off too easily like when she stopped functioning in the middle of our ordering baby equipment and left me to finish the job. I never complained or said a word about that. And when Harry screwed me by arriving a month early, I had to scramble to rush the deliveries. It was so insane.

"Claire Bear, do you like this shade?" Mads holds a lipstick up to the screen, but through the phone, it's almost impossible to tell the color.

"What's it called?" I ask.

"Guaranteed Boyfriend Magnet. Ha. Ha. No seriously, it's Summer Pink Haze. When Chad and I are a couple, I'm going to ask him to set you up with someone."

"Hard pass on that. Don't need to be dodging some punk's gropey hands right now, and I'm not sure I can even go out on weekends when Harry isn't in day care. My life is too complicated for a boyfriend."

"But senior year is supposed to be wild."

"For you. Any dish on the new boy?"

She puts down the lipstick, gets on her bed, and hugs her pillow. "Well, we already know he's drop-dead gorgeous, plays football, and is a senior. That's practically half his bio."

"But what about the other half of his story?" I ask, trying to pierce the rarified bubble she's been in since she met him.

"I do have some dish."

I clear my throat with an I-know-what-you-did noise and attempt to cross my eyes. "Have you been snooping again?" I ask. "One day you'll get caught."

"Hmm...snooping. Who me?" Mads teases as if she's sweet little Miss Innocent.

Her mom sometimes brings work home and might leave her computer open. She trusts her family. Mads isn't above feeding her curiosity, and she has first-rate detective skills, very stealthy. She never leaves "fingerprints," so to speak, and she's careful about who she shares her stolen information with so she can maintain plausible deniability about the source of the gossip.

"His file has a lot of password-protected papers. One doc hinted at serious trouble at his old school. Maybe he is officially a bad boy. Exciting, isn't it?" she asks.

"What kind of trouble? Not all trouble is the same." Failing a course is one thing, but if he stole a test, that's a whole other level of trouble.

Mads claims I'm way too rational and cautious, and compared to her, I am.

She rolls her eyes. "Whatev," she says, in her best middle school swagger. "I bet it's nothing terrible. I really like him."

"Slow your roll, sister," I advise.

"Ergh, Claire Bear, you're such a downer. You've been playing parent to Harry for too long and now you sound like one. Get over yourself."

A parent! That's not the image I want.

Mads says, "I'm asking Nando to make sure Chad sits with us at lunch. Great idea, huh?" She sighs, "I want this hunky guy."

Any more cautions from me will spoil her Chad vibe, and I'm not that kind of "parent." *The fact I can even joke about that makes me so weird.*

"Yes, great. See you tomorrow, Mads."

I shut my light, and I'm about to queue up a playlist on my phone when I see the text from Unknown daring me to acknowledge its presence. I channel a dose of Mads's bravery and recklessness and restrain my good judgment before opening the text.

Hi

A gif of a waving hand accompanies the text, which seems innocuous, but they warn you against being suckered into things like that on social media.

I text back.

Hi

But I don't add an emoji, which might be considered too friendly with a stranger.

Unknown replies immediately as if his or her finger was at the ready, anxiously awaiting my response.

I thought you weren't going to text me back.

A sad-face emoji is added to those words.

Who are you?

> Guess. Someone told me you are whip smart.

I smile. I do have a rep as a superpower in the brains department that offsets my lower status in the beauty department, but mix the two together, and it gives me a better than average grade.

> 20 questions or three guesses? Pick your game of chance.

Now the unknown person adds an emoji with one eye closed and its tongue hanging out.

I decide to play along.

> Only have time for three questions and one guess.

If my questions are strategic, I might be able to sus out this mystery person.

> Go.

> Are you male?

> Yes.

A bit surprising because girls are more prone to emoji overuse. But once again, I chastise myself for falling into the trap of making incorrect assumptions. I don't like that in me or anyone else.

I ask my second question.

> Do I know you?

> Yes.

That's a relief. I'm not dealing with a creepy internet stalker who wants to meet me in a secluded spot or send me offensive photos of body parts. I only have one more question. Most of the guys I'm close to are into sports, so I go for a two-part question and hope he lets me slide on that violation.

> Do you play a sport? Which one?

> I'm a football man.

That reply is accompanied by an emoji of a football, a trophy cup, and a flexing bicep.

Snap! The only football player on the Tigers' team who isn't in my contacts is Chad.

> You are too easy, NEW BOY.

> And we have a winner! C'mon down and collect your prize.

> What's the prize?

> A frozen cappuccino at Annie's Donuts or a place of your choosing.

Is this dude asking me out? He belongs to Mads.

> Impossible.

> Why?

> Not sure it's a good idea.

> But you won that game fair and square and never even used your hint.

> Were you hiding that rule about being able to get a hint? Not fair.

He sends an emoji of a guy doing a face plant.

> Gotta go.

How did he get my number? Did he also text Mads? New Boy, what are you up to?

CHAPTER 4

No rolling over in bed today for another five minutes when the alarm rings. The first day of senior year will be kickass! I'm working in warp speed and planned for extra time to get Harry and me ready. My outfit from Taylor Imports is set. I brush my straight brown hair into a ponytail, dab on silver eye shadow and pink lip gloss, and then finish packing Harry's things for Sunny Acres. From the list of stuff they want him to bring, he could move in there permanently.

Today, I have him in blue pants and a red onesie with every sports ball imaginable on it. Pretty sharp for a butterball baby. Once I hear he's only sucking air from the bottle, I lift him out of his baby seat. In a nanosecond, he expels all that milk back like he's a firehose locked on me.

"Harry! You tyrant!" I exclaim. "Why would you do that? Couldn't it wait until you got to day care? Isn't cleaning you up what we're paying them the mega bucks for?" And what yanks my chain is he's beaming with pride, as if he has been awarded the prize for the largest quantity of barf in a single explosion. I shake my finger in his face. He smiles and laughs at me.

My brand-new blue tunic is probably stained forever. I bet I have gunk in my hair too. "Do I vomit all over you? No, I don't," I yell at him. Now he understands I'm raging. He whimpers before breaking into a gusty bawl. I bring the crying heap into Mom and order her to change him.

"I have to clean myself too," I say and check the time. No chance to re-shower. I towel off my hair, wash my face, and sniff myself but can't tell if I have puke odor on me. I'll have to keep my distance at school, so no one gets close enough to pin the bad smell on me. It will be like a fart in the wind without an owner. At least I'm not going on a college interview today, grabbing for good news wherever I can these days. I toss the tunic in the laundry and wonder if it will ever be wearable again. No time to deal with that now. I put on a black-and-white striped shirt.

When I return to Mom's room, Harry's half in and half out of his barf clothes. *Give it up, Claire. Why do you expect anything different from her?* I finish dressing him and hope his scent will blend in with all those other hurling and pooping babies at Sunny Acres. Before I leave, I say to Mom, "Remember, you promised to make the appointment. If you don't..."

What do I threaten her with? Usually, parents have lots of options when they're dishing out the perfect punishment, but I'm drawing blanks. Should I pull out a Bible and insist she put her right hand on it? It would take me an hour to find a Bible, so I'm not doing that.

"I will," she says.

"If you don't, I'll be angry. This is my first day of senior year. I deserve it to be a good one."

"You do. I'll make an appointment." She gushes at Harry. "He's so cute." On the rare occasions she can rouse herself to show interest in him, I'm overjoyed. Too often, she avoids him, and I'm thinking that might be her way not to get too attached. But in my heart, I believe she loves him.

Then she adds, "And you too, Clarry. Very cute outfit. Clarry and Harry."

CLAIRE, I screech in my head, but my inner editor warns me this is a terrible time to make a case out of this. I've told her repeatedly not to call me by my baby name once she decided to use rhyming names for me and Harry, like we're twins. She thought it would be so adorable, but it's nauseating.

"Senior year. Good luck." She motions for me to come closer and gives me a one-armed hug. It's been forever since she made a gesture like that to me, and I wish I had time to lean into it, but I don't.

"And take a shower," I shout over my shoulder as we leave. Now I have to hurry because I've lost at least ten minutes from the barf incident.

"I'll try," she says.

"No trying. Just do it." Repeating Mads's mantra that trying is a wimpy word. Mom's promises are hit or miss, sort of like playing roulette. Red, she'll take a shower, and black she won't. Place your bets, people. You've got a fifty percent chance of winning.

I push the stroller with one hand and eat my peanuts and salty caramel bar with the other. Maybe Mrs. Sample will give me a hug for being the best sister ever. She kind of reminds me of my grandma before the Alzheimer's set in, when she could make me melt in her hugs like a toasty marshmallow.

The day care starts at 7:30, and we're right on time. Ha. Ha. Why does a baby have to be at day care on time anyway? It isn't like he'll have to make up first period goo-goo class if he's late. Harry has that goo-goo business down cold.

Mrs. Sample greets us and calls for someone named Amelia. A young woman not much older than me skitters in, wearing a shirt with zoo animals, a multicolored beanie with a propeller on top, and star stickers on her cheeks. This must be a typical day care worker's outfit. I hope Harry appreciates it.

She takes the baby from me and lifts his chubby hand to wave and with the cloying voice of a two-year-old, she says, "Say bye-bye to your mummy."

Today, I'm not letting stuff like that bother me. Mrs. Sample will have to straighten her out. Everyone here has to know: I. AM. NOT. THE. MOTHER.

I return Harry's wave, but he's focusing on a bunch of red balloons in the corner, so my waving gesture is only for Amelia.

Mrs. Sample says, "You can pick Harry up after four, but not later than six."

"I'll be on time, Mrs. Sample. Thanks. Bye."

I fly the rest of the way to Newton North; pretty sure my feet never even touch the pavement. I'm fired up to be a bona fide senior and one step closer to flying out of here to college.

As I cross Walnut Street, I join a throng of noisy kids and let their energy push me through the open doors. The principal and Mads's mom stand on either side of the entrance, greeting everyone as they come through. When Mrs. Sunday says, "Hi," the traditional response is "Happy Monday, Sunday" or whatever day it is. Freshmen find the play on her last name clever, but by senior year it has lost its charm.

I bounce up two flights to my homeroom, eager to see the great Mrs. Gillespie. How will I ever manage in college without this funny, brilliant woman?

"Hey, Mrs. Gillespie."

"Welcome back, Claire. I hope you had a wonderful summer."

"I did," I lie. A more correct reply would be "I survived," but, of course, that would generate a host of questions I don't want to answer.

I take a desk next to Nando, near the back of the room.

"Hey, it's been forever," I say to him.

"Hola, bebé."

"Did college football recruiting start yet?" I ask. Before he answers, Mrs. G. claps three times: the time-honored signal for us to shut up.

"Hello, my fine friends," she says, removing her glasses and letting them rest on her bust, which is sizable enough to serve as a shelf. "Here you are on the first day of your senior year. You've made it this far, so there's no reason to think you can't make it to the end." Everyone laughs as if cued. "Please direct your attention to the board."

She rises out of her seat, moves in front of her desk, and rests half her butt on it for support. On the whiteboard behind her, Mrs. Gillespie has written three cryptic things, and that's why I love her.

Friday

Yes

$180 = 90$

"Mysterious you are, Mrs. G. Keep us on our toes, you do," I whisper.

Nando laughs at my Yoda impression and says, "Nice one, Jackson."

Mrs. G. lands her pointer on the word *Friday*.

Then she says, "By this Friday, you should all have made your first appointments with your college counselors to discuss applications. If you are late doing this, you will find yourself at the end of a long line of seniors who are steps ahead of you."

Next, she points to the word *Yes* and says, "The answer to your question 'Do grades still matter?' is yes, and do not let anyone tell you differently or you'll be sitting in this homeroom again next year, my lovelies."

I say to my friend Alvene who's on my other side, "And lovely you are, Ms. Alvene. Missed you."

"Right back at ya, sugar plum," Alvene replies.

Mrs. G. continues, "And last on my list is a math equation. You have 180 days of school until graduation, but I guarantee it will feel like ninety when you're bopping across the stage to get your diploma. You will be wondering where the year went."

Oh, Mrs. Gillespie, come to college with me. Maybe at graduation, I'll dare to hug her and lose myself in her as if I'm being wrapped in a warm tortilla.

The bell rings and kids scatter. In the hallway, I bump into Chad. His deep-brown puppy eyes tell me he's lost.

"Need some help, New Boy?" I ask.

"Hey, Claire."

"Where are you supposed to be now?"

He hands me his schedule.

"Okay, *parlez-vous francais?*" I show off one of the few French phrases I know because Latin is my language of choice.

"Huh?"

"You have French on the second floor. I'll walk you there."

"You'll be late for class and get in trouble because of me," he says, giving me the full frontal of his incredible smile.

"I don't have a first period class. I'm on my way to make my appointment with the college counselor. You should make one soon. These appointments are like tickets to a Taylor Swift concert. They go fast. You could wind up with a seat in the nosebleed section if you wait."

"I'm still figuring out my plans for next year."

"Does that mean you're not going to college?" I ask, immediately regretting being so intrusive. After complaining all summer about people sticking their noses where they don't belong, I want to swallow my words back.

"It's complicated," Chad replies with a frowny face as we arrive at the door of his classroom.

Before he goes in, he asks, "Can I text you if I get lost again and need a guide? Did you put me in your contacts list?" He sticks out his phone to show he has my name and number. It's one of those très expensive, latest-model iPhones.

"Nice phone." I stare at that beauty.

"Yup, a gift from the king."

"The king of phones?"

"AKA my father."

"So does that make you Prince iPhone?" I tease.

"Nope. I'm a mere serf in the king's castle."

I have not put him in my contacts' list in case his name would pop up when Mads is around. "Your schedule shows second lunch today. Madison and I have the same one. She'll save a seat for you. Find us in the back of the caf."

"And we need to make plans for that coffee I owe you. You have to collect your prize. It's not optional."

"Not sure if I can," I reply. If he hasn't texted Mads yet, this won't be good.

"Aw... I'll keep asking until you say yes."

Got to give him props for persistence. If I don't agree now, he may bring it up in front of other kids, and everyone will get the wrong idea. So, I'll go with him for coffee and use the time to perfect my wingwoman skills and push him to hook up with Mads.

"Tomorrow after school is okay," I reply.

He takes one step into the classroom and then says, "Tomorrow. Meet me in the parking lot after school. I'll be the guy in the bright red Mustang."

"A Mustang?" I repeat. That's a high-end car. No one at Newton North drives anything better than an ancient Toyota Corolla. That car screams "notice me." It would generate wild gossip if anyone saw me get into Chad's car and would for sure get back to Mads. She'd kill me. Heck, I'd kill me if I was her. "I have one condition," I say.

"Lay it on me."

"I'll meet you at the corner of Commonwealth and Walnut. I don't want to get stuck riding the Newton North High School gossip wheel like a dopey old hamster. Once you get on that, it's a bitch to find an off ramp. People get the wrong idea around here."

"Getting the wrong idea could be fun, but okay. I'm not going against any of your rules while I'm the new kid here."

I add, "And don't mention this to anyone. I'll explain tomorrow. This has to stay on the down low."

"Got it."

He goes into the classroom, and I'm off to schedule my appointment with the college counselor to kick-start the rest of my life.

CHAPTER
5

Those energy bars I had on the way to school don't hold me, and by lunchtime, I'm famished. After a summer of listening mostly to baby gurgles interspersed with the chirping birds of Cold Spring Park, the noise in the cafeteria is deafening. I head for our usual table in the back. Mads loves this vantage point so she can scope out the action in the cafeteria. It's sort of like she's in a gangster movie where they face the door on guard for approaching enemies.

"I'm nervous," Mads says, as I put my tray down.

Her eyes dart in every direction, trying to spot Chad. I rest my hand on hers to tamp down her fidgets.

"He'll come, won't he?" she asks. "Does he know anyone else here? Why aren't you wearing that blue tunic we picked out?"

"Harry christened it with his best barf before we left this morning. Do you think he's crying at the day care? Should I be calling to check on him? Do people check on their kids?"

"I bet he's having a ball, and he's not actually your kid. They'll call you if anything goes wrong, which it won't. You wanted your normal life back, and there's nothing more normal than being in the caf and inhaling the smell of plastic food being cooked."

"That's why I stick to the salad bar. Eyes left. Here they come. Take a breath, Mads."

Nando and Charlie arrive with that stunning black guy trailing behind them. I scoot to the other side of the table, hoping Chad takes the hint and sits next to Mads. He does. *Way to go, wingwoman,* I applaud myself.

Once again, as soon as she sees him, Mads gets lockjaw. I stretch out my leg to kick her out of her marble statue imitation: gorgeous but frozen.

It's awkward waiting for her to loosen up, so I get the party started. "So, how's your first day?" I ask Chad and gag at the utter lameness of that question. It makes me sound like someone's grandmother. Good thing I'm not the one trying to impress him. "And here's the money I owe you." I put the cash for the burrito on the table.

"Straight up not taking that," he says.

"So leave it for some lucky kid to scoop up."

"You are persistent. Okay, I don't want you breaking your rule number seven or number two." He stuffs the money into his jeans pocket. I'm surprised he was paying such close attention to my rule numbers, which I was making up as I went along.

Chad grins at me, and for the first time I notice a slight groove in his chin. It takes your breath away. Only a master craftsman could've designed that chin. It's square, but not hard. That dude has scored a sensational set of genes.

Charlie says, "You'll like it here."

"I have no choice about that," Chad replies. "Changing schools again isn't an option." Then, as if the two of us share a special secret, which we don't, he tilts his head toward me with a smile that's almost too large for his face. What-the-what does that look even mean?

"Do you change schools often?" Charlie asks, flipping his black bangs off his forehead in what he's convinced is his signature sexy move, but really, it's just cute. He'd be crushed if I ever told him that.

"Nope. This is my first time." Chad bites into a hefty sandwich.

Finally, finally, Mads reboots and speaks. "Where did you go to school before here?"

Chad gazes at his sandwich as if the answer is written on the bread. Is he embarrassed to say where? He blinks, displaying the full effect of those luscious lashes, and says, "West Concord Academy."

"Holy crap," Nando says. "Are you Richie Rich?"

Chad's lips tighten into a firm straight line, and his eyes narrow to match. He's annoyed. "None of your business. Eat your lunch."

Nando sometimes has no filter, but he drops it and moves on.

"Chad, you should get a ticket to the Senior Supper and Dance. It's real soon, for seniors only, like me," he says while slamming his finger into his chest in case we forgot he's a senior too. "We own the school, and now we will do to others as we were done to."

"What kind of dance? Do I need a date?" Chad asks.

"Nah," Nando says. "There'll be plenty of single girls there. You'll bag someone in no time. Didn't you ever look in the mirror, bro?"

Charlie snickers and covers his mouth. Guys pretend they aren't obsessed with looks like girls are, but it's so not true.

"Just don't accept a date from Vivian." Nando adds with an idiotic grin.

Chad's body goes rigid and his nostrils flare. He glares at Nando. "Now why would you say that about any girl?"

"Because she's built like a block of cement. You can't tell where the boobs stop and the waist begins. You wouldn't want to be caught dead with her as your date."

"You're a tool, man," Chad says. "You have no idea what type of girl I like, and size doesn't matter, except in your case because you're a little dope. I want to meet her."

Nando's diss of Vivian is middle-school manure, but most boys would let it pass and not confront him. Charlie concentrates on feeding his face to avoid having to get into this.

"I'll introduce you to her," I offer. "She has a wicked sense of humor. And she's smart. Follow me."

As Chad follows me, he loses the angry expression, and his righteous beauty is restored. When I find Vivian, I avoid hugging her in case I reek from Harry's smell, but Chad throws his arms around her. He doesn't seem like the hug-any-girl type.

"Vivi," Chad says.

She flutters her eyelashes at him. "Can't believe you've returned to me after all these years. You have lifted our status at Newton North by your mere presence."

In this threesome, I feel like a tree stump until Vivian says, "Hey, Claire. I didn't know you knew this guy."

"I don't."

Chad clutches his heart. "Oh, but you do know me, Claire. Did you forget that burrito we shared?"

Is he joking? He might be joking. "I mean, I just met you. I don't really know you."

"I'm going to fix that."

Desperate for him to stop talking about me, I ask, "Vivian, how do you two guys know each other?"

"We went to pre-K together," she replies. "Before you take off, Claire, are we doing the voter registration this year?"

"Of course. Who else, if not us? These clowns have to get engaged in the political process. It's a presidential election year; everyone should be pumped. Let's meet with the city clerk and put the plans in place."

"Perfecto," Vivian says. "Will your mom help us again?"

"Um...not sure...she's working a lot...if she has time... I'll ask. Got to finish my lunch before I faint on day one of senior year," I say, not wanting to talk about Mom anymore. I've kept her pregnancy and the baby with no father a secret, except for Mads. I'm afraid people will judge Mom in not nice ways. I've heard too much slut-shaming around the school, and I don't want any of that directed at my mother.

I'll have to find someone else to fill in for Mom; she was our voting guru and chief advisor about voter registration, candidates' debates, and all things election.

Mads whispers when I sit down. "Was Chad weird about what Nando said?"

"Maybe. Not sure." I turn to Nando. "Dumbass, clean up your act."

Nando's usual strategy when someone calls him on his BS is on full display. "If it isn't Claire Jackson with another of her lectures that I didn't sign up for."

Before I can pounce on him, Chad is back. "Vivi's cool."

Nando lowers his eyes. He has embarrassed himself completely.

Mads says, "Chad, come with us to the senior dance. I'm buying my ticket later, and I'll get one for you too."

Cool it, Mads. Buying a ticket for a guy you hardly know isn't a great first move.

"It will be my treat," she adds while sunbeams aimed at Chad shoot out of her eyes. "To celebrate your arrival at dear old Newton North High School."

Too soon, Mads, I want to tell her, but it's too late. Her offer is already out in the ether. She'd better tread carefully, or this guy will assume she's an easy mark. And she is not. Mads and I made a pact to watch out for each other so neither of us gets caught up in a situation we don't want to be in. It's the I-have-your-back rule. Plenty of girls at school would like nothing better than to "catch" Mads in a reportable offense and bank some chits by passing that information to her mother.

"Claire, are you going to the dance?" Chad asks. "I'm not buying you a ticket because that's probably your rule number eleven or twelve: no free school dances." He gives me a broad, delicious smile.

I smile back and say, "Wrong! That's rule number three, high on the list of life's important rules."

I glance at Mads to gauge her reaction to Chad and me joking, and she seems unfazed. After all, Chad and I only exchanged smiles, which is just an automatic response. It means nothing.

As I WALK to Sunny Acres after school, I note this is the longest I've gone without seeing Harry since he was born. It feels strange, but also good. When I don't have to take care of him, my life is my own. This was an excellent first day. I even snagged an appointment with the college counselor for tomorrow during my free period.

I'm buzzed in, and someone directs me to a back room where

Harry's waiting with other babies. At least he's not the last one here. *Kudos to Claire.* He made it through the day without getting socked by another kid, at least not where it would show, anyway. I put on his sweater and sit him in the stroller.

"Hope you got your money's worth, bro," I say, buckling him up. "At these prices, you should ask for extra milk." I laugh, but that twenty-grand check is forever seared in my brain.

Our homecoming is a major disappointment. A part of me expected Mom to be waiting for us, eager for our report on the first day. That part of me is delusional. Harry and I are on our way upstairs until I spot Mom's legs stretched out on the recliner in the living room. She's still in the same sweatpants, so I'm assuming no shower or hairbrush today.

"Hi, Mom. Harry liked the day care."

"That's good." Her voice has as about much enthusiasm as mine does before the dentist starts to drill.

"And did you do what you promised?" I ask.

"I made an appointment. They had an opening tomorrow." Her eyes plead for a pat on the head or a high five, but you don't get rewarded for doing what you're supposed to do.

"Glad that's done. Can we order Thai to celebrate?"

"Whatever you want."

"That reminds me, Mom. The credit card didn't work yesterday."

She unlocks the recliner and sits up, and those eyes, puffy from crying, wreck me. She replies, "I'm juggling some money around. Possibly, I forgot to pay that bill." She takes a tissue from the side table and wipes her nose. "I have another card in my nightstand. Go get it."

Fortunately for me, Harry isn't crawling yet, so for now he'll be safe on his mat under his arch thingy, while I go upstairs. Google should know when babies get moving. That will change so much around here and not for the good.

I find the credit card in her drawer, and it still has the sticker on it, indicating it hasn't been activated.

I trot downstairs and say, "This card is brand new. You should pay the bill for the other card."

"The money's kind of messed up now while I figure out a few things."

"Messed up how?"

"It's complicated."

"Are we broke?"

"No, there are savings."

It's enough I have to take care of Harry. I so don't want the responsibility of our money too. But what if she's sliding us into bankruptcy? This isn't supposed to be my life. I don't want to be my mother's mother, but from the time she told me she was pregnant, our roles started to reverse. My first question to her was, how did that happen? God, I sounded just like a parent trying to understand their teenager who got into trouble.

"Well, you know how that happens," she replied.

"At seventeen, I don't need a sex ed lesson, and please spare me the graphic details that would scar my teenage brain. I meant, how did you let it happen? Alcohol?" I asked, but I've never seen her drink anything more than some wine, and I never saw her drunk.

"One or two glasses of wine, but no more."

"Drugs?"

"Never!" she shouted.

"Do you like the guy?" I asked. It seemed like a logical question, but it caused a flood from her eyes.

She said, "I couldn't see him again."

"Why not?"

"I shouldn't have let it happen, but it did."

It was all so mysterious. It left me assuming he's married or a real bad dude. She claimed she didn't know his last name and left the line blank on Harry's birth certificate where it asks for the father. This baby has an unknown father. He clearly wasn't the result of one of the great romances of the century, or even of a blockbuster romance of an hour. She says the encounter was a mistake. Tough gig for

Harry when he grows up and wants to know who his father is, but that's Mom's fault for abandoning her good sense one night with a rando.

"You have to activate the credit card," I tell her.

"You do it, Clarry. Go to their website and put in my social security number." She rattles off a bunch of numbers.

I take the card, get my laptop, and follow the activation instructions, which were written for a third grader.

Once it's done, I ask, "Do you need help to remember to pay the bills?"

"Can we talk about it another day? I can't today."

"Okay. The card is activated, and it's ready to lose its virginity on a takeout order from Lemon Grass."

CHAPTER 6

My appointment with the college counselor the next day is the first step on my future path. I can picture me doing a happy dance opening college acceptance emails. The anticipation of meeting with the gorgeous Ms. Hernandez gets my adrenaline flowing. This must be what candidates feel on Election Day while waiting for the results. Someday, that might be me running for office.

Outside Ms. Hernandez's office, I park myself on the wooden bench and wait. Her door opens, and Rob, whom I've known since kindergarten, comes out gray-faced, eyes unfocused, and slightly hunched. His meeting with the college counselor was definitely not the highlight of his day. Poor guy. He struggles, but he's sweet. I like him.

He almost walks straight past me, so I call out, "Hey, Rob. How ya doing?"

His head jerks toward the sound of my voice. He attempts a smile, but it's weak. His facial muscles seem beyond his control at the moment.

"It wasn't great," he says. "I mean, there's some hope for me, but I can't walk right in to any college like you."

I stand and lay a gentle it-will-all-work-out punch on his shoulder. "You'll find your happy place. Hernandez is a master college matchmaker."

"I guess," he mumbles as he leaves with his face still scraping the floor.

I take a seat in the office, and the radiant Ms. Hernandez busts out a gigantic smile, probably relieved not to have another student like Rob next. It's a mystery why someone like her chose to spend her life maneuvering seniors like chess pieces into colleges when she could've had a career strutting down the fashion runway or posing for a magazine cover. I'm surprised the guys who meet with her can concentrate on college stuff while she sits opposite them.

Our meeting flows like a gentle, babbling brook, and I leave with three to-dos: get one more recommendation, finish my essay, and complete my list of potential colleges.

The rest of my day is perfect, and when the last bell rings, I join everyone flowing toward the escape route before anyone nabs them back for something. The sun pokes out of the clouds, but it doesn't give off the same warmth as in the heart of summer. Fall is advancing.

Mads startles me when she pops up from out of nowhere. "Hey, babe, come over this afternoon."

"I can't."

"Want me to come to your house?"

"Uh, no, I have get the car and go grocery shopping before I pick up Harry."

Lying to Mads is wrong in so many ways. I am not that person, or I wasn't that person. But this lie is excusable because I'm meeting Chad to give Mads an alley-oop in the romance department. It's puzzling why a stunner like him isn't picking up on her obvious cues. That only underscores how important my plan is. Mads will thank me later.

"Bummer. Okay, call me," she says, and we hug. But now I can't leave, or she'll know I'm not going straight home. I have to stall until she's out of sight.

"Forgot my econ book. Talk later," I say and head back into the building, this time going against the current of bodies. The lies are adding up, and I feel like even a bigger a-hole.

I wait inside the school for a few minutes before I move outside again to look around and make certain the coast is clear. I go to meet Chad. This coffee date—I mean coffee meeting—is such a nothing burger. I don't even bother to redo my ponytail or put on lip gloss or check myself out on the phone camera for leftover lunch stuck in my teeth. This coffee is about Mads, not me.

An exquisite red car with the top down is parked at the corner. A convertible! They cost a fortune. I bet you could go to college for an entire year for that kind of money. I get in and rub my hands over the smooth leather seats before I buckle up.

"Do you want me to put the top up?" he asks.

"Definitely not!" This is my first ride in a convertible, and I want to savor the wind whirling around me even if my hair is blown to bits as if I stuck a wet finger in an electric socket. "Also, can we go to a coffee shop outside the city?"

"Why?"

"Because I don't want anyone from school to see us."

"You mean because someone might think this is a date."

Precisely, but I wish he hadn't said that word. "Yeah, sort of that," I say, while he types into his GPS.

Chad drives us to a place named Coffee and Bagels a few miles past the city line where we won't run into someone from school. That lowers my stress level.

Inside the coffee shop, we order our drinks from the barista. I make it a point of going first to prevent any argument about who's paying. I can buy my own coffee. When Chad gets to the register and finds out I've paid, he hands the lady a twenty from his stash of cash with a pouty face. We head for a table in the back. As soon as I sit, I remove my hair elastic and use my fingers to comb through my hair and redo the ponytail. Although I don't need to impress this guy, I don't want him to gag when he sits across from me.

Chad has a bagel and cream cheese and offers me a bite, which I decline. Sharing food is a bridge too far. I dive right into my mission and say, "Madison is the most beautiful girl at school, and she's the queen of nice. We've been besties forever, and I guarantee you'll love her."

If I can goose the Chad-Mads ship successfully, this outing will be a huge success, and someday Mads and I will laugh about my role in getting them together. She might promote me to wingwoman first class.

"She's pretty," he says, and wipes a blob of wayward melting cream cheese that created a white goatee on his brown chin. "If you go for that," he adds. What does he mean? I was expecting him to grill me on all things Mads to get up to speed before he makes his move, but he seems uninterested. I'm mystified why he isn't jacked up about the magnificent Madison.

"Most dudes would do anything to get into striking range of Madison," I say.

"Do I seem like most dudes? You aren't the only one with rules." He slaps on a goofy grin.

"Okay, you've got rules too, but you two would be perfect together." Am I stereotyping here because of how amazing they would look as a couple? This summer I learned that the assumptions you make about people can bite. I still have teeth marks on my butt from the number of people who were so sure they knew my story.

Chad sips his cappuccino. "I know she's your best friend, but can we talk about something else?"

"Sure." I'd better ease up before I bungle my matchmaker task. "Okay, new subject. My rule number four is I have to know the person I'm having coffee with."

He raises one skeptical eyebrow. "You made that rule up."

"You don't know all my rules, and it's my word against yours. This is legit rule number four."

"Lay it on me."

"Why did you change schools for your senior year? That's never done. Breaking new ground, Chad?"

"It's a complicated story. I'll give you a sliver of the why, but you'll owe me in return."

Oh. Oh. Here it comes. Deals with boys are the hot potato of relationships. He'll probably ask for something I don't want to give. A large *No* flashes in my brain. I can do without knowing his life's story.

"No deals," I reply.

"Which rule is that?"

"No number. It is given from on high, and it's not negotiable and not amendable." I say it as if I'm making a motion on a new resolution at a student government meeting. I love parliamentary procedure.

"But it's only fair," he says. "I'll tell you about me, and you have to tell me something about you."

Ah, he only wants to talk. And I thought... Well, I can agree to that.

I say, "I'll make that deal under one condition."

"Bring it on. You're one heck of a negotiator. Are there always conditions with you?"

"I want you to text Madison. She's amazing. The best. So fun."

"Text her what?"

This guy is confusing me. He had no trouble texting me, and now he needs a instruction manual to text Mads. But because I know her so well, I come up with an idea quickly.

I put down my cup. "Ask her what you should wear to the senior supper and dance. Fashion is her wheelhouse." I'm going to dust off my cupid wings tonight, so they're ready for the dance.

"Do you think I dress bad, or something? Do I *need* advice?" he asks.

"No, but this will be great."

"Okay, what's her cell number?"

"Give me your phone, I'll put it in, but don't tell her I gave it to you, or she'll want to know when we were talking about her. It would be better to leave me out of this."

He slides his take-your-breath-away expensive phone across the table without hesitation. When I see the screen, I'm presented with a picture of him standing on a boat, wearing a low-slung bathing suit and no shirt. I shiver at the sight of him half naked and suck in a gulp of air to cool the heat rising in my face. After adding Mads to his contacts, I hand him back the phone.

"Nice boat," I say.

"Yup."

"Is it yours?" I ask.

"My dad is a big-shot commercial real estate developer, and this 'boat' is one of his toys."

"So that's why you drive that car?"

"That car was my consolation present for changing schools."

"So why did you come to Newton North?" Going back to my original question.

His shoulders slump. "Don't judge me. I had to punch a guy at my last school. He was relentlessly making fun of a girl who was easy pickings. You know the type—too quiet and shy. When he tried to kiss her against her will, I lost it. I knocked him down and got booted out of my fancy prep school."

"Why did you get thrown out? He was the bully."

"Yup, but it never works that way. My dad was pissed I wouldn't be getting the prestigious diploma, and at first, he threatened to ship me off to some remote boarding school in Utah. But I knew he was ginning me up because he was so angry. My dad wants me near him all the time. I mean all the time and all my life. He doesn't let me breathe. Only son and all that crap. Heir to the business. Blah, blah."

"But he bought you a beautiful car."

"He gave me that car because his friend told him awful stories about bad dudes who ride the bus. He didn't want me hanging with the wrong crowd. He has mapped out my whole life: what to study at college, where I'll work. All I'm expected to do is nod and 'yes sir' him."

"Your father's right. The bus is a minefield on wheels wrapped in a pukey odor that a thousand cleanings can't kill. The punks on the bus are always on the hunt for easy prey. It's the worst."

"So, are you suggesting I ride the bus and knock a few heads? And for the record, the kid I hit was fine, only a chipped tooth, but his parents made a big deal out of it. They were lucky I didn't bill them for special tutoring for their son." Chad grins, satisfied with himself.

The vision of Chad punching someone doesn't compute. He seems so measured and more mature than most guys at school. But he felt he had to protect that defenseless girl, so I guess it was justified. He reacted the same way when Nando ragged on Vivian, but he didn't hit him.

I smile. "You don't want to be knocking heads with the bus crowd and getting expelled again in your senior year."

"Expensive private schools don't expel, they request you leave," Chad explains.

"Newton North must be a comedown for you but glad you're slumming it with us."

"So far, it's okay. Now it's your turn. That's the deal."

And I can't explain it, but I trust this guy. Maybe it's because I hardly know him and didn't grow up with him like I did with Nando and Charlie. My instincts tell me it'll be okay. I may be a fool, but I'm going to share the thing that's heavy on my heart.

"I should tell you about Harry."

Chad almost elevates off the chair, and his hands lurch forward, knocking my latte into my lap. Luckily, I'm wearing dark wash jeans that hide everything.

"No problem," I say, as Chad plies me with more napkins than I need for a mop up.

"My fault. You took me by surprise. I didn't know you had a boyfriend."

Why would he be upset if I did have a boyfriend?

"Yeah, right, I have a boyfriend who pees on me." I expect him to laugh, but instead he clenches one fist and pounds it into the other palm.

In an impassioned tone with eyes facing some unknown horror, he asks, "You let your boyfriend pee on you?"

OMG, does he think I'd be okay with that? A giggle wants to escape, but I squelch it because his rage seems real.

"You're overheating for nothing," I say. "First of all, I didn't say anything about a boyfriend, and Harry is four months old and my brother. Second, I figured out how to stop him peeing on me after the second time he sprayed me."

Chad's fist unclenches, and the tension in his face dissolves. He might've been on the verge of storming out to hunt down this "boyfriend" to protect my honor.

"I was gonna... I was gonna," he stammers and then says, "Whew. That was funny." He struggles to regroup.

"Actually, when I said I wanted to talk to you about Harry, I wasn't trying to be funny. You never gave me a chance to explain before you semi-lost it. Harry's arrival was a huge shock. My mother couldn't handle it and crumbled. She can't work. I had to step in and do most everything for the baby, but at least now he's in day care."

"I'm so sorry, Claire. That must be rough for you."

"Only Mads knows about all this. Please don't tell a soul."

"Never."

"Can we leave? I have to pick up Harry. They're hardcore at that place about not being late."

Chad gives me a small, warm smile. "Don't want you to be late for your not-boyfriend Harry. I can drive you both home." He picks up his plate and our cups and puts them in a plastic bin on the counter.

"You can't drive us," I say.

"Why not?"

"Duh, no car seat."

"Oh yeah, I forgot about that. My bad."

"Besides, I leave his stroller at the day care, and it's only a few blocks to my house."

I give him the address for Sunny Acres and remind him about texting Mads.

"Mads?"

"I mean Madison or Maddie. Don't call her Mads under any circumstances unless she tells you to. Only I call her that, and if you do, she might assume we've been talking about her."

When Chad parks in front of the day care, he sticks out his hand for me to shake, saying, "Deal. I'll text Mads—I mean, Madison—tonight. Promise."

His grip is perfect, not too tight and with no awkward squeezing. A warmth comes through his skin as I gaze into his deep chocolate eyes.

I step out of the car, and he adds, "We have a special game on Friday afternoon with Wellesley. I could use a cheerleader there."

"I'll come for a while until I have to pick up my 'boyfriend,'" I laugh.

"You can bring the dude. I bet he's clickbait."

"I don't want anyone at school to know about his existence and ask me questions I don't want to answer."

"Got it."

He drives off, and I go inside to claim the clickbait.

On our way home, I stop to phone Dad.

"Hey, Dad."

"Clarry, so good to hear your voice."

My snark wants me to offer a sharp response like if he misses my voice, he might try calling more often when he's not so busy in his new marriage, but I keep it cool. I want to share all the news from my meeting with Ms. Hernandez.

"How are you?" I ask, sounding ridiculously formal for a father and daughter and more like neighbors bumping into each other in the supermarket.

"I'm fine. I wish you could come and visit."

"Yeah," I say.

"So, one more year of high school and then college."

"Yup."

"Where are you going to apply?" he asks.

"Not sure. Most people are applying to at least ten schools, or I could go early decision, but if I don't do that, Wisconsin will be on my list. Ms. Hernandez, the college counselor, recommended the University of Wisconsin as a good safety school if I wish to live in the snowy, frigid cheese state."

"That would be great. We'd love to have you here. Come visit and I'll show you around the school." His reaction surprises me in a good way. I'm happy he'd want me nearby, but Stanford is my first choice.

Dad says, "I miss you, honeybun. When are you coming to visit?"

Dad has no clue what life is like for me, or he wouldn't ask me to come, but I don't tell him any details about Mom's state of mind or that she leaves me with all the responsibilities for the baby. It'd be impossible for anyone not living with this to understand. Plus, they're divorced, so he doesn't have to know. He called to congratulate Mom when the baby was born, but I avoid all Harry talk with Dad.

When my parents informed me of their split, they spouted slogans from every self-help book ever published on the subject of what to tell children about divorce. They should've asked for their money back because I didn't buy a word of their feeble reassurances that my life would be as good as before. The only thing I hung on to was they both said there was no one else in their lives and Dad got a great job offer in Wisconsin—both of which were true. Their divorce was civil, at least for them. It took months for me to re-glue my broken pieces after I finished mourning my old life.

The idea of getting out of Newton for a while and going to Wisconsin is tempting, but I can't abandon Harry. Who knows what catastrophe could happen while I was away?

Then Dad spoils his offer by saying, "We can use another pair of hands around here with Bella. She's a cutie-pie with mischief as her chief occupation. I forgot taking care of a toddler is a full-time job. Maybe I'm too old for this baby business. Your mom is lucky to have you there. We want some Claire time too." And with those words, his sweet invitation to visit turns sour.

So, my father marries a woman with a little kid and it's on me to provide free babysitting? My parents have made some questionable choices, and somehow they expect me to pitch right in like the ultimate good sport. But his request for help with his wife's daughter pushes my buttons. Once upon a time, my parents believed I could be a doctor, or a professor, or an engineer. Now, evidently, I should aspire to a bachelor's degree in wiping baby bottoms.

Really, none of this matters. I can't go anywhere right now and leave Harry defenseless. Mom might decide if she can't take care of him without me, she should ship him off.

"Got to go back to work, Clarry."

"One more thing, Dad. I'll need about $750 for the application fees. Will you send me a check for that, or do you want to message me the cash—"

"Clarry, your mother already has all your college money.

According to our divorce agreement, I gave her my share of it. You should ask her for the application fees."

"I didn't know that."

"Now you do. Got to go. Staff meeting in five. Talk soon."

"Bye."

I resume pushing Harry's stroller down the sidewalk when my head turns into an exploding emoji. I raise my eyes, expecting to see my brain matter disintegrating into gray, mushy bits. My hands rush to the top of my head to save as much of me as possible.

I recite out loud in a continuous loop, "Two and two are four. Two and two are four," as if I might forget the answer to that equation if I don't keep repeating it.

Claire, get a grip! She couldn't have done that, could she? But the answer is four. Two and two are four. There's no other possibility than the one staring me in the face.

My knees buckle, and as I'm collapsing to the ground, the stroller rolls away. When did I let it go? I run at top speed, and the pavement's downward slope only increases. I pray for a miracle to reach Harry before the stroller crashes.

A few feet from the corner, I stretch out my arms as if they're made of elastic and manage to grab the handle. Harry's fine, but tears fill my eyes, and I can't see in front of me. I'm shaking off a vile wave of nausea, but this time I press the lever to lock the stroller's brakes in case I pass out. That lapse can never happen again. I swear to whoever is watching over us.

My own mother has driven my future off a cliff.

CHAPTER
8

My breathing is erratic from running and panic. I inhale deeply to regain control and then start for the house. Once inside, I park Harry on the living room floor and go upstairs to declare war on my deceitful mother.

As expected, she's lying on her unmade bed in a T-shirt and oversized sweats.

"Wake up!" I shout. She murmurs, but her eyes stay closed.

"I have to talk to you *now*." Red-hot fire shoots out of all the openings on my face as if I've been infused with dragon blood. "You stole my money!" My accusation ricochets off the ceiling and fills the room.

She props herself up on an elbow and reaches over a slew of pill bottles on her night table for a tissue. "I'm sorry. I had no choice." She doesn't even ask what I mean. She knows damn well what she did.

"What do you mean, no choice? What kind of sorry excuse is that? 'Oh, I just had to shoplift that exquisite necklace. It was too beautiful not to steal it. I had no choice.' How stupid does that sound?"

"This is different. Everything crashed. It's all my fault. I'm so sorry."

"Sorry. Sorry. That's all you've got! You steal my college money, and I get a 'sorry.'"

"When I start working again, I'll make it up to you," Mom whimpers. "I'll fix what I did."

"That will be too late! How am I going to college next year?" Indignation squirts out of every one of my pores.

"You shouldn't have to take care of Harry all the time. He had to go to day care."

"I shouldn't have to, but I do it, and in return you betrayed me!"

"I got some new medication," she says in the soft voice of a scared child trying to deflect an incoming scolding. An hour ago, I'd have been overjoyed she took the first steps to getting better, but now there's a sick irony in seeing the stack of amber vials on top of the box I made in sixth-grade woodworking class with the etching *Best Mom Ever*. What a joke.

There's no use talking to her. I storm out and before I know it, I'm flying out the door and running down the street. My ponytail slaps the sides of my head as I run in a frenzy until I stop abruptly, almost losing my balance and make a sharp turn toward Mads's house. I bang on her door repeatedly with both fists, an expression of my hysteria.

Mads opens the door. Her eyebrows flare. "What's up, Claire Bear? Why are you crying?"

I push past her and go into the kitchen, helping myself to a glass of water, which I empty in one gulp.

"I almost got Harry killed today," I blurt out.

"Ah, what?"

"For a second, I let go of the stroller. It rolled. I chased it and managed to grab the handle before disaster struck. I'm still shaking." I show her my hands as proof that I'm wrecked.

"Sit down. Take a breath and tell me exactly what happened." I follow her instructions. We sit at the table, and she asks, "Is he okay?"

"Yeah, he's fine. That's the lucky thing about being little—he won't remember this, and I swear it will never happen again."

She responds as if she wrote the how-to-be-a-best friend handbook. "Crap happens, and Harry's okay. So, forget it."

"I couldn't think straight."

"It's not like you to lose control."

"I got really bad news," I say, before exhaling a loud, sorrowful sigh.

Mads tightens her jaw and appears frightened by that sound. "Is it your mother?" she asks.

"Yes, but not in the way you think. I can't go to college next year." My elbows rest on the table and my head sinks into my hands. Not going to college—I can't believe I said that out loud. It's unreal.

"You're joking. Of course, you're going to college unless you're planning to go on an around-the-world trip, or you've won the lottery and never have to work a day in your life."

"My mother drained my college account."

"What the hell?"

"She spent it all on Harry's day care."

"You are not—did she cop to that?" Mads asks.

I refill my glass, but this time only drink half of it. "She admitted it. She even thought I might forgive her because she finally went to a doctor and got new medication."

"That's a positive step."

"I don't think one thing offsets the other."

Mads says, "Why not tell your dad and ask him for the money?"

"He told me he already gave my mom his share of my college money. That's what she used for Harry's day care tuition. She's probably spent her share on other things since there's no money coming in. We're probably eating my college money one meal at a time."

"Wow! That's awful. I'm so sorry, Claire. What can you do? You can't sue your own mother."

"Nobody's suing," I say weakly.

"Do you want me to talk to my mom? She could help you," Mads says.

"Definitely not!" Having people involved in our lives is my worst nightmare. No matter what my mother has done, I have to shield her and Harry from the outside world. If anyone thinks she's not fit to care for the baby, some authority might step in and take him away. I'm pretty sure my uncle is pressuring her to give up Harry. That's a non-starter for me. She has betrayed me. I won't let her betray Harry, too.

"Don't tell a soul, Mads. I mean it. Promise me."

Mads crosses her heart and sticks her pinky out like we're five. Not wanting to insult her gesture, I wrap my finger around hers. She says, "I promise. You can trust me. You know I trust you. You're my true sister. This is totally unfair. I want to help you. There must be some solution."

"Right now, I can't even think straight."

"Well, at least you were able to come here and leave Harry with her."

I jump up. "Harry! No, I didn't exactly leave him with her. Well, I sort of did. He's home but on the floor in the living room. I didn't even tell my mother where I left him. Holy crap! I'd better get back."

"Do you want me to go with you?" Mads asks.

"No. FaceTime me later." I hand her the glass.

"Love you," she says, and we hug. "I wish I knew what to do. If you don't want to talk to my mom, you should talk to Ms. Hernandez."

"Maybe."

I race home with my damaged heart.

BACK AT THE HOUSE, I open the door to Harry's pitiful pleas coming from the living room where I left him. He rolled part way under the sofa and got stuck. I maneuver him out slowly so he won't bonk his head and squeeze him to my chest. He and I are joined in this mess, each in our own way.

I kiss the brown fuzz on his head and tell him. "We're the miserable Jackson kids, buddy. You're the poor dude with no father, and I'm your big sister, the victim of an embezzlement."

We go into the kitchen where I can easily pacify him with milk, but there's nothing there to relieve my hurt.

If I could ignore Mom, I would, but she's too fragile. I should tread carefully around her. She's still my mother.

But before I go upstairs, I order takeout from Pino's. Pizza is my go-to food for the sads, but I'm not sure all the greasy goodness and spicy sauce in the world would cheer me up.

Harry's drunk from all the milk he had and weighs a ton as I carry him upstairs. I guess being wedged under the sofa for a while gives you a hearty appetite.

As we get closer to Mom's room, I hear her talking, which is rare these days. Since the pregnancy and birth, she's a quasi-hermit and rarely communicates with anyone, preferring to feast on her overcooked agony.

I lean by the door to listen with no regard about violating her privacy. Under current conditions, I'm entitled to know what's going on with her. Maybe this is why parents read their kid's diary, check their search history, and keep their cell phone tracker on. But for Mom and me this is inside-out or upside-down or just plain effed up. We are living in an alternate universe because I'm not supposed to be the parent here.

"Pat, please, we need your help." There's a tremor in her voice.

Why does she expose herself to Patrick, brother or not? He constantly berates her. When he heard about her pregnancy, he had the stones to tell her the baby was her biggest mistake ever.

Mom's silent for a while, listening to a ton of shit. When she does speak again, she says, "Maybe, if you're sure it's the right thing to do. That would help a lot. Yes, I understand what you want me to do. I'll watch for the mail."

I expect whatever he's helping her with will be as welcome as the worst case of diarrhea ever. He's that kind of guy. Her conversation ends, and I enter the room.

"Why were you talking to your brother again?" I ask not caring if she knows I was eavesdropping.

"Uncle Pat called to ask how I am," she replies.

Liar. Covering for her brother pisses me off.

"Did you tell him how great Harry's doing?" I ask.

Her eyes lower, and her cheeks drain their last molecule of color. "Of course."

Liar. Liar. Her brother treats Harry like an unwanted pest you have to flick away. He never came up to see her or the baby.

"Uncle Pat doesn't give a damn about Harry," I say.

"He cares in his own way. Sometimes people who don't have their own children don't understand all the complexities of families. Life presents you with complicated choices. I asked him for a loan," Mom says.

"You shouldn't have done that." Asking him for a favor is as risky as stepping in front of oncoming traffic. You might make it safely across, but you might also get hit and die. Either possibility leaves your heart pounding as you dodge the cars.

I bet he was ready with his quid pro quo. She takes time to reply, and I suspect she's hunting for her own inner editor to compose her response. My BS detector senses a major lie coming, so I jump in to thwart her attempt to concoct a story to protect her brother. I ask, "What did Uncle Pat say about lending us money?"

"He said he'd give us the money on one condition."

"Which is?" Jeez, I have to extract every last little detail from her.

She heaves out a guttural groan, followed by a sigh. "He said I have to change my situation. Perhaps I shouldn't have called him."

It's impossible to stifle my rising hostility, but I don't want to cause another panic attack, so my brain holds up a yellow traffic sign: proceed with caution.

"Mom, what's the condition? After what you did with my college money, you owe me the truth."

Her tone develops a robotic quality, neither loud nor soft, not happy or angry, she sounds more defeated like a wounded soldier on the battlefield waiting to bleed out. "The condition is to give up Harry, and he'll give us as much money as we need for your college and everything else until I can work again."

"What a colossal prick! Uncle Pat had two choices: either give us the damn loan with no conditions or don't. He's coming after Harry. Did you hang up on him? Did you tell him to bite you?" I already know she didn't even shout at him. I heard her. She shrank into a quivering ball of Jell-O rather than light up that arrogant gorilla who shares her DNA.

"I shouldn't have called, but I don't know what else to do, and maybe Harry would be better off with someone else. And you'd have all the money you need for college."

Would Mom trade Harry for my college funds? I don't want to believe that's possible, but I have to make my position crystal clear. "I won't go to college if Uncle Pat is paying for it. I'll never take a cent from him. He's not buying me. Period."

Is it possible to disown an uncle?

"I'm sorry," she says, which is fast becoming the most overused word in her vocabulary.

"Enough with the sorry! I'll come up with a plan, and Uncle Pat won't be part of it. Harry's not going anywhere. Come down to eat in an hour. I ordered pizza."

Harry and I retreat to his room, and I get him ready for bed. *I'll come up with a plan.* Who do I think I am? There's no magic wand under my mattress I can wave to produce a stack of money. I'm like Jack in the movie hanging onto the raft in the frozen sea as the Titanic sinks. He doesn't make it. On top of having no money for college, I have to make certain Mom keeps Harry.

Mom comes down to eat, and I put a slice of pizza on her plate. She picks at the pepperonis. We sit there together, each in our own misery. I can't forgive her. She should've trusted me enough to talk to me before she emptied her "special account." I'm not a child. Maybe we could've worked something out, but she never included me.

And I'm scared she'll compound her bad act by letting her brother take Harry. My uncle might want Harry to be the son he never had or he's only a way station until he ships Harry off to another family. Either way, it doesn't matter, because I'm not letting Harry go.

Mom says, "Patrick is sending a check and some papers for me to sign."

"Did he say what kind of papers?" I ask, wiping away the warm oil running down my chin.

"I'm not sure. Maybe it's for a loan."

"Promise me you won't sign anything before you show it to me. I think he's trying to persuade you to give Harry to him."

"I want to avoid a confrontation."

"And why I should give a damn about him getting mad?"

"You know, he was always there for me when we were growing up. Maybe he's right about what I should do, and if I don't agree, there could be payback."

She's been brainwashed. I stop eating and say, "I refuse to let you borrow money from him. He could offer us a million dollars, and I'd tell him to bury his sour dough."

He's such a friggin' big shot when everyone knows it isn't even actually his money. He struck gold marrying a woman whose family owns a chain of supermarkets down south. She's nice but a jellyfish. He probably bullies her too. I doubt his type has a shut-off switch.

"Mom, you shouldn't trust him. He does not care about Harry at all. We have to stick together on this."

"He's my brother."

"A sorry excuse for one. I hope my brother doesn't grow up to be like that. Promise me you won't sign any papers that have to do with Harry," I demand. Maybe I should introduce Pat to Chad, who's an expert on schooling bullies.

Mom gets up and brings her dish to the sink. "Clarry, will you clean up? The new pills make me sleepy. Dr. Goldstone says it will take time to get used to them."

What a stupid question. Don't I do most of the cleaning around here? After she leaves, I push my plate to the side, and my head drops to the table, which serves as a hard, unforgiving pillow.

I need for this day to end.

CHAPTER
9

I awake to discover Mother Nature and I are both in the dumps. She has decided to paint this day in shades of gray with a giant cloud cover that blocks every speck of blue sky. Drab and gloomy captures my mood completely.

I plunk Harry down on Mom's bed, hoping the stink of his loaded diaper will work like smelling salts and force open her puffy eyes. It works, and she leans in close to kiss him. Too bad he can't live off of those kisses, but he has a one-track mind and waits for her to produce a bottle. When none appears, he loses control and gives us his most heartfelt wail. I don't have time for Mom to get herself in gear, so I hoist the baby and his extra five smelly pounds so we can get ready.

Once he's fed and dressed, I bring him back to her. Now that his stomach is full, he may enjoy the kisses. I shower, dress, and eat some granola and yogurt, and then go get the baby. He's so happy with Mom, too bad he can't always get that from her.

When we get to the day care, Harry seems to be in a fine mood. I hand him over to the ever-cheerful Amelia, who is decked out in fire engine red from top-to-bottom. Harry is mesmerized by the color.

I'm almost at school when a weird sensation comes over me. *Does school still make sense the way it did only yesterday?* I probably already have almost enough credits to graduate, and there's no need for A's if the end is a job as a check-out person in the Stop and Shop. Pity overwhelms me, and I reverse direction to head for the main library to lick my wounds.

I text Mads not to wait for me at The Case, our usual meeting spot along with a hundred other kids. Someday, I'll have to find out who started the tradition of hanging out by the trophy case on the first floor. A bunch of us created a special Zoom group pretending we were at The Case when we were learning remotely.

> Not going to school today. Figuring stuff out now that my plans have been set ablaze in a massive bonfire.

> Are you okay?

> Fine.

> Are you sure? I can meet you later. Big English test this morning.

> I'm really okay. Call later.

A row of heart emojis ends my message.

In the library, I head upstairs and claim one of the empty study rooms that give people privacy to work or read or (even though you're not supposed to) sleep. I take out my notebook and write $20,000 on the top of a page, but I'm guessing our financial problem is a lot bigger than that.

I start my list of options. Number one: get a job. A job isn't a problem, but how much money can I make part-time? I power on my laptop to Google jobs in Newton. Most of them offer $15 an hour. Multiplying that by the number of hours I can realistically work and still go to school in the mornings is puny. At that rate, it'd take years to earn even half the $20,000.

So, I write number two: get a day care refund. I don't know if this is possible, but it's worth considering. If Mrs. Sample refunds half of our money, Harry could stay there until noon while I'm in class. But this plan means I definitely can't work. We'd have the $10,000 refund, but then there'd be no way of getting the rest of the money I need. That trade-off kind of sucks.

I add a number three and stare at the words, stumped. I don't have an inkling of a third idea. I highlight the words number three in yellow as if that might give me inspiration, but it doesn't. The ping of my phone breaks my agony. It's a text from Chad.

Are you sick?

No.

Mental health day?

Sort of. I'm at the main library.

I'm on my way.

Don't ditch school for me.

I'll do it for me. Where are you?

Second floor. Study room.

Coffee?

Oh, yes, please.

I add an emoji of a donut.

Got it. Don't move.

No place to go. I'm sinking fast.

Perhaps a kiss from a handsome prince will save you.

Did that dude use the K-word?

Very funny. No kiss needed.

While I wait for him, I start a new search for "make money fast."

I learn you can buy boxes of make-up for hundreds of dollars and try to sell them to your friends at a profit, or you can make telemarketing calls but you only get paid if someone buys something from you. I'm shocked by how many unbelievable schemes there are. I wouldn't get involved with any of those. Instead, I start doodling, waiting for the caffeine and deciding if Chad was trying to be funny about the kiss. He couldn't think I'd let him kiss me. It would be like cheating on Mads.

Chad opens the door to the study room and puts two cups of coffee and a bag on the table. I open it immediately and dive into a glazed donut, hoping the sugar will lift my mood. Chad sits opposite me and cranes his neck to read my notebook upside down.

"What's all that?" he asks, sipping his coffee.

"This is my attempt to fix my sorry life. I had everything mapped out for college, and now I have to regroup. I don't have any money for college, not even for application fees. My mom used it all for Harry's day care."

"That sucks. But you can get student loans."

"My dad would plop out a brick if he thought I was taking loans for everything. He's a madman about not going into debt, and you know how much I hate owing people."

"You've made that evident from day one. Can I read what you wrote?" he asks. I nod, and he turns the notebook to study my laughable attempt to make new plans.

He turns to a blank page in the notebook and says, "You don't have the big picture. Your mom may have equity in the house. That could make a difference."

"Equity in a house? Is that equity like equal rights? I need money, not fairness."

Chad laughs. "So, equity has another meaning. It's, like, your assets. Your house is equity, but it may have a mortgage too. Does your mother have a mortgage?"

"How do you know all this?"

"My father's desperate for me to work in his business. He's

always on a tear teaching me about real estate, but that's his passion, not mine."

"And what is your passion?"

"Not marketing and finance." He makes a face like his donut was dipped in vinegar. "I want to study anthropology. I have lots of questions rattling around in my head about diversity in humans and how they developed their physical and social traits. How did different groups adapt to life and survive, or didn't survive? I want to understand what happened to people hundreds or thousands of years ago. My dad claims that's a rubbish subject and insists I need a practical education. He lays down decrees for the rest of us, and we're supposed to obey."

"We?"

"Three younger sisters who, by the way, think I'm the best thing that ever happened to them. I'm the god-king of big brothers."

"So, even families with a gazillion dollars have problems."

He picks up the pen and writes on the blank page: Mortgage? Retirement funds? Savings? Other assets? "You need to ask your mother about this."

"I'm not sure she's in the right frame of mind for me to bring this up. Her head's not in the game."

A series of pings from my phone. I know what they are without looking. Mom has been sorry-texting me all morning. "Sorry." "Forgive me." "Please call me." "Are you okay?" or "I can fix this." I delete all of them. Melanie Jackson is on her great apology tour, but I'm not hopping aboard that train. I don't reply.

"My mother." I look up at Chad.

"Aren't you texting back?"

"Not now." I know that makes me look bad, but I can't help it.

"I understand. You need time. That happens to me with my dad. Come to school tomorrow and to the football game?"

"Did you text Mads like you promised?"

"I did," Chad replies, "And she's coming to my house Saturday to find something in my wardrobe for the senior dance. Happy?"

"Yes. You two will have fun."

"Did you buy your ticket for the dance?" he asks.

"No, and I probably won't. I feel like high school is kind of over for me. Besides, I should be careful about spending money we might not have."

Chad makes his adorable frowny face. He's not happy with my answer, but he drops it and so do I.

I pack up my computer and stuff. We clean off the table. Chad drives me to Sunny Acres because I decide to bust the kid out early today.

Chad asks if it's okay for him to wait and meet Harry. That's sweet.

"Sure."

I wheel Harry out in his stroller, and Chad crouches beside him and lifts the baby's hand to high-five him.

"Hey, little dude, wassup in day care land?" He leans his head closer to Harry's and whispers in his ear. Harry grins, probably from the feel of Chad's hot breath.

"What did you tell him?" I ask.

"Buds don't snitch on each other, woman. That's rule number one in the brotherhood. Ask any guy."

"Thanks again for the coffee. We've got to get home."

"Get some information on your finances, and I'll try to help you understand what it means and if there are options to get some money. Hang in there, Claire."

"No other choice."

HARRY and I enter a dark house. Maybe they shut off our electricity. Perhaps Mom forgot to pay that bill too. I glance into the living room and she's in the chair. I flick the light switch, and she raises her arm to shield her eyes from the sudden brightness. At least we have electricity.

"Why are you sitting in the dark? You're scaring me." I put Harry down on the floor and move in closer to Mom.

"Look at me, please," I beg. "I need to know you're okay."

"I'm sorry, Claire. I have no right to ask to be forgiven."

"Please look at me," I repeat. She does, and her blue irises are surrounded by pools of red. I fling my arms around her neck and hold on to her, as if she might vanish if I let go. "Mom, it's all right. I'm okay. We'll figure something out. I promise." I reassure her because staying angry will only make everything worse. I wipe the rivulets on her cheeks, before I spot a box of tissues nearby and give her a bunch. Lucky Harry has no idea what's going on. I glance over at him, wishing we could switch places just this once.

Mom replies, "That's what Dr. Goldstone said. We had a session today, and I confessed my sin. He told me not to get bogged down on those problems until I'm better, but I want to make things right for you. I feel so much guilt; sometimes it doesn't let me breathe."

Harry does his did-you-forget-about-me whine. "I'll get his bottle. Hold him for a minute." I put him on her lap and hope I don't hear a thud while I'm in the kitchen. I come back and take him from her and sit on the sofa.

Since her hyperventilation incident, I've been worrying about her driving to her appointments. This is as good a time as any to deal with that. Maybe she feels guilty enough to agree to anything I want.

"From now on, I don't think you should drive. You aren't steady. I can take you to appointments or you could take an Uber."

And once again, the long tentacles of this role reversal Mom and I are acting out wrap us in a tight bundle. I hate hearing myself as the parent lecturing her kid about driving carefully or not getting into the car with someone who's impaired. But maybe lots of Ubers are a luxury we can't afford.

"Okay," she replies without argument. Either she realizes I'm right, or her guilt makes her agree. Who the hell cares? It's done.

"Mom, do you have a mortgage?"

"Why do you ask?"

"The econ teacher was explaining equity. Do we have any equity?" My lying is improving. The lies flow so effortlessly these days.

"There's a small mortgage. Most of the house is paid off. I don't remember how much is left."

"Did you use up all of my college money?"

"There's a little left, but we need that to pay bills, too. Pat will give us a loan."

"Not happening. I'm going to find a solution that doesn't involve him. In the meantime, you have to get better."

While Harry's on my lap, he squirms and twist his neck about forty-five degrees so he can stare at Mom. Usually, his focus stays on his bottle in case it might disappear if he diverts his eyes, but today he must sense something isn't right. Maybe he understands more than I give him credit for.

⚏

LATER THAT EVENING, I research equity and mortgage. It's confusing, but what's clear is if you don't pay your mortgage, they can take your house away. Foreclosure, it's called.

Maybe number three on my how-to-get-money list should be to sell the house and move into an apartment somewhere cheaper than pricey Newton. I could get my college money back, and we'd have enough to live on until Mom can work. I write this option down; seeing it on paper makes my head spin. The thought of leaving my friends and finishing high school in a different town is painful.

To make myself feel better, I add a number four to my list: win the lottery without buying tickets with money we don't have.

CHAPTER 10

"You look like cold shit," Mads says the next morning when we meet at the side door before school.

"Thanks."

"Seriously, babe, you've got a ton going on, but that hair and outfit are *not* acceptable." She makes a motion with her finger, instructing me to follow her. When I don't move fast enough for her, she grabs my arm and drags me to the restroom by her mother's office. Students avoid this bathroom because it's too easy for Mrs. Sunday to slink in for a quick check. No one wants to be chatting behind a stall door with the vice principal present.

"I'm behind on the laundry," I say, defending my choice of clothes today. "Harry keeps spitting up on me, and I have to change all the time."

"I can't give you any clothes, but I can do a few things to help. Mads breaks out her hairbrush and a scrunchie from her bag and starts to pull through some painful knots.

"It's not just the no money thing," I say. "My uncle is threatening to make my mother give up Harry in exchange for a loan. She never could stand up to him. My dad used to run interference with him, but now she has only me."

"Why does he want Harry?" She questions me while applying lip gloss. I'm savoring the luxury of being taken care of for a change. I've forgotten what that feels like.

"I don't know if his plan is to keep Harry for himself, or if he's only a stopover until the baby is shipped off to another family. He wants my mother to resume her before-Harry life, but that can't happen. I think she'd never forgive herself if she agreed to that. Harry and I might have to run away."

"Are you demented? You have no money, and you want to hide out with a baby? Get real. Why don't you talk to your mother's doctor and find out what's going on with her? And talk to my father, too."

"Why do you think I need a lawyer?"

"Stop trying to go this alone. My father's a great lawyer, and he loves you."

Mads finishes me off with some blush.

I say, "I'll ask about seeing her doctor. There may be privacy issues, and I have no money to pay your father."

"My dad wouldn't charge my best friend."

"Thanks."

"You should've been here yesterday. Every girl in school managed to hang at The Case, circling Chad like sharks after chum. I wanted to kick their butts. But at least he asked me for a date. Who do you think gave him my number so he could text me?" she asks.

"Probably one of the football guys."

She puts away the make-up.

"A date," I say, pretending to be surprised, but hating myself for the deceit. "After all, you are irresistible, Madison." Once they're a couple, I can tell her everything, or maybe I'll have to take this secret to the grave.

"Aw..."

A few freshmen enter the restroom but flee when they see us. In the beginning of the year, the ninth-graders are jumpy about encroaching on seniors' space. I was the same way. All I could do was gawk at the upperclassmen.

Mads continues, "This is the first positive sign from Chad. He lives near the country club in Waban, probably in a mansion. I can't wait to get my hands on him and..." Her voice trails off, but her meaning is made obvious by her blush. "I'm bummed I've got to miss the football game today. I'll be in the dentist's chair with his metal torture tool stretching my lips into the next state. Are you going, babe?" she asks.

"Yup, until I have to jet out to do my Sunny Acres run."

"Tell me if Chad says anything about me."

When we get to her homeroom, Mads says, "You could apply for student loans."

That is a suggestion I expect to hear a lot, but being in debt isn't part of my future. I steel my spine, knowing what I'm about to say next will freak her out. "We might have to move to save money."

"Out of Newton!" she screams as her eyeballs pop out. "You *cannot* do that! I won't allow it!"

"Believe me, it's the last thing I want. The whole idea gives me a migraine."

"Claire, find another way. Talk to Ms. Hernandez. There may be a ton of options to get college money. You have a great GPA. Promise me you'll make an appointment with her immediately."

She stares at me until I promise, and then her eyeballs retreat into their sockets.

⚏

Lunch at our table is different today because none of the guys shows up. Without the dynamics they bring, the girls let themselves get silly.

When our lunch period ends and we're at the door, Charlie, Nando, and Chad cruise in. Chad bumps into me, and I'm sure it was intentional.

"Hey, you dropped your dance ticket," he says to me.

"Ticket?" I ask, bewildered. I didn't drop anything, and I didn't buy a ticket.

"For the dance," he says and picks something up off the floor.

Mads is beside me and laughing. "Oh, babe, take good care of your ticket. It's a valuable piece of paper."

"That isn't mine," I say.

"Then why are your initials in the corner?" Chad sticks the ticket in front of my face, and sure enough, the letters CJ are in red in the corner. Chad's eyes have an extra dose of glitter and a heap of mischief. Again, he pushes the ticket toward me while tipping his head to one side as a signal for me to take it.

"Put it in your bag where you won't lose it," Mads orders.

I don't want to make this into a bigger deal, so I take the ticket "I dropped." During the ticket transfer, Chad's and my hand touch, and in a flash, he twists his hand so our palms come together. He wraps his fingers around my hand. I want to pull away, but I don't. I luck out that Mads and Alvene are too busy dishing about the new young English teacher, who graduated college about an hour ago, and they don't notice what just happened. The feel of his skin leaves my hand warm and tingling all the way up my arm.

"Madison is right," Chad says. "This ticket is special. Don't lose it."

"I won't." I put it in my backpack. Now I have a ticket, but it's a toss-up if I'll be able to go.

LATER THAT AFTERNOON at the football game, I choose a seat on the top row of the cold metal bleachers next to Alvene and Chloe, wishing I'd brought a blanket. It's not supposed to be this frosty so early in the fall. My legs are freezing through my jeans, and my butt is two giant ice cubes. At least my orange-and-black beanie is keeping my head warm.

Wellesley is one of our main rivals, which accounts for all the noise coming from both sides. Depending on who has the ball, everyone's either yelling for a touchdown or screaming for defense as if shouting alone could make it happen.

Chad's football number is ten. A coincidence? I think not. My eyes follow him, running the length of the field on long, muscular legs. He isn't afraid to mix it up and is often at the bottom of a pile of players. He's a fierce competitor.

During halftime, I stroll around with Alvene and Chloe, warming my muscles. The game is tied, which makes it seem as if the first half didn't even exist and the game is starting over. We return to our seats, and this time, I take out a couple of notebooks from my backpack and sit on them to separate my lower cheeks from the icy bleachers.

Charlie has the ball, and a Wellesley player tangles his legs with Charlie's and face-plants hard. When the Wellesley dude gets back on his feet, he brushes dirt from his pants and body-checks Charlie, who loses his balance and also goes down. Other players step in to separate them, and the refs ignore it. There are no penalties.

In the last few minutes, the Tigers challenge the Wellesley team close to the goal line. I hold my breath when Chad gets the pass and scores. Everyone on our side of the field is on their feet, shouting, and high-fiving each other. The Wellesley side is silent.

We won! The other guys try to hoist Chad onto their shoulders, but they can't quite get him up there, so they settle for the usual back and butt slaps to express their excitement.

When the teams line up to shake hands, I notice that Chad changes his place until he's standing next to Charlie. The Wellesley player who mixed it up with Charlie passes by and leans in to say something to Charlie and then the Wellesley guy falls down. It's weird. From this angle, I can't be certain what happened. Chad offers the opponent his hand to get up, which the kid refuses. The lines break up, and everyone returns to their bench.

Defeating Wellesley is epic. This win may send our team to the play-offs, and Chad's the hero.

I hang by the fence, waiting for the coach to release the players from what seems like an extra-long after-game huddle, and I'm running out of time

When Chad does jog over, I only have a couple of minutes to talk.

"Great game," I say.

"Those Wellesley guys are bums," he says.

"What happened?"

"One guy was going off on Charlie the whole game."

"Like how?"

Chad stares at me intensely. "Like racist shit I'm not repeating."

"What a jackass."

"Exactly. I wasn't having that. He and his puny pine nuts needed a lesson, and I supplied his instruction."

"Huh?"

"When we lined up after the game, that mother—, I mean piece of scum, was still coming in hot, so my foot might've stretched out too far while we were shaking hands. Perhaps the kid tripped over my size twelve cleats," Chad smirks. "Accidents do happen."

"Aren't you afraid?"

"Afraid of some snotty Wellesley kid? Are you joking?"

"I mean, aren't you scared you'll get in trouble?"

"I thought you knew me," he says in a tone I've never heard him use. "I'm not taking crap from anyone. Good trouble. Do you know what 'good trouble' means?"

"Yes, but I don't remember whether it was James Clyburn or John Lewis who said that."

"It was Lewis, a great man. He told us to get into good trouble, necessary trouble. I'm not going through life timid. That's one thing I learned from my father: be strong and let no one get by you. I'm not hiding in the corner when injustice is obvious."

"You're right, of course. But why didn't Charlie stand up to him?"

"Good question. Some people can't or won't confront. When Charlie let it pass, I had to deal with the ignorant fool. I put him on the ground, but hell, I didn't punch him."

"So, this is like what happened at your old school?"

"Oh, that guy I actually punched, but only once. Another Chad Williams lesson, free of charge."

"You are an engaged teacher. Lucky students. And you put the win in Newton's column."

"If someone tells Coach what I did, he might suspend me for a few games. Unsportsmanlike, blah, blah, blah."

"Why would he suspend you? You won the game." I can't wait

around for Chad's reply. "I've got to dash before Harry gets tossed off the Sunny Acres team. Call me later."

"Can I come over this weekend?"

"Sure. Give me your phone. I'll give you my mom's address."

After the divorce, I started referring to "Mom's house" and "Dad's house" as if I no longer had "my house."

"It's a date," he says. What is with this guy? He said the D-word again. These sly comments have to end. He's supposed to be focusing on Mads. I'll have to be more aggressive with him about dating Mads.

I speed-walk to Sunny Acres, rehashing in my mind what Chad said about the game. I'm not into violence, but maybe sometimes it's justified even when it isn't technically self-defense. As my English teacher would say, "This requires more deconstructing."

I make it to the day care just in the nick of time. That was too close. There's only Harry and one other baby still there. Mrs. Sample is singing to them and stops when I enter.

"Sorry if I'm late," I say. I'm sure she can hear I'm out of breath.

"Not late, dear, right on time," she replies.

I put Harry's backpack under the stroller. "Mrs. Sample, in case I have to be late sometime, could I have my friend Mads, I mean Madison, pick up Harry?"

"For security, the only people who can pick up a child have to be approved by the parent or guardian. Your mother is the only one with the legal authority to do that for Harry. She'd have to submit a form for your friend. Shall I get you one?"

"Maybe another time. Thank you."

I thought it would be the smart and conscientious thing to do to have an alternate pick-up person. It's unfair I do all the bringing and picking up for day care and can't make the simplest decisions for Harry. For now, I put the idea of Mads on the pick-up list on hold, because discussing it with Mom might ramp up her anxiety if she thinks she can't rely on me. But the beginnings of a solution to all these problems are taking shape, and Mads is right: I need a lawyer.

CHAPTER
11

My weekend is filled with grocery shopping and laundry and even having to wash the sticky kitchen floor. I bring in a basket of clean clothes to Mom's room, and my eyes are drawn to the array of pill bottles on display on the nightstand. It's hard to believe that all these chemicals are good for you. They'd be worth it if they helped, but whatever she's taking isn't working.

This morning, I'm waiting for Mads to call and report on her night with Chad. Her call probably won't come until noon. I remember those luxurious days of staying in bed late on a Sunday, but Harry forbids sleeping in.

The Facetime call comes at about 12:30.

"It was perfect, babe," Mads gushes and even just awake with her hair all over the place, she's still fab. Messy chic in her cute polka-dot short pj's.

"I'm calling it our first date. His closet is a walk-in, almost the size of my whole bedroom. His parents were out, and we had tons of privacy, but he never made a move on me. Isn't that strange?"

"Yeah, you'd think he'd be a playa." I laugh when I hear myself use that slang, but Mads has a point. Chad has a beautiful girl in his bedroom with no parents around and doesn't try to score. Baffling. Most guys would be panting at their good luck unless they go another way.

"Maybe he got burned by a girl at his old school," I say, trying to provide a possible explanation. "Or he doesn't get involved during football season so he can keep his headspace clear for the games. Forget about it for now. I have positive feels for you two."

Mads props her phone on her pillow and holds her hands

together in a prayerful pose in response to my comment. "And I think pink."

"Pink what?"

"Chad and I will wear pink to the dance. Some guys are hot in pink, and it's a great color for me, too. Matching announces we're a couple."

"He agreed?" This doesn't sound like Chad, but perhaps I've misread him.

"I didn't mention the matching thing to him. I told him his wardrobe was lacking a pink shirt. After all, that's what a good consultant does. Find the holes in his wardrobe and fill them. We're going to go shopping together for the dance. That'll be our official second date."

"Way to go, girl!" I reply and breathe easy. *Mission accomplished, Claire.* "Mads, you know, it's the twenty-first century, and he may be waiting for you to get things rolling. The age of consent has arrived."

"Ya' think? If nothing happens soon, I'll go on the offensive. You and I can evaluate the sitch at the dance."

"If I'm there."

"No trying, and no ifs. You must be there!"

"My mom isn't reliable. If she was Harry's nanny, I'd fire her."

"Can't you get someone to stay with her?"

"If she agrees."

"Make her agree, Claire Bear. She owes you a ton after what she did. Did you ever tell your dad what's going on with your mother?" Mads asks.

"No. This isn't his problem."

"But you are."

"He's busy with his new family and adorable little Bella." Ugh, I sound snarky about a toddler. *Check yourself, Claire, that isn't worthy.*

"She's not his kid." Straightforward as always, Mads never holds back.

"But Bella lives with him, and he loves taking care of her. If I bother him, his wife will classify me as the typical spoiled stepdaughter, demanding attention."

"What are you doing today?" Mads asks.

"Laundry and homework."

"You are getting so boring, Claire."

"Here's the good news. My mom agreed to let me talk to her doctor and set up an appointment for this week."

"Well, halla-hella-luyah. Now you're talking. Meet Chad and me at The Case tomorrow before homeroom." Mads drags out his name as if she wants to keep it in her mouth as long as she can.

"Okay."

We hang up, and for the rest of my Sunday I do adult stuff, even waking Mom to get her to eat. After I take Harry's clothes out of the dryer, I cut off the footie parts before his toes permanently curl. I've wanted to do that for weeks. If the credit card works, I'll order him some larger clothes. I should ask Mads to help me pick out his clothes. She can be Harry's fashion guru too.

Chad texts about coming over later. I thought he'd forget about that after his evening with Mads. I'm not sure I want him to observe my chaos at home. Before Harry, having someone over was not so friggin' complicated. But I say yes. Maybe he'll give me the low down on why there was no action with Mads last night.

I tell Mom Chad's coming over and stress that if she wants to meet him, she must fix her hair and be in mom-suitable clothes and that doesn't mean baggy sweats.

"I'll try," she says.

Mushy answer, as expected. Asking her to meet Chad is a real crapshoot. Sometimes she seems better, but most often she doesn't have the energy or focus to carry on a conversation. I wonder if the problem isn't that the pills aren't working, but that she isn't even taking them. I once saw a movie where a patient stashed his medication in the cuff of his pants. He didn't get caught, but he didn't get better either.

"And one more thing," I say to her. "The fall senior dance is next

Friday. I want to go, but I don't think you should stay alone. Maybe Becky can come over?"

Oh, hell, now I'm effing arranging a babysitter for my mother. How much worse can things get here? I'm not sure how much Becky knows about Mom's condition, and my guess is not a lot, but I want to go to the dance, and Becky is Mom's closest friend in Newton.

"I owe you that. There's so much for me to make up for."

"I forgive you, Mom." What else can I say? She's my mother, and she's suffering. If I stay angry, I'll feel like a dog.

CHAD SHOWS up around eight and hands me a brown bag. "Open it."

The aroma of chocolate fills the air. I stick my nose inside and inhale the sweetness. "Hmm, so you're a baker too," I say.

"Me? No. These are my grandma's special, amazing, life-altering brownies."

I take one out and finish it off in about two bites. "You do not exaggerate. They're amazing, but life-altering? Whatever do you mean? Are these spiked with substances?" I ask, though I'm pretty sure Chad isn't into that poison, and I better not be wrong. I'm paranoid about that stuff, because I don't want any photos of me with my eyes unfocused at half-mast surfacing when I'm running for office.

Chad reaches in the bag for a brownie and says, "I want you to meet my grandmother. She's special."

"So is mine."

"Don't want to argue, but my gran will stack up against anyone's."

"This isn't a competition, Chad. Just setting the record straight, but you can't meet my grandmother. She's in a home for old people in New York and often doesn't remember who I am. She confuses me with my mother. But before she got sick, she was the best grandmother in the world."

I linger in my warm memories of my grandmother cooking my

favorite foods, sewing my Halloween costumes, and singing to me in languages I didn't understand, with melodies I'll never forget. I lost her, and in a different way, I'm on the verge of losing my mother.

"Where is the future all-star?" Chad asks.

"Asleep. And about that ticket to the dance," I begin.

"You mean *your* ticket?"

"You can drop the pretense. I didn't buy that ticket."

"Actually, no one said you bought it." He smiles. "Just said it was yours and had your initials on it. Do you dispute that?"

"Uh...no."

"And do I get a 'thank you' for having Madison pick out my dance clothes?"

"Yeah, I heard it was a big success and you are going to the mall together."

"You're welcome."

"Why am I welcome?" I ask.

"Because I did that for you, or did you forget that you made me?"

"But you had fun."

"Madison is great. We laughed a lot, and now I've got a pile of clothes to give away. Some of them are from middle school when I was short and skinny."

"Someone will be lucky to get them. Glad you two are on track."

"On track for what?"

"For being a couple."

"Hang on, I didn't say anything about that." Chad wags his finger in my face. "So, I ask you, Claire Jackson, don't I get a say in who I want to be with?"

"Of course you do, but everyone wants to be with Madison. You'd be the envy of lots of hungry Newton North dudes."

He wiggles his chair to be closer to mine and says, "You asked me to text Madison, and I did. I invited her to my house to investigate what's in my closet. I'm letting her pick out a pink shirt for me, but you can't dictate who my girlfriend should be. I do have free will, you know."

"I know that. And people shouldn't tell other people who they can or can't love or dance with."

"And I can play at that too, so if you want me to set you up with someone," he snickers, "I'll gladly do that for you. I can play matchmaker too. I even have a brother in mind."

Is he riffing or serious?

"Don't tell me who you're thinking of. My life is already an over-packed suitcase that can't close. Adding in a relationship will break the hinges forever."

We both take a second brownie, and I don't know how, but it's even better than the first one. Perhaps there's a secret ingredient in them after all, because as I swallow each bite of fudgy goodness, it releases bits of tension in me. These brownies could be addictive.

Mom comes into the kitchen and joins us at the table. I offer her a brownie, but she refuses. Her hair is brushed and pulled into a neat bun. She's wearing jeans and a plaid tunic that hides how thin she is, but her clothes are fresh and clean, and I'm grateful for that. I introduce her to Chad.

"I understand you go to school with Clarry," she says, pissing me off because I asked her not to call me Clarry anymore for obvious reasons.

Chad chuckles. "Clarry and Harry. You're the rhyming sibs."

I shoot him a stink eye and say, "Claire to you, buddy."

"Got it," he says, but he doesn't lose the grin.

Mom asks Chad some boring standard questions adults ask: how do you like school, where are you applying to college, do you have any brothers and sisters? Chad replies respectfully, and when Mom runs out of steam, she makes an excuse about having to go to return some emails.

That went more smoothly than I anticipated, which proves there is a regular mother lurking in there somewhere.

"Your mother seems nice."

"She is, but before Harry arrived, she was more fun, talkative, and friendly."

"Maybe someday I'll meet your dad. Does he come here often?"

"Actually, since he got remarried, he comes much less. He's busy. I go there when I can, but not now. Harry needs me."

"Does Harry ever see his father?" Chad asks. It's such a logical, straightforward question, but I hate it. With anyone else I'd stonewall but talking to Chad is getting to be easy, like with Mads.

"Only Mads knows the truth about Harry's father. I'm going to tell you, but I have to swear you to secrecy."

"Shall we make a blood oath? I'll cut my finger. I'll do whatever you want to prove you can trust me."

"No blood. I'm going to trust you, New Boy. Harry's father is unknown," I say. "My mother left that line blank. You know, the line on the birth certificate that asks for the father's name? I know what you're thinking, but I swear my mom isn't like that. This was some idiotic one-night stand, and she doesn't remember the guy's full name if she ever knew it. How pathetic is that? Harry's dad is a phantom."

"Not judging," Chad says. "That will be rough for the dude when he grows up."

"That's his fate, and life's rough sometimes."

"Yes, it is. And I've been suspended from football for a few days. Someone on our team sold me out to the coach for tripping the Wellesley kid intentionally."

"Why would anyone do that?"

"I'm still the new guy, and dragging me might be part of my initiation. Also, there are some guys who believe they can only rise to the top by stepping over others in their way. They treat people like those little fake rocks you put your feet on at a climbing wall."

"They sound like my uncle, who's a lifetime—no, actually a founding member—of the back-stabbers club, and guess who his latest target is? Forget it, don't guess. It's Harry."

"What can he do to a baby?"

"He can pressure my mother to give him up for adoption. He thinks Harry is a gigantic mistake."

"Your uncle sounds like a snake."

"He is, but I've been working on a plan that will wall off Harry from falling into his clutches."

"What is it?"

"It's not quite ripe for the telling. Let's get back to you. Why didn't you tell your coach what the kid said to Charlie?"

"Not my style to ruin someone's life if I don't have to, even if he is a bigot. Coach would get our parents involved, and before you know it, the incident would become a missile with no guidance system. Plus, what if Charlie doesn't want this spilling into the public arena? I sent my message to the jerk, and if it was received, he won't be spewing that garbage again. There are boundaries to acceptable trash talk. No slurs. Period."

"That never occurred to me. What a nightmare if parents and principals, and who knows who else, had to get involved. Much better that you settled it." I slap my palms together as if to signal "case closed."

"Say a prayer this doesn't get over-blown and make Coach feel compelled to mention it to my father. He won't be pleased if I'm in trouble. I didn't realize how late it is. I've got to get home. And now it's your turn to meet my family. I'll check with my father on the best day."

"Your father? I would've thought your mother would handle things like that."

"My father rules, and she's his loyal subject. Besides, his schedule is jammed with tons of business meetings."

"Are you his loyal subject too?"

"Sort of. He can't make me do anything legally because I'm nineteen, but he's a force, and it's tricky to find a balance with him. I just want my own life."

"Nineteen and a senior? How did that happen?"

"Some rich parents start their sons a year late in school so they'll be taller and bigger than the others in their class, and they can dominate in sports."

"That assumes their kid even has athletic talent," I say.

"When you travel in the rarified circles of the wealthy and mighty of Newton, everyone's supposed to be born with talent. It comes with the money."

"Conventional wisdom says that everyone in Newton is rich, but it's bunk. My uncle's brain works the same way as those people. He believes having loads of money grants you special powers. And by the way, I'm not even eighteen yet."

"A seventeen-year-old baby," he says with a laugh.

"Yup, I'm a baby taking care of a baby. And if I come to your house, I'll probably have to bring you-know-who with me."

"My sisters will go bonkers for him. Harry must come."

"Do you want to ask Mads, I mean, Madison, too? She'd love it."

He loses the smile. His eyes narrow and his nostrils flare. I've never seen him so upset. Whoa, baby, I touched a live wire.

"Enough with pushing Madison on me. If I want her to come for dinner to my house, I'll decide, not you," he snarls. I was only trying to boost their relationship. I wasn't expecting a slap-down.

"No. I was suggesting—"

"If it isn't a rule or a condition, then the answer is no. Free will, remember?"

"I'm sorry. I just thought—" I pause there and then say, "You're right." I back off, recognizing how furious I'd be if Chad insisted he'd only come to my house if he could bring Nando or Charlie with him.

Chad opens the door to leave, glances back, and his amazing grin has returned. "No worries, Clarry." He waits for me to explode on him for using that name, but I can't. It's too sweet the way he says it.

I go upstairs to thank Mom for coming down to meet Chad, but she's not there. I call for her, and there's no answer. I glance in Harry's room. No sign of her. I check the living room, and she isn't in her recliner. Then I notice the door to the dreaded basement is open. I negotiate the narrow stairs that threaten to send you tumbling with the slightest misstep. The place is soaked in dinginess and discharges a musty odor that's permanently built into the walls.

This was a no-go zone for me when I was small. I was afraid of the dark corners and the shadows and the creaky noises that meant someone was hiding, waiting to jump out and kill me. Dad tried lots of techniques to trick me into going into the basement alone to cure my fears, but it usually made everything worse. I hated that he thought I was such a coward.

Mom's sitting at the bottom of the stairs. I join her. I'm not sure what to say, so we sit quietly without an inch of space between us. We stay like that for a few minutes before I take her hand and lead her upstairs.

Back in her room I ask, "What were you doing in the basement?"

"Nothing... I forgot. I think I was looking for something."

She doesn't ask me anything about Chad but cooperates when I help her get ready for bed and having to do that makes me feel awful. Dr. Goldstone, I have a lot of questions for you.

CHAPTER
12

On the day of my appointment with my mother's therapist, my gut morphs into an atom collider and whatever is bombarding my insides hurts. I'm angry at myself for being this nervous when technically this appointment isn't about me. I'm determined to find out whether Mom has been honest with her doctor, or if she's given him a glossy, edited version of her reality.

I leave school before lunch and follow the GPS's instructions to go south on Route 1, the old highway that's now a two-lane road chock-a-block with strip malls on both sides. I drive into the parking lot in front of a three-story nondescript building. It's a big brick box with boring windows and no style. This place is too depressing for the already depressed.

I'm early, so I wait in the car, trying to stay calm. At precisely 1 p.m., I knock on the door of suite 15, and a welcoming, if muffled, "Come in" greets me.

Dr. Goldstone is a white-haired man whose shirt is one size too small and has gaps over his belly. His untidy appearance makes me uneasy until he lifts his chin and I'm sucked in by warm, blue eyes that could only belong to someone kind. They're a lot like Mom's before all her crying cost them their captivating glow.

Dr. Goldstone points to the chairs in front of him, and I sit, scanning the room discreetly to get a sense of this man. The shelves behind his desk overflow with books crammed in without order. I'd love to ask if he's read them all or if he's trying to impress his patients. A corner of his humongous desk is filled with the kind of things people collect on their travels to remind them of where they've been. I'm tempted to pick up the giant conch shell and listen for the ocean's roar, but the doctor might start analyzing my actions too. Maybe he uses this stuff to jump-start a conversation with a reluctant patient.

"Claire. Claire, I'm so happy to meet you," he says with way too much enthusiasm. I hope he doesn't add the trite line, "I've heard so much about you," which leaves you feeling exposed, almost naked.

But he can't resist. "I've heard a lot about you," he says with a broad smile. If I were keeping score, and I may be doing just that, I'd say strike one against the doctor.

"So how does it feel to be a big sister?" An unimaginative opening question. Strike two on the doc.

Why didn't he ask me how it feels to have a mom who gets pregnant with a mystery guy, who uses my college money for the kid's day care, and frosts that cake by sinking into profound despair? I'd say those are the questions he should be asking.

But if I don't answer, my silence might be misinterpreted, and I may be judged as much by what I don't say as what I do. I run through a quick internal debate whether to rattle on about how Harry's the best thing that ever happened to us or throw him under the bus and blame him for stealing my future.

Instead, I find a middle ground and reply, "It's fine. He's cute."

Asked and answered, Dr. Goldstone. He writes on a pad, ensuring my comment will become part of the file for all time.

"Yes, indeed," he says. "I've seen his picture, and the resemblance to you is remarkable."

"Maybe he's a double of his father, but we'll never know that, will we?" I say, shooting an arrow into the heart of the problem.

"Does not knowing who the father is affect what you think of your mother?"

Now he's making this about me. Why does he care about my opinion? I don't want you probing my mind, Doctor. Strike three.

"Shouldn't it bother me?" I grumble. "Would it bother my mother if the situation was reversed, and I had no explanation about what I had done and with whom?"

"Yes, I can understand your feeling. Your mother mentioned you have questions for me, and she gave consent to discuss her treatment, and if we step into an area of patient confidentially, I'll let you know."

"I don't see any improvement with all the medication."

He replies, "With some people, the medications take longer to achieve maximum effectiveness. The psychiatrist who prescribes her medication and I are in constant communication. For the time being, we have to be patient, but if your mother doesn't improve, we'll make some changes."

"She's definitely not any better. She sleeps a lot, picks at her food, and has lost weight. Did she tell you how anxious she gets when I leave Harry with her for a few hours?"

"No, but you should tell me."

I give him the highlights about life with Mom and Harry. The doctor makes notes and says, "You're right to be upset. It isn't easy to understand what's going on. You probably expected she'd be able to care of her baby, but she can't. Not right now. What else is on your mind?"

"What can be done to help get her back to work? We need the money. I'm sure by now her clients have found someone else to handle their websites, and she may have to start her business from scratch."

"Yes, that's a problem, but she needs to regain her equilibrium and confidence first. The medications and our sessions should help with that. Your mother says you do a lot for Harry and around the house. Can you keep that up until the pills kick in?"

"Do I have a choice? If I don't do it, who will? There is only me to take care of Harry until Mom is better."

"Do you have enough money for food and bills?" he asks. "There are resources available for help in these situations unless you have family or friends for that."

"We're okay for now. My best friend's father is helping us, and my mother's friend is always around. We have lots of support," I white-lie. I'm hyper-afraid to involve "resources" that could claim Harry should be taken out of the house.

To prove I'm not an ignorant child, I say, "I'm studying our finances, and we might sell the house and move into a smaller place."

The doctor puts down his pen. "Claire, if you can wait on talking to your mother about moving, you should. A major change at this time might be more than she can handle."

"Okay," I say, kind of embarrassed I never considered that angle. *Doc, I'm removing one of your strikes.* If Mom got worse because I made her sell the house, that would be on me. And I'd be joining her wallowing in guilt.

Then, for a reason I don't understand, except perhaps I need a brief distraction from the intensity of all this, I pick up the conch shell and put it to my ear. The roar of the ocean makes me smile. The doctor watches me. This might be one of those priceless do-not-touch objects people own. I replace it gingerly.

The doctor removes his half-frame glasses and lets them hang from a cord around his neck. "I have a question for you. Would you describe the day Harry was born?"

Why is he asking about this? Maybe he wants to compare Mom's birth story and mine to see if we agree? I have no problem with that and begin from the moment the nurse came to find me in the waiting room and bring me to Mom's room.

"She was so pale," I tell the doctor, "And her hair was matted with sweat. No birth glow here. I remember rushing to her side, hoping she was okay.

"When Mom blinked her eyes open, she said, 'Clarry' and fell back into silence. It was like she was testing her memory to be sure she still knew my name.

"'Are you okay?' I asked her repeatedly."

I recall the hospital scene to the doctor, hoping some detail will unlock a clue so Dr. Goldstone will know how to fix her.

I continue, "I'd never been around someone who just had a baby, and I had no idea what to expect after the ordeal. What I saw wasn't a pretty picture.

"'Ti...er...ed,' Mom answered me, drawing out the word into three syllables. I assumed they pumped her with a massive amount of drugs. Popping out a baby must be traumatic.

"But I was worried about the way she appeared, so I persisted in questioning her."

The enormous dread I felt then sweeps over me now as I tell the story.

"My mom reassured me she was okay, and I pushed some damp hair off her forehead and noticed her skin was clammy. 'Can I get you something to drink?' I asked her."

I'd seen enough movies to know this is a standard question to ask someone in the hospital.

"'Juice would be good,' she answered."

Dr. Goldstone interrupts to ask if Mom mentioned the baby, and if he was in the room with her.

The doctor won't trip me up on any of the details because that day is now a memory tattoo. I continue to describe the hospital scene.

"At first, when I saw Mom, I didn't give it, I mean him, a second thought. He could've been there. It was quiet, and I never surveyed the room. Dr. Goldstone, you have to understand all I wanted was for my mother to be okay and come home. I never wondered where the baby was until I was on the way to the nurses' station to get the juice."

I skip the part of the story about the rooms I passed in the hallway filled with balloons and menageries of stuffed animals, some as big as a horse. My poor baby brother didn't even have one tiny stuffed animal to come home to. So, in addition to all the other work I had to do to get things ready, I made a mental note to order a couple of toys. I bought him a musical mobile and a stuffed white dog with floppy ears that were pink on the inside. Later, I found out the dog made a noise when you pressed its belly.

I continue my description for the doctor. "When I got back with the juice and helped my mom sit up to drink, I did ask her about the baby."

Dr. Goldstone stops writing and shakes his hand, probably to loosen a cramp. I wonder if he does so much writing during all his appointments, or if my words are especially valuable pearls he wants to save forever.

Anyway, I resume my sad story, and he starts writing again.

"'He's in the nursery,' Mom replied to me. 'I need to rest. The nurse took him out. I can't take care of him. He'd be better off with another mother.' Wasn't that an odd thing to say on day one?"

The doctor gazes at me with those soothing eyes and says, "Not everyone responds in the same way to birth, and some people need more time to adjust. Did you go see the baby in the nursery?"

I begin the retelling of scene two of Harry's birth story. "I did go to the nursery, but if you're asking if it was a wow moment, it wasn't. Any of the babies could've been Harry. I didn't feel a connection. If the nurse hadn't pointed him out to me, I could've settled for another squealing kid."

Then I stop. I have to be sure I have time to ask my final question before this appointment is over. "Dr. Goldstone, I have a question. Do you believe my mother is capable of hurting Harry?"

He sits upright and stops transcribing my words, attesting to the seriousness of this question. He stares into my eyes as if he can see all the way back to the retinas. It's unnerving. And then he throws my question right back at me. "Do you think she might? Are you afraid of that?"

"Listen, she kisses him and sometimes does the feedings, but most times she's too tired, too sad, and too out of it to do much. To be honest, I have a hunch she's trying to avoid getting too attached to Harry in case she decides to let him be adopted. Did she tell you her brother is pressuring her to do that?"

"Claire." The doctor's voice gets even softer, and I suspect this is part of a therapist's training for calming people. He says, "Your mother has a lot to work through, but I don't believe she would ever intentionally harm the baby. Would you support her if she decides to give him up for adoption?"

So, he answers my question with a question, and I'm guessing there's a strong possibility adoption has been discussed in this cramped office.

In the firmest tone I can muster, I reply, "No adoption. That's a hard no. Not letting that happen. I'm getting a lawyer to make sure I can fight any dirty trick my uncle pulls. He's bullying and threatening my mother. Did she tell you that?"

"I'm sorry I can't discuss what your mother says when we meet, but she has talked about her brother. I'll leave it at that. Although we have to consider the possibility that unintentionally, your mother might not take proper care of the baby. For example, if she didn't sleep well at night and is extremely tired all day, she could fall asleep and be unavailable to him. We've got to get things fixed before Harry is more active. Then whoever watches him needs to be attentive to make sure he doesn't get hurt."

So bottom line, Claire, you're still responsible for Harry all the time, and you have no choice but to get legal authority to keep this family together at any cost. I won't let Harry live under the constant threat he could be shoved out. Mom, Dr. Goldstone, and my uncle will soon learn how far I'm willing to take this.

The doctor stands, the universal signal the appointment is over, and ushers me out, saying, "I encourage you to reach out for resources."

And then, as if he can't stand to let me leave feeling somewhat reassured, he says, "Call me anytime, but especially in an emergency."

E-effing-emergency! Why would he use that word? Does he anticipate some horrible thing happening? I don't ask what he means because I don't want to know. It's a matter of self-protection. If I know what emergency he's thinking about, I wouldn't ever be able to unknow it. I'd be afraid to close my eyes when I sleep in case I miss an emergency. The anticipation alone could bury me.

I walk to the parking lot like one of the living dead. Be patient and hope the therapy and pills kick in before a disaster strikes.

In the car, my palms slap the steering wheel. The thudding makes my ears vibrate and my bones jangle all the way to the elbow. I stop and squeeze the hard rubber cover on the wheel until my knuckles are white and demand that I release my grip. I lower my forehead onto the steering wheel.

CHAPTER
13

By Friday I'm mostly recovered from Dr. Goldstone. He was really nice, but the whole scene unnerved me. At least today, there'll be a huge distraction from my problems and that's evident the minute I'm inside the hallowed halls of dear Newton North.

The buzz about the dance tonight is like an earworm. Alvene's in a gaggle spilling the tea about which couples will be made tonight and which will be broken. Mads struts over, wearing an oversized grin that practically shouts "tonight's the night."

"Hey, girls. Ready to rock 'n' roll?" Mads asks as she shakes her booty. "Help me decide. Dangling silver earrings or my fake diamond studs?"

No one offers Mads advice about her jewelry choice because we're way out of her league on decisions like that.

The day of the senior supper and dance is a half day, supposedly for teacher prep, but I think because some wise administrator understood it can take people hours to do hair, nails, and makeup. Not me of course. I don't have the luxury of time to agonize over those details. The little prince does not allow that.

At noon, everyone rushes for the doors, and the school empties fast. I pick up Harry on the way home, and the two of us bound upstairs to Mom's room, or I bound and Harry jostles in my arms, which he finds hilarious. I plunk him on Mom's bed, and then I crawl in next to her on the other side, trying to re-create the days when we'd lie in her bed and talk. I don't expect that to happen now but being close works almost as well.

My doubts about going out tonight linger, and though Mom said I should go, I'm compelled to make sure, risking the possibility I'll get a different response this time.

"Mom, are you sure it's okay for me to go to the dance?" I ask and promise myself this is the absolute last time I'm going to do that. "I'll have Harry fed, bathed, and in the crib before I leave," I add.

"Yes, you should go," Mom replies. Bingo! I don't need additional reassurance. Becky will be here, and everything will be fine.

"Would you like me to fix your hair before Becky comes?"

"Okay, but you don't have—"

"I want to." I get her brush and pull it through her hair, being careful not to tug on the few knots, which reminds me I keep forgetting to buy conditioner. Stuff like that was never my job before. All I had to do was write something on the shopping list on the refrigerator and it would appear.

I wrap Mom's wavy hair into a messy bun and notice a few grayish-white strands mixed with the brownish blonde ones. Maybe those gray hairs are the reason she avoids Sunny Acres, afraid someone might mistake her for Harry's grandmother, just like they assumed I was the baby's mother.

When I finish her hair, I give her a hug, and she seems a bit floppy, not toned like she used to be. She hasn't exercised or done yoga in months. I swear I can feel her backbone protruding.

Her phone rings, and the caller ID shows it's Pat.

"Aren't you going to answer?" I ask.

"I have no energy for him right now."

But I do. I take her phone and rudely yank the pacifier out of Harry's mouth. In a few seconds, he's beet-red and screaming his head off. I snap a photo of him and text it to my uncle and then focus on quieting Harry and apologizing for what I put him through. He rests his head against my shoulder, and I pat his back like Mom always did when I was upset. It's a proven technique.

"What did you do?" Mom asks.

"I sent your brother a photo of his nephew. After all, he never came to see him. What are we, yesterday's trash?"

Mom takes her phone from me with shaky hands and sees the photo of Harry. "He'll be angry with me about that picture."

"I wanted to send a message. Who cares if it pisses him off? What can he do to you? If we're lucky, he'll stop talking to you."

"He's strong-willed and gets angry when someone doesn't do what he wants."

She's wrecked, and that's on me. I acted on my frustrations but didn't consider the consequences for Mom. I should know better. Dr. Goldstone was clear not to push her while she's trying to get better.

"I'm sorry, Mom. But I do have a plan that will stop Uncle Pat from pressuring you to do something you'll regret. I'm going to get legal advice from Mads's father. We'll have our own lawyer, and Mads said we don't have to pay him. How great is that?"

"Why do we need a lawyer?"

"I'll explain everything after I meet with him, once I'm sure my plan will work and get your brother off our backs. I mean, off Harry's back."

Mom worry-rubs her hands together. "Oh my God, Clarry, do not take on Patrick. I will deal with him. This is my mess. I have to fix it. Can you bring me a glass of water? It's time for my pills."

"I suppose I shouldn't have sent that photo. It was childish." I get the water for her.

One by one, her handful of pills disappears. You'd think the odds would point to some of them helping, but there's no evidence of that. Dr. Goldstone should decide soon whether these pills are duds.

Within a few minutes, her eyes close. I take Harry and get him ready before I dress. I refuse to give him an opportunity to unleash his usual horrors on my outfit tonight.

⚓

BECKY ARRIVES RIGHT on time and greets me with her usual bear hug. She claims I'm the daughter she never had. She used to joke she's sharing me with Mom. Her son is much older than me and has been out on his own for quite a few years.

"How is she doing?" Becky asks, as she hangs her coat in the hall closet, completely at ease in our house.

"She has new pills and a new doctor."

"So better?" Becky's eyes get squinty, which is her tell for scoping out a lie. Years ago, she caught me fibbing about something stupid, and I got "the look." Her uncanny sense for spotting liars could've given her a stellar career in law enforcement, but she chose journalism. I suppose that profession also has its share of liars.

"Not really," I answer truthfully, and I'm rewarded when Becky drops her eye-squint.

"She never calls me and rarely replies to my texts. Since Harry was born, she sort of cut me out of her life. I'm happy she asked me to come tonight. And it's good she isn't relying solely on her primary care doctor for this problem. She needs a specialist. Who is she seeing?"

"Dr. Goldstone is her psychologist, and he arranges with someone else to prescribe the medication."

"Good. That's a step in the right direction. Fab skirt, Claire."

"Thanks," I say, pleased I chose my twirly, black velour skirt, which is great for dancing. My silver sweater has sparkle threads, and if they have strobe lights in the gym, they'll bounce off the fabric and I'll shine. I didn't ask to buy anything new for the dance because I don't trust Mom's got a handle on our finances. A new outfit for me might mean a bill won't get paid.

Becky and I go upstairs, and she heads to Harry's room. When she comes out, she says, "He's luscious. His hair is darker than your mom's—more like yours. Those cheeks are adorable. Have a wonderful time tonight. Any last-minute instructions?"

"Harry should be out for the night. There are bottles already made in the fridge. You should call if you need me. And Mom hasn't eaten since lunch. You could order something for the two of you."

"Got it. Don't worry. We'll be fine. Have fun. Your mother and I have a ton of things to catch up on."

Good luck with that. My guess is Mom will close down after a few sentences, but I'm not sticking around to find out. I tell Mom I'm leaving and scoot out before anything happens that would prevent me from going.

⚓

THE PARKING LOT at Newton North is pretty full. I find a space at the far end, shut the motor, and just sit, savoring the fact I made it to the dance. One more look-see in the mirror to admire my fairly decent makeup job. The lavender eye shadow, black mascara, and warm, subtle rose lipstick are perfect. I add some gloss to my lips.

Inside the gym, the decibel level is roaring, and there's no lingering stink of sweat thanks to our marvelous custodians who perform miracles. Orange and black streamers provide a canopy over the dance floor, and bunches of balloons in those school colors are in every corner. The Tiger colors have nothing to do with Halloween but at a dance in the fall, who could tell? A large, silver sparkling ball rotates overhead and sends streams of color to the walls and floor. Very festive.

I circle the room hunting for Mads and stop often for hugs and fist bumps with other classmates. The senior dance is a big deal. Alvene puts her hands on my shoulders and takes a step backward, eyeballing me. Then she does her coolest finger snap with her side-to-side head movement.

"Ooo, Claire, you're smokin'!" she says. "That skirt is amazing. Where did you get it?"

"Taylor Imports, naturally, but it's not new. You look fantastic too."

"Who me?" She puts her hands in the air pretending to doubt me, laughs, and spins around so I can admire the back of her shirt, which spells out "Ready for *Love*" in sequins. That girl knows what she wants.

"I'm going to miss you next year, Claire."

"Hey, we've got lots of time until graduation. You'll see me every day."

"We should go to the same college and hang together."

"Not going to college next year."

"Snap! You're full of surprises, aren't you, darlin'. Since when no college? What are you gonna do? Hey, there's Maddie," she says and doesn't wait for my reply. She loops her arm around mine and drags me with her.

The music heats up, and lots of people rush onto the dance floor. Kids are getting their freak on. I even spot some twerking. I'm not doing that, though Mads and I have spent hours in her room in front of her full-length mirror perfecting our twerk.

Charlie leads Alvene away to dance, and she yells above the crowd noise: "A gap year sounds exciting. I'm soooo jealous. I bet you're going to Washington to work for some congressman."

She knows me. My old plan was to work for Congressman Samuels's reelection campaign this fall and then ask for a summer internship after my freshman year in college. Now I'll have to tell Alvene my gap year destination is the City of Newton, working a dead-end job. No one will be jealous of me.

Mads is her usual spectacular self in tight dark pants, white canvas slip-ons, and a pink crop top that highlights her navel ring. I bet her mother was shocked to see that shiny souvenir from her summer away. Magnificent.

Mads hugs me. "At last, you're here!" she says. "I was getting worried you wouldn't show."

"How was the supper?" I ask.

She nudges me to the side of the room and whispers in my ear. "Excellent. I put my hand on his knee, and he didn't pull away. I'm trying the make-the-first-move approach like you suggested, but what is this dude is waiting for? An engraved invitation?"

"No idea."

"So, only the knee? No stealthy roaming?" My mouth twists into a smirk.

"No cap. I kept the brakes on," she answers as Nando and Chad join us.

Chad is stone-cold hot in his light pink polo. I predict he and Mads will go down in Newton North High School history as the most beautiful couple ever. Chad smiles in my direction, and I flash it back to him. He positions himself between me and Mads, the same way he maneuvered himself at the football game to be near Charlie.

"You seem relaxed," he says to me.

"Because I actually made it here." My feet are bouncing like I'm ten years old.

The DJ announces the next song, and Chad stares at me with a magnetic hold. He grabs my hand, and in a split second I'm deep in the middle of a mob jumping and gyrating to the beat on the dance floor.

As we rotate, I scan the room at each turn trying to find Mads, but it's hopeless. We're moving too fast.

Chad clasps my hands tight, as if he's afraid I might run away, and I might. Mads will be pissed Chad didn't choose her to dance with. Why didn't he? I have drummed it into him that Mads and he belong together. Does he think it's a coincidence she also wore pink tonight? And she had her hand on him during the supper. He isn't stupid. He knows he's supposed to be with her. How did his brain scramble something this simple?

By the time the music stops, his arms are around my waist, and my hands are on his shoulders. We're closer than we need to be, and I gently step back. Chad's grin extends from his full lips into his eyes.

"I have to find Mads," I say and dash over to ask Alvene if she knows where Mads is. She doesn't so I make a beeline for Nando, who's chatting up Chloe.

"Did you guys see Mads? I can't find her."

Nando points to the exit and says, "Pee time."

Panic boils in my veins, and my heart rises and stops in the back of my throat. I head for the restroom and find Mads sitting on the radiator. Her face is red and wet, a deadly combination of angry and crying.

"You have no reason to be mad at me," I stammer, opening my arms to hug her. She twists her body to the side and crosses her arms in front of her chest to prevent me from getting close.

"Why you and not me?" Her question is more accusation than curious.

This dance with Chad wasn't what I wanted, but I suppose I dug myself into this hole. I should've come clean straight away after the first text from Unknown. I never dreamt one simple text could cause all this. Chad did everything I asked him to, but I never mentioned he should dance exclusively with her. That should've been obvious to him. I screwed up, but I did not encourage him to pick me.

"Chad and I are just good friends. No romance, I promise you."

"What do you mean, good friends?" she asks, sniffling.

"Um...we spend time together."

"Duh. We all spend time together. So?"

"We've gone out for coffee, he's been at my house, and..." I pause. Do I have to confess everything? Is that in anyone's best interest? But the sneaking around has proven deadly, and I have to regain her trust.

"Chad invited Harry and me to his house for dinner." Perhaps mentioning Harry's coming with me will soften the blow and reassure her this isn't a date.

My words hang in the bathroom's air and mingle with the odor of a powerful disinfectant. Every second waiting for Mads to reply is an eternity.

"WTF, Claire? What the? Forget it. My back is already bleeding from the stab wounds." The ground underneath me rumbles as if I'm standing on an earthquake fault line. There's fury in her eyes, and her voice is raised. "How could you do that? You knew I wanted him. You went behind my back. You pretend to be my best friend, and you betrayed me!"

Her words are hot and sting like alcohol on an open cut.

Betrayed! It must've hurt Mom when I accused her of that very same thing after she stole my college money.

"It isn't like that, honest." What else can I say to convince her? My brain is oatmeal. I know "It isn't like that" is a lame thing to say, but I'm not functioning. I can't think straight and wind up saying, "It just happened," which sounds even worse.

I'm struggling to explain. "I did *not* make a play for him. It was me who got him to ask you to help with his outfit for the dance. Ask him."

"Are you serious? He didn't even do that on his own. He was pretending to like me."

"He does like you, but maybe not the way a boyfriend would. I don't know. I never asked him how he felt."

"I guess you're the Chad expert around here." Her words drip with scorn and spite.

A bunch of girls burst into the restroom, shouting and snickering about boys, mostly. They hog the mirrors, redoing hair and makeup and spewing lots of senior gossip.

I lower my voice and whisper, "Can we talk somewhere else?"

"Traitor!" Mads shouts, not caring who hears her. The others girls turn to us but know better than to get involved. And Mads isn't finished yelling at me. "You're a lying bitch. You should've told me the two of you hooked up."

"Shush, please," I urge her, knowing this juicy story will be common knowledge in no time.

"We aren't a couple!" I insist.

"Don't tell me to shush." She stomps her foot, but her canvas shoes make no sound on the bathroom floor, so it's sort of a stomp in name only. She races past me and out the door. Gone.

I start to go after her to tell her I love her and beg her to forgive me, when my phone buzzes. I pull it out of my little purse, hoping it's a text from Mads that she has forgiven me or wants to meet, but I'm not that lucky. There are two texts and one missed call from Mom. With all the noise in the gym, I didn't hear my phone.

I read the last text.

> This is Becky on your mom's phone. No emergency, but could you call as soon as possible?

As fast as my heart rose, it descends with a hard, painful thud. The only time someone writes "no emergency" is when there *is* an emergency.

I dash out the door and into the gym. I grab Alvene by both her arms and say, "I have to get home. My mom isn't feeling well. Tell Mads I left and I'm sorry."

"Sorry for what?" she asks.

"She'll understand. Got to go." I don't want Mads to think I'm leaving because of our fight, but I have no time to find her and explain myself.

"Is your mom okay?" Alvene asks.

"Just the flu." Whatever is happening at home, it isn't good. I text Mom's cell as I sprint toward my car.

> On my way.

I pass a group of kids sitting in a car with the windows rolled down.

"Hey, Claire, is someone chasing you?" one of the boys shouts. "We've got something here to help you slow down."

"Can't stop." I huff and a whiff of whatever they're smoking follows me the rest of the way.

Another text from Mom's phone:

> Becky again. Drive carefully. Everything's going to be fine.

Going to be. Going to be. It's not fine. It's *going* to be fine. My body shudders.

I unlock the car door and hear footsteps. I say a silent prayer it's Mads coming to find out why I'm leaving the dance early. She should know I'd never hurt her intentionally. This won't be easy to fix; I have to convince her there's nothing between Chad and me. If I lose Mads, I'll be devastat...

I rotate 180 degrees and discover the footsteps behind me belong to Chad; I'm not surprised.

CHAPTER
14

Chad stands under the streetlight like a rock star in the spotlight.

"What are you doing here?" I ask as I open the car door.

"I saw you rush out. Did you and Madison fight?"

"We did, but that's not why I'm leaving." I get in and lower the window. "Something's wrong at home. I got a strange message from my mom's friend who's there. I'll text you later."

He stands to the side, and I drive off, trying not to press the gas pedal into the floor. How did the distance between school and home become longer since I drove to the dance a short time ago?

At the back door, I again hear someone behind me. This time I have no doubt it's Chad. He jogs up the driveway and follows me inside. Becky's at the kitchen table, waiting for me. She seems okay, and I don't hear any screaming baby.

"Who are—" Becky says, peering over my head at Chad.

"He's a friend. Is it Harry? Is he all right? Did something happen to him?" My words race out like they're passengers on a burning train.

"Harry's fine. Your mom isn't doing well. Sometimes it's hard to see what's really happening when you're so close to a situation."

Oh, I saw it all. Becky stands and envelops me in her arms. My emotions are wrecked.

"Stay calm, Claire, so we can help your mother together. Did you notice she's sleeping way too much and when she's awake, she's fuzzy? I used her phone to call her doctor so he wouldn't think it was a wrong number. He answered right away. He wants her to go to the hospital to get checked out."

"Hospital?" I might vomit out my insides. This is penance for dancing with Chad. Should I have refused to dance with him? It all happened so fast. Maybe I was secretly excited he chose me, and now I'm being force-fed a giant scoop of karma because my mother is going to the hospital. This is the nightmare on Ivanhoe Street.

"That's the best place for her. She needs help." Becky says this so matter-of-factly, but perhaps that's an act for my benefit.

"When is she going?" My voice is low, and I sense it might be barely audible. "I have to see her," I say, and head toward the stairs. Becky trails me. I assume Chad is behind her. My body shivers as if someone cranked the AC to deep-freeze levels.

Becky continues talking, and it's difficult to concentrate on her words. Dark thoughts flash in and out of my mind, and I can't make them stop. She says, "The doctor said we should bring her tonight. I told your mom, and she didn't balk, but who knows how much she's absorbing. Take it easy, Claire. Your mother is fragile and vulnerable. Tread lightly with her."

Does she have the right to tell me what to do with my mother? I've been dealing with this every day for months. Becky waltzes in and wants to take charge. She has great intentions, but she should respect that I'm the one who's been on the front lines this whole time, keeping out the enemies and guarding my family fort. She's not in charge here. I have a plan to deal with this as soon as I make certain it is all legal. I gulp. Now who knows if Mads will find a way to cancel that meeting with her dad? If that happens, I'm dead.

Mom's face is gaunt in the dim light of the night table lamp, and her eyeballs have sunk farther into their craters. Becky could've been shocked when she saw Mom, and this is all her overreacting. I've had time to get used to this. Maybe Becky's ringing the alarm will prove to be totally unnecessary.

"Hey, Mom, Becky says you're okay with going to the hospital. I guess Dr. Goldstone thinks it's a good idea."

"Uh-huh," Mom says.

I wobble, and Chad comes up next to me and holds me around

the waist for support. I don't want to crumple and let anyone believe I'm not strong enough to take care of my family.

Chad whispers, "Do you want to sit?"

I shake my head. "Go downstairs and wait. We'll help my mom get ready." Chad obeys and leaves the room.

"I'll drive your mom, and you stay with Harry," Becky says.

"But I should bring her," I protest.

"Listen, Harry doesn't know me, and I don't know his routine like you do. There's nothing for either of us to do at the hospital once she's settled in a room."

I guess she's right, but I don't like being relegated to a passive role. I get a wet facecloth to refresh Mom. She's wearing her sweats, which will be comfy for the hospital, so no need to get changed. I brush her hair again and put it in a ponytail, making her presentable enough so the people at the hospital don't make wrong assumptions about her. They don't know how she used to enter a room on a magic carpet, radiating beauty and peace. It wasn't long ago that she'd be the person who could calm any storm, unlike Dad, who'd often enter a situation like crashing waves. They made a good pair until they didn't want to be a pair anymore.

Becky says, "Mel, how about a pit stop to the bathroom on the way, and you can brush your teeth? Do you want one of us in there with you?"

"No," Mom says and steadies herself with one hand on the wall for support.

"But don't lock the door, hon," Becky reminds her.

Becky and I wait near the bathroom, ready to spring into action if necessary.

"It's the guilt, the doctor told me," I say. "Why is Mom consumed by so much guilt? Why can't she forgive herself and accept the fact she made one mistake and move on?" I'm just venting and not expecting Becky to respond, but she does.

"Your mom was pumped when she came back from that D.C. work trip. I thought she met someone special. She was upbeat and happier than she'd been in a while. But by the time she found out she was pregnant, that good feeling vanished. She never mentioned anything about the guy, and when Harry was born, I wasn't sure about the timing anymore. Your mom said he was early, but maybe that was a deflection."

I should ask Becky if she tried her squinty-eye technique to evaluate Mom for lying, but I'm not going there now.

"Why did she ghost the guy?" I tell Becky. "She gave me the impression she didn't know how to reach him and maybe didn't even know his last name. He could've been an anonymous sperm donor for all I knew."

"I think she knows who the father is but refuses to say and doesn't want him involved with Harry."

Maybe Becky knows more than she's saying. That shouldn't surprise me. I tell Mads things I'd never tell Mom.

"Claire, she must have a reason if she's keeping that secret."

She might be right, but Becky's no therapist and could be running cover for Mom. In this delicate dance of the secrets, I'm not sure who can be trusted.

"Do you swear," I ask Becky, "she never told you who he was?"

"She never gave me any details." My questions have to stop when Mom emerges from the bathroom. I notice a drop of wayward toothpaste on her lips and retrieve the facecloth to wipe off the blue paste.

Chad's standing on the bottom step, a sentinel guarding access to the second floor.

"Chad, walk in front of my mother as we come down, just in case." A big, powerful guy like him should be able to prevent a spill if she falters.

By the time Becky and Mom are in the car, I'm drained. Becky promises to call me as soon as she knows anything. Chad and I go back inside. I flop onto the living room sofa, and my head falls on the armrest. I want to sleep and sleep and shut off my brain; it's too busy conjuring up awful thoughts.

My eyelids close, and the pictures aren't pretty. The video opens with Uncle Pat carrying a screaming Harry out of the house while Mom lies in a hospital bed hooked up to machines and tubes. Then the scene shifts to Mads's bedroom, where she's shredding and trashing every reminder I ever existed in her life.

If I keep my eyes open, maybe I can shake off these horrible images. Chad sits silently on the recliner.

I don't remember falling asleep until my body jerks upright at the sound of my phone. Chad's sleeping on the floor near the sofa with one of the toss pillows under his head. I guess he was zonked. He stirs, also woken by the phone.

Becky says, "Your mom is settled into a room for the night. Her vital signs are fine. The doctors here said Dr. Goldstone will be by in the morning, and they'll make a plan for your mother. That's all I know."

"Is she upset?" I ask and press on my thigh to stop the leg jitters.

"No. She's mostly out of it. On some level, I think she's glad to be here and feels safe and taken care of. There's nothing more for me to do here. Bringing her to the hospital was the right call. Do you need anything? I'm going home unless you want me there."

"We're fine," I say. "And thank you."

"Call me any time, and I'll be there. I'll text you tomorrow. Keep in touch with me," she says.

"Thanks."

I hang up, and Chad rubs the sleep out of his eyes. I share what Becky said, and he says, "What can I do?"

"What can anyone do? My mom is sick. She probably belongs in the hospital, but I'm scared this is the beginning of the end of my family."

"They will help her. You need to believe that."

"I'm trying." I'm upset at myself using these weasel words. Mads would scold me for that. I can't prevent the tears and cry openly without shame. Chad gets off the floor, joins me on the sofa, and puts his arm around me. My head falls to his chest.

"My mom being in the hospital will be a gift to my uncle. He'll use that against her and may declare her unfit or something to take Harry away. He can't know about this. What if Mads hates me and cancels my meeting with her father?"

"Why would she hate you?"

"She's in love with you. You have to tell Mads we aren't in a relationship, and I didn't take you away from her. I didn't, did I?" Now I'm second-guessing myself, which can complicate everything.

Chad lowers his arm and puts some space between us. "I'm going to set this straight once and for all. I'm not her boyfriend and never said I was. I didn't deceive her and never promised her anything."

"She's pissed because you danced with me."

"In case you didn't notice, girl, I'm my own man. I can dance with anyone I want to. It's not my fault she freaked. I have nothing to apologize for or explain."

"But she had an elaborate blueprint in her head for the two of you. She expected to be an official couple after tonight. She was sure—"

His nostrils flare. "Don't I get a say in this? I get pushed around enough at home with all my father's demands. Can you believe that now I have to take golf lessons after football season so someday I can do business deals at country clubs? He makes me sit at the table in a suit and tie when he invites business associates. Do anthropologists play golf? Do I want to fit in with those blowhards at the country clubs? But I don't get a vote. Every man should get a vote, but I guess not me. Mads thought I shouldn't have the freedom to decide who to dance with, and that's not how this is supposed to work. Now you're angry with me too?"

"I'm not angry with you. You're right. You're free to do what you want and with who you want."

"Damn straight," he replies, and his pinched eyebrows return to their normal position. "What can I do to help, Claire?" he asks again.

"My mom's friend hinted my mom may know the name of

Harry's father and refuses to say. All this time I thought he was a one-night stand without a name."

"Isn't it better if she knows, even if she won't tell you? Are you desperate to find out who he is?"

"Do I want to know? What if he's a lowlife? What if he finds out about Harry and also tries to take him away?"

Suddenly, I can't draw a deep breath. I open the front door and step outside. The night sky is disappointing, with thick clouds blocking the stars. It isn't fair. A sky with no stars seems so hopeless. Even if I could see one star poking out of the clouds, I'd say a prayer, or just gaze and wonder what's going on out there in the vast universe.

The chilly night air opens my lungs, and I breathe easier again. I hold the fresh air in my lungs for a while before time forces me to let it out.

"It's cold out there," Chad calls to me.

I come back in, put my hands on my hips to make my declaration. "I don't give a hot damn who Harry's bio dad is. Harry is staying with me. We are on the same team."

"Is your team recruiting? I could try out for a position," Chad jokes.

"Strength and speed are requirements for the Clarry and Harry team. Perhaps I should see some push-ups or sprints first," I quip, happy to puncture the tension for a moment. "I'll never let my mother allow Harry to be adopted even if he's a pain in the butt. He's her pain in the butt. I'm sending Mads a text to beg her to forgive me."

"For dancing?" he asks.

"For dancing, for coffee, for dinner at your house, for texts, for everything."

I debate about adding emojis for emphasis and decide they'd detract from the seriousness of my message.

CHAPTER
15

Chad reaches into his pocket, takes out his phone, and places it on the coffee table. He taps on the screen, and John Legend's voice fills the room. I'm sure it's him, but I don't recognize the song. Must be a new album. Legend's voice is dipped in warm oil and cradles my soul.

Chad guides me up from the sofa, puts his arms around my waist, and we sway to the rhythm. "We only got to dance once tonight."

I put my hands on his shoulders. With those strong brown arms, he pulls me in tighter. Why does this gorgeous hunk want to dance with a skinny white girl? Our bodies flow together, and the closeness comforts me. The music enters me, and for now, I refuse to let Mom or Mads spoil this moment. When the song ends, I'm disappointed. Chad seems reluctant to lower his arms, and I keep mine on him, waiting for him to move first.

"I love me some Legend," he says, finally releasing his hold on me.

"That music is sweet," I reply. "Thank you."

"Thank you for what?"

"For being here. I can't imagine what tonight would be like for me with only Harry here. He isn't much use in times like this, in case you hadn't noticed. Do you want to see how Harry sleeps with his tush in the air?"

We go into Harry's room to admire his baby yoga position. Chad snickers, and Harry fusses after he jettisons his treasured pacifier. It mystifies me why he spits out the thing that comforts him. Hunting for a replacement is a time-sensitive job because you have to get it done before he starts to scream like a maniac. We have tons of those buggers, but when you're desperate for one, they gang up and scatter to their secret places to make your life miserable.

"Look in the dresser for a pacifier," I whisper to Chad. "Those things control our lives around here."

"I'm on it," he says, opening and closing drawers, rummaging for one of those priceless pieces of chewy plastic. I check the changing table, and as if we're synchronized swimmers, we dive to the floor to continue the hunt. I run my hands under the crib, and Chad does the same under the dresser.

He strikes gold first. "Got one," he announces, as proud as a fisherman landing a trophy fish. He hands me a grungy pacifier full of dust and hair and a crumpled envelope.

"What's that?" I ask, taking the gross pacifier from him.

"Dunno. Found it on the floor." I shine my phone's flashlight on it. The return address is Uncle Pat's. My instinct is to rip it to shreds, but what did he send to Mom and how did the envelope wind up in Harry's room? Maybe he sent us a check. Why didn't Mom mention she got something from her brother?

I say, "Gotta wash this thing off. Be right back."

Time is of the essence to get the wet, clean pacifier back into Harry's mouth before he loses it.

Once Harry's relishing his pacifier again, I tell Chad, "Let's go to my room," hoping Chad doesn't misinterpret that invitation, but he was alone with Mads in his bedroom and nothing happened, so I'm probably being weird. I leave my door open and sit on the floor, avoiding the bed for obvious reasons. He joins me and stretches out his long legs.

There's no check inside the envelope, but Mom might've taken it out. There is a piece of paper, which I remove and read. I never believed that even an a-hole like Uncle Patrick would dare send such a hateful thing to his sister.

My worst fears stare at me in black and white.

I hand Chad the paper and raise my hands to cover my ears from a piercing wail that sounds like a wounded animal, but the howling is coming from me.

As Chad reads, his jaw goes slack. "Why would he send your mom a surrender for adoption form?"

I take the paper from him; it feels toxic in my hand, as if it's been doused in poison. I re-read it. My uncle sent her The Commonwealth of Massachusetts, The Trial Court Probate and Family Court Department Surrender Form and highlighted the lines for her to fill out and sign.

"It's a dick move," Chad says. "But look at it this way. Your mom crumpled the form and shoved it back into the envelope. She didn't sign it."

"Yes, but getting this might be the reason she's in the hospital."

"What are you going to do?"

"Mom being in the hospital changes everything. It's not a choice for me anymore. I'll do whatever it takes to keep Harry with us."

"Don't give up. I don't give up ever. I don't accept any obstacle in front of me, and that includes what my dad wants. You need to do that too. Never abandon your dreams."

Pretty words, but reality isn't pretty. I understand my feelings more and more. "I had so many plans for my future, but now I only have one," I explain. "I have to admit I love that little nugget. If my mom agrees to adoption, she'll regret it for the rest of her life, and her guilt will mushroom until she never recovers."

Still my phone shows no reply from Mads. My heart sinks like the Titanic going to the bottom of the ocean.

"Mads is freezing me out. I should've told her you and I were texting and went for coffee. I didn't, and that's on me. She has every right to be angry."

"She's your best friend. She won't abandon you, and neither will I."

Ever the gallant knight. I smile at him, but it's a sad smile, and I can tell he knows that.

Even though I dread having to be alone, I say, "You'd better get home before your parents put out an Amber Alert for you. I don't need the police showing up at my door."

"I'll text them I'm staying at Nando's tonight."

Is he demented? That's the worse idea ever.

"What if they call Nando to check up on you?" I ask.

"I'll get him on script. He'll cover for a teammate."

"Oh, New Boy, are you friggin' serious? Nando will think we're— that we're doing the... A piece of gossip like that is so hot, it would take weeks or months for it to die down enough to become embers."

"I don't care if he thinks we're cuffed."

Is Chad clueless or does he secretly want everyone to assume we're a couple? "I care, and I don't want to give Mads one more reason to be mad at me."

"So, you're saying there's nothing between us?" He twirls those words into a question, accompanied by his frowny face.

"You and I have become close friends, but Mads thinks I stole *her* man."

He puts his shoes back on and heads for the door. "Can't believe a friendship like yours and Madison's can break over one dance."

I lock the door after him and head upstairs. One dance that Mads knows about and another that happened a short time ago that was utterly perfect.

⚐

THE NEXT MORNING Harry unleashes his standard wake-up call, and I'm still in my senior dance outfit. Even though Mom's usually asleep this early, knowing she isn't here this morning is haunting. I pass by her room on the way to get Harry and avoid the sight of her empty bed.

Harry has his usual stink on him, and I gag as I change him. From the contented noises coming from him, it's clear the poor guy doesn't have a clue his mother is in the hospital.

"Everything's going to be okay," I tell him because that's what parents are supposed to say when their kids are certain life's bungie cord has snapped. "I'll protect you," I promise him, but from his expression, it seems he couldn't care less. Only your constant admiration of the wonder of him means anything to that baby.

After Harry has his bottle, I put him on the floor and check my text messages. Nothing from Mads. I know she won't be awake yet, but I text her again anyway.

> I'm sorry. You have to forgive me. I love you. Please, please, please text me back.

She'll have my message the second she opens her eyes. I put Harry on the floor with a couple of toys, and he surprises me by rolling over. He whimpers and moans as if something awful happened to him until I flip him back the way he was. What a doofus.

In the middle of making piles of clean pj's and overalls, my phone rings. All I want is for it to be Mads, but it's Dr. Goldstone. I'm on that call before the second ring.

"How is she?" I ask without a hello.

Dr. Goldstone's voice is like being immersed in a bubble bath. "How are you doing, Claire?" That his first question is about me is surprising under the circumstances but so kind. He continues before I reply. "I know this is difficult for you, and I want to assure you having your mother come to the hospital was the right thing to do."

"I'm okay. Is she very sick?"

"In some ways, yes, but her immediate problem was too many pills. We don't think she was abusing them intentionally."

"You mean...she might've tried to ki—" My mouth freezes. I can't say the word. I won't say it. She'd never do that to me. Never in a million years would she leave me.

"It's too soon to be sure. I want to be honest with you, but you should not get locked into one possibility until we are certain we know how this happened. The main thing is she will be fine. Her friend was right to call me. In the hospital, they're regulating her medication, but it will take a while for her body to process that extra medicine. On a positive note, she's more aware of her surroundings."

"Can she come home? I can give her the pills, and I promise this will never happen again."

"I know you can, but that's not a solution. She has to get better. She's going to spend some time in the psych unit to regain her equilibrium and get control of her life."

"For how long?"

"We can't tell yet. The pregnancy and birth caused a lot of turmoil she couldn't handle, and she has to come to terms with the guilt she's carrying."

My fingers find a loose thread on my sweater, I tug at it, and it gives way. "Can I come visit her and bring—"

Dr. Goldstone interrupts, "The protocol is not to have visitors for the first couple of days to give patients a chance to get settled. I'll let you know when you can visit."

"I can't come today?" I whine like a bratty toddler.

"Not today. But she's okay and not in danger, I promise you. Can you manage with Harry?"

"I always manage with Harry. Mom knows that." I study the hole in my sweater that's the size of a quarter.

"She does. Call me around one o'clock tomorrow, and I'll give you an update."

"Can I call her?"

"No cell phones in her unit, and right now she doesn't have phone privileges. She needs to concentrate on getting better."

"And that must mean not speaking to her brother either."

"Yes, we'll keep the outside world at bay for a while."

"Tell her I want her to be okay, and she does not have to feel guilty about me."

"I will."

"And tell her Harry and I love her."

"Of course. I'll call you if anything changes. Stay calm."

He hangs up, and I sink to the floor, clasping my bent knees and rocking on my bottom, hoping the motion steadies me. I should be relieved she's getting the help she needs, but this is all soul crushing.

I stay like that until Harry objects to the lack of attention. I pick him up and press him close to me.

I text Mads again.

> Forgive me. Please talk to me. What can I do? I love you.

This time I yield to the emoji world and add a bunch of hearts and an emoji of blowing a kiss.

I toss my sweater with a rather large hole into the trash. I put on a T-shirt and hoodie and put a sweater on Harry. We have got to get out of this lonely house.

CHAPTER 16

Harry and I headed to Newton Centre for no particular reason. I walk like a mindless automaton down Waverly Ave. and then onto Grant. Once we're on Beacon Street, we turn right toward Langley Road. A few steps passed the Diamond Hair Salon, I surprise myself and stop, reversing direction to go inside. Within a minute, I'm in a chair, and a woman with intricate tattoo sleeves on both arms and blue hair past her shoulders is hovering around me, studying my hair.

"What's it going to be?" she asks, and the funny thing is I know exactly what I want even though I hadn't planned this at all. I glance at Harry, who's almost sitting up in his stroller, taking in these new surroundings. Too bad his hair isn't longer; I'd ask for a two-for-one discount. Only joking, Harry. You can grow it long and wear a man bun for all I care.

I tell the hairdresser what I want. She nods and does an earth-around-the-sun circle to see my head from every angle. "Are you sure?"

"Yes, I am."

She picks up her scissors and comb and gets to work. About a half hour later, a shaggy brown rug of my hair covers the floor near my chair. I wasn't expecting how much this new style would confirm everyone's impression: Harry is a mini-me.

"Do you like it?" the stylist asks, holding a mirror so I can see the back. I don't reply immediately, so she asks again. This time, I detect a flutter in her voice. Perhaps she's nervous I'll hate it and sue her for hair malpractice, assuming that's a thing, but I wouldn't, because I love, love, love it.

"It's perfect," I say, "Thank you."

"Hon, do you want some gel to make it spiky?"

"Sure!" I thunder because today I'm announcing the new Claire: bolder and braver. I stare in the mirror, hardly able to recognize myself.

Outside, the breeze on the back of my neck amuses me. We cross the street and enter the Sunlight Bakery.

The scent inside is heavenly, or what I imagine heaven might smell like: all sugar and melted chocolate with hints of cinnamon and, of course, the aroma of fresh-baked bread. This bakery should bottle their scent as a comfort perfume you can use on your down days.

The bakery lady in a white cap and flour-covered apron asks if she can give Harry a cookie. I wish I could say yes, but he's on a strictly mashed diet until his teeth come in. Right now, they're only bumps on his gums. I inspect each cake in the case with the utmost care, asking the lady what's inside the ones whose frosting and toppings make it impossible to guess what kind of cake it is. Each one she describes sounds delicious. I could buy the entire store and drown my spirit in the sweetness.

Indecision isn't normally an issue for me, but today, picking the perfect cake looms as a life-or-death choice. It's unlike me to make a big deal out of such a minor decision. I do one final examination of each creation and hope the bakery lady doesn't think I'm a cake stalker who's wasting her time.

"The lemon one," I say and point to it, as if she wouldn't know which one I mean.

"Want me to write anything on it?" she asks.

"Yes, write 'Happy Birthday Claire' and put the number eighteen in the center. Can you fit on all that?"

"Sure. We'll have it ready in five minutes." She carries the cake into the back room.

I pick up a package of birthday candles from the counter and hand it to her. "Add these, please." The new credit card is accepted, but who knows for how long until it's also maxed out. I still have to do more digging into our financial stuff, but now my priority is keeping Harry safe legally. For that, I need Mads's father.

No texts from her as if my wishing could actually produce one. That would be some strong magic.

No message from Mads. And nothing from Chad all day either. I was sure he'd be in touch first thing to see how I'm doing, but I guess he needed a break from the messy life of Claire Jackson.

I text Mads again.

> Will you come over later? WE NEED TO TALK.

I add three rows of the praying hand emojis.

Harry and I take the long way home because there's no rush returning to an empty house. As I push the stroller, my mind is on Mom lying alone and weak in a hospital bed. Maybe my uncle isn't the only family member who's pressuring her. It's not like I haven't been laying on my demands about keeping Harry. Between her brother and me, we've got Mom in a tug-of-war game, being pulled in opposite directions, probably to the breaking point. My uncle and I are both convinced we know what's best for this baby. I guess we have that in common.

Should I back off for Mom's sake? My eyes fill. I can't accept that she'd want to give Harry away, but that's her right. He isn't my baby.

Once we're back home, I turn on all the lights to make the place seem cheery. Then I recall Dad's lectures on the high cost of electricity, retrace my steps, and shut off most of them. Last year, my biggest worry was whether to major in government or political science at college, and now all I can think about is adoption and money.

By 7:00, I have Harry in the crib and shift my attention to the cake sitting in the middle of the kitchen table. I put eighteen candles on it, and then add one more for good luck like Mom always does. It should be quite spectacular when lit.

I grab the lighter out of the drawer just as a FaceTime call from

Dad comes in. He has Isabella on his lap. "Hey, Clarry, happy birthday. We all wanted to—quiet, Bella, I'm talking to your big sister."

Um...she's not my sister. She's Susie's daughter, unless he's planning to adopt her. I don't need another baby in my life. I raise my phone so my face is dead center on the screen and say, "I gave myself a birthday haircut."

"What did you do!" The veins on his forehead bulge. He could be on the verge of a stroke. "What if you have a college interview?"

"I can talk to an admissions officer with short hair. The stylist didn't cut off part of my brain. And there are no hair length requirements for applying."

"I'm shocked. You've had long hair since you were two. What did your mother think of this?"

I'm tempted to say it was her idea, but this isn't a good day for a prank. I stick to the truth. "She hasn't seen it yet." For now, I'm keeping the fact she's in the hospital on a need-to-know basis. "And, Dad, I'm planning to take a gap year and postpone college."

His wife sticks her head next to his, so she's on the camera too.

"Happy Birthday, Claire," Susie says. "Love the new you!" Her smile is genuine. She and I haven't had a lot of time together, and our conversations are still brief like two people just getting to know one another.

"Thanks, Susie. Bella's so adorable," I reply.

"Next time we call, we'd love to meet your little brother," she says and disappears from the screen.

"And is a gap year a good decision?" Dad asks. "What are you going to do for the year?"

"My college counselor suggested it." Lie. "She's checking programs that would bolster my credentials." Lie.

If I tell him Mom spent my college money on Harry, he'll blow up and try to drag me to Wisconsin. How could he understand that the family ship here is taking on water, and I have to be here to haul Mom and Harry onto the raft like Jack did with Rose in the movie

Titanic? But I need a bigger raft than he had to make sure the three of us can fit on it. In my movie no will be left behind.

"So many changes, Clarry. Hard for your old man to adapt." He puts Isabella's face against the phone and says, "Give your sister a birthday kiss."

The kid clearly failed her class in kissing because she licks the screen. Dad's face reddens. This is all too funny.

"Got to go, Dad. Thanks for calling."

I take a photo of the cake and send it to Mads with no message. She knows it's my birthday. I light the candles and blow them out and totally forget the part about making a wish. Figures. I shove a hunk of cake into my mouth and taste the self-pity baked in and text Mads one more time.

> My mom is in the hospital.

All that sugar brings on a brain fog, and I wallow in the sweet loss of my ability to have a coherent thought.

My eighteenth birthday will go down in history as the suckiest day ever. No Mom, no Mads, and no Chad. If it wasn't for Harry, I'd be going out with friends and even opening some presents. But I suppose this is good practice for when I become Harry's temporary legal guardian and give up the me part of my life. It will be a mountain of responsibility. There'll be many more lonely days like this.

If I have full authority of the baby, my uncle has no way to get control of him and put his plan into place. Uncle Pat doesn't love him, and he's dead wrong that Harry is a mistake.

The doorbell rings. It's late. I peek through the peephole to see that gorgeous hunk showing off his magnificent smile. I open the door.

"You didn't say you were coming. You didn't text me all day." I'm sort of annoyed, though I have no right to expect anything from him. But still, yesterday's dance, his arms around me, and his gallant words made so much difference. Today, he squashed those feelings when he went missing.

"Whoa, baby! What did you do?" Chad exclaims.

"Whoa, what?"

"Going gangsta?" he asks, staring at the top of my head.

In response, my hand automatically touches my head. I forgot for a moment about my birthday haircut that declares there's a new Claire in town. I smile and joke, "I had to keep myself busy when you didn't call, didn't I?"

"I had a lot to do," he says and steps to one side, revealing Mads standing behind him. I almost lose my balance. I'm deliriously happy to see her and also afraid of her anger. Mainly, I don't understand why the two of them came together.

"Mads," I say, stating the obvious as I process the scene. I'm trying to gauge her mood, but it's unclear, so I go back inside, and they're right behind me.

"Did you lose your mind?" she asks with the same wide-eyed astonishment as Chad.

"Do you like it?"

"Who are you? I used to know a Claire Jackson. You stole her face, but not her hair."

"I'm still me."

Giving me the once-over, she says, "Kind of punk. A trendsetter. Once again, you surprise me."

"I had to mark the day like you did on your eighteenth birthday, but this isn't as wild as what you did."

"No, it's hella cool, Claire Bear. You need big hoop earrings to go with that haircut. I have some you can borrow." She runs her fingers through my short ends. This haircut is definitely going to be the hot new topic with my friends, and secretly I'm loving the shocking effect.

"Why are you here?" I ask, "I mean, I'm happy you're here, but I thought you might never speak to me again. Did you two come together? Or—"

"Chad came over," she says, "and we had a long talk."

Harry picks this moment to interrupt, and I dash upstairs to get him. I hold him against my shoulder and his body vibrates from a humongous burp.

"Heck, Harry, manners," I fake-scold him.

Chad grins. "Way to go, dude." He lifts Harry's hand for a high-five. "You'll have to show them whose boss of the burps by the time you're in kindergarten. Start practicing early, kid, but pay attention to the babes at day care. Girls don't understand the value of a loud, throaty burp."

"Stay with him," I tell Chad and hand Harry over before I drag

Mads to my room. I sit on the bed, but she remains standing, a few feet from me.

I jump into my apologies, mimicking all the times Mom went heavy into apologies and guilt confessions. "I'm so, so sorry. There's no excuse for not telling you Chad and I were hanging out sometimes. It was wrong, wrong, wrong. You have every right to be mad at me, but please know how sorry I am and how much I wish I could get a do-over."

She's not yelling at me, not staring me down, and not red with anger, so I keep going. "You always have my back, and I deceived you. I kept this secret because I was trying to convince Chad you two should be together, but I guess I didn't do a great job. The whole thing got away from me. But I swear I was stunned when Chad dragged me to dance." I raise my right hand as if I'm taking the witness stand. "I wasn't sure what to do."

"I know. I know," Mads says. "Chad called me today and asked to come over. I didn't want to be a jerk and blow him off, so I agreed. He explained you did nothing to encourage him and were on his case about me all the time, but he was adamant he makes his own decisions."

"But you wanted him."

Mads joins me on the bed, and we sit shoulder to shoulder and knee to knee as tight as ever. She says, "I guess I acted spoiled and like an entitled bitch, convinced he'd have to like me. Who wouldn't fall in love with Madison Sunday if they had the chance? You know that arrogance isn't the real me, right?"

"I know that, Maddikins. But sometimes we all get caught up in stuff." I put my arm around her.

"I thought I could make it happen between Chad and me and didn't imagine he might like someone else. From the moment I saw him, my brain got fried. I just wanted that handsome boy."

"But except for that dance, there was nothing going on between us. He followed me home after the dance when I got the call from my mom's friend to come home. I didn't ask him to follow me, and when I cried about my mom being in the hospital, he hugged me. And we did dance again in my living room, but I swear that's everything. Chad and I are just friends. You have to believe me."

"Now it's you who isn't facing reality, babe. He's gaga over you."

"He told you that?"

"No, but I'm not stupid. You were wrong about hiding your coffee dates and texting from me. If you had told me right away, I wouldn't have wandered into this la-la land imagining Chad and me were a couple when we never were."

Whatever Mads had envisioned with him was intense, and she fell from a great height when she realized it wasn't going to be.

"I don't think he likes me like that," I say. "He wants to help me because my life's blowing up, and I need saving. Please tell me you forgive me. I betrayed you and feel like a dirt-eating worm. Will you forgive me?"

"When you both disappeared from the dance after our fight, I was sure you were off somewhere getting it on with him, and my anger rocketed off the planet."

"What?! I told you there was no boyfriend-girlfriend thing happening. He's never even kissed me. I'm in a bad place, and I need you more than ever with my mom in the hospital."

"I know. Chad filled me in. What happened to her? Is she okay?"

"She has to stay for a while, and they won't let me visit for a couple of days. That makes me so panicked, not knowing exactly how she is. It dredges up the feelings I had after Harry was born, and I was worried sick about her then."

"I'm here for you. You know that," she says.

"I need for you to say you forgive me so we can be like before. That would be the best birthday present ever. I can't live without you. I love you so much."

"Me too, you," she says. "Happy birthday, Claire Jackson. I forgive you." She hugs me, and I squeeze the life out of her.

"Let's go down before Chad assumes we're in a death match up here."

Chad eyeballs Mads and me carefully to make sure we didn't give each other black eyes. He puffs out his chest in a proud victory pose, definitely claiming credit for fixing what I broke. He can have all the glory. I'm beyond grateful for what he did.

As soon as Harry sees me, he whimpers and his eyes fill up. I understand his message: take me. Sometimes he pretends to be a big shot and is willing to go to anyone until he isn't. I bring him back upstairs, give him his leftover bottle, and he's out again.

When I finish, I hear Chad and Mads in the kitchen and join them. Chad has set out plates, forks, and napkins. "I found a discount cake sitting here. The candles seem to indicate this might be a birthday cake."

"Hey, that's no discount cake," I say. "It cost a lot of money."

"You were cheated. A huge hunk is missing, or maybe you have mice in your kitchen."

"I'm the mouse with a big mouth."

Mads says, "We should sing and then gorge ourselves to celebrate."

"Yes, exactly," he says, "and I guess you remembered I love lemon."

"I did remember," I say, and my cheeks get hot that he made the connection. Subconsciously, maybe I was buying the perfect cake for Chad. His eyebrows elevator up a few floors, and he says, "So, you knew somehow I'd be sharing in this cake. Very intriguing." His mouth shifts into a full-fledged wise guy smirk.

When they finish singing happy birthday, Chad steps over to me, leans his head down a bit, and kisses me. My lips melt like warm wax from his slightly parted, moist mouth. Yikes, what am I doing? Mads is right here with a front-row seat. I ease myself away from him.

"That's our first kiss, Mads, I swear. I didn't lie about that."

"So you both say, but get real," she says. "What's going on with you two?"

"Hey, for your information, that was an innocent happy birthday kiss." Chad teases.

I cut Chad an enormous piece of cake.

"Half that size for me," Mads says. I cut hers and take a small slice for myself. I'm kind of sugared out.

While we eat, I give them the Mom update and share how scared I am they'll find out she took too many pills on purpose. "I'm praying this was a fluke that could happen to anyone."

Chad says, "It's important not to get ahead of this. You'll know soon enough and then you'll deal with whatever you have to deal with. You're tougher than you think." He gulps down a glass of water before he tackles the last of his cake.

My phone buzzes with a number I don't recognize, and I pounce on the call, assuming it's the hospital. When Uncle Pat booms, "Hello?" in my ear, the wind is sucked out of my lungs. My heart thumps, and my hand rushes to press into my chest to stop the fierce beats. I wish it was the hospital calling.

I grab a pen and write "uncle" on a napkin and show it to Chad and Mads.

"Put him on speaker," Chad whispers, and I do.

"Claire, my favorite niece," he says, and I stick my finger in my mouth, pretending to gag. "I heard your mother is in the hospital. I'm sure you're upset."

He wasn't supposed to find out. He could seize this as his opportunity to prove she can't take care of a baby and he should take Harry. "Who told you she's there?"

"The hospital called me."

"Why would they do that?" I'm spinning out of control but try not to come across as unhinged. I can't let him think he can get to me like he does with Mom.

"I'm listed as her next of kin," he says matter-of-factly, as if the entire world knows that.

He's her next of kin? What am I, a bowl of pudding? This will not stand.

"Your mother and you need my help. She can't manage her life."

I suspect my inner editor may be trying to step in and make me play nice, but I'm in no mood for nice. I give her a swift kick to keep her from interfering and making me sound weak.

I tighten every muscle in my body, hoping that firmness will extend into my voice. "You're not the boss of her or me, so back off. I'm warning you. And you'll never get your hands on Harry."

Chad nods at me when I say that.

"You're getting hysterical," my uncle says condescendingly, treating me like I'm the infant.

"You are confusing hysterical with strong," I reply.

My uncle chuckles, which infuriates me. I could jump inside the phone and strangle him.

He continues, "You're young and you need help. Your mother would agree, and she wants me to be involved. I'm flying there to see her and settle this situation as soon as the documents are prepared. I'll take Harry off your hands so you can go back to your normal life."

Chad's pacing. His eyes are hot and glaring. And Mads is on the verge of crying.

"My mother wouldn't agree to that," I say without knowing whether that's true. "And for your information, Harry and I are doing just fine here without you. Do not come. We don't want you, and you'll never get your hands on that baby."

My inner editor must be having heart failure, wondering what's up with this version of Claire. Maybe I'll fire her permanently. I don't need her controlling what I say.

"Nonsense. You shouldn't have to care for your mother's baby. He needs a stable home. I'll text you when I arrive. No need to thank me. This is what brothers are for."

I end the call without a goodbye and drop my phone as if it's scorching my hand.

"My uncle is evil on steroids!" I shout at the ceiling. "He blames Harry for my mom falling apart. I'm no dope. I know she's having a rough time, but that doesn't mean we're kicking the kid to the curb."

Chad says, "Your uncle sounds like a douche. Classic rotten. I could deliver a return message to him hard and fast if you want." Chad punches one fist into the other.

He'd better calm down. This isn't his fight. I keep my tone more measured and say, "Leave him to me. My uncle, my responsibility."

Mads looks shaken. I take her hand in mine and give it a squeeze.

Chad says, "I love that you protect Harry. I stick up for my sister, too."

"Do you also have a vile uncle?" I ask.

"No uncle. Her bully is closer to home. My old man is determined to send Angela away to boarding school next year. I'm her defense lawyer arguing before the almighty judge that she should not be shipped out against her will. She wants to go to Newton North."

"You're a good brother," I say.

"I am, and you're a good sister."

I peek at Mads, and her eyes are ready to overflow. If she starts crying, I will too.

"Um... I haven't always been a good sister," I tell Chad. "There were many times I wished Harry wasn't here disrupting my life. That's a horrible thing to think, like wishing he'd never been born. I was so upset that I had to give up my summer, then my college plans went to hell, and to be honest, I resented him for everything that's making my mother not well.

"When my mother first told me she was pregnant, I couldn't see straight. I was angry at her for being stupid. Why would she do that to us? I thought someone her age knows how to handle that type of situation. No one needed a baby around here. But life didn't give me a choice, and I had to stand by and watch my mom disappear down a deep, dark rabbit hole."

"But you love Harry," Mads says and sniffs back some potential tears.

"I do. Everything that's happened has shown me how much I care about him and that there are no limits on what I'm willing to do for him."

"You're more a parent to Harry than anyone. My dad is going to help you, and I'll always stick by you and Harry," Mads says.

And Chad joins in. "And I'm on your team, remember?"

Harry's army is taking shape.

"I love you guys." We stand and group hug. I never want to forget how that feels.

"Got to fly. I'll drive you, Mads," Chad says and side-eyes me when he calls her that. I think the three of us are well passed the stage when we have to be so cautious around one another.

Before Mads leaves, she kisses me and says, "Happy birthday, Claire Bear. I've got you."

"Uh, one more thing," I say and pause, nervous that what I'm about to ask will be a bridge too far after everything that's happened between Mads and me. "I was wondering, since Chad is on the team too, can he come tomorrow when I meet with your dad? It would help to have another pair of ears there." I don't want to push her buttons, but I really want him there.

"Sure. We'll have a legal party. I'll make the popcorn." Her forgiveness sounds genuine and not one of her Academy Award-winning performances.

I close the door after them and head to the kitchen to clean up. After the dishwasher is loaded, I toss the rest of the cake in the trash. I've had enough sugar and calories to last me for some time. I probably need to brush my teeth for half an hour so they don't rot away overnight.

I study myself in the bathroom mirror, still jazzed about my new haircut, which has transformed me from a kid to an adult, strong and ready for the fight ahead.

CHAPTER
18

I climb into bed, prop myself up on the pillows, and put the laptop on my raised knees. I plan to demonstrate to Mads's father that even if I'm a non-paying client, I do my homework. I don't want Mr. Sunday to imagine me as the same child he took out for ice cream or hosed down in his backyard on hot summer days while Mads and I squealed.

Before I start my research, a loud whoosh rattles my window, and I get up to make sure the window is secure and observe strong gusts whipping the tree branches into a frenzied dance.

Tomorrow the lawn will be strewn with debris, but I refuse to add yard cleanup to my never-ending to-do list. Unless I stumble onto a secret stash of cash for a cleanup crew, whatever lands on our property will remain there as a permanent Jackson art installation.

I resume my position in bed and Google adoptions and guardianship issues. Right off, I learn these things are handled state by state, and the laws and procedures in Massachusetts might be different from other states. Once I click my way to the Massachusetts government website, it directs me to the Middlesex Probate and Family Court, which has jurisdiction over these matters in the City of Newton.

From there I link to the Massachusetts General Laws Article 5, Section 5–204, which deals with guardianship of a minor. Some of the legal language is beyond me, but I get the gist of most of it, I think. The first paragraph makes it clear that if Mom agrees to let me be Harry's temporary guardian, the process will be smooth. We might not even have to go before a judge. Being Harry's guardian seems like the best option. It will give me the legal credentials that only Mom has now. And while she's in the hospital, she can't do much of anything, which makes this all the more urgent.

With that authority, I'll be able to put Mads on the pickup list for Harry at Sunny Acres and not have to be concerned whether Mom signed a form so Harry can get his shots at the pediatrician's. I'll be able to make these decisions without having to involve her so she can concentrate on getting better.

As I continue reading, I learn there's also a "caregiver status" I could apply for. Mr. Sunday will help me decide which option is best to get control of Harry and neutralize Mom's dear, darling, despicable brother, Patrick the Prick. It's not that I'm against adoption in general. Sometimes it's pretty great, like with my friend Alvene. Her parents are wonderful, and she loves them to bits, but she plans to search for her bio parents when she goes away to college. Adoption doesn't have to be Harry's fate. And the beauty of my plan is that it's temporary until Mom is all better.

As my eyelids get heavy and the words blur together, I close the computer and conk out, as the storm brewing outside is like white noise background. I sleep until a monstrous thunderclap wakes me. The sky lights up and sounds off again. It's only 2:30 a.m.! I'm pissed. I'll be a zombie tomorrow.

Before the storm spooks Harry, I get him. He's still sleeping when I put him in my bed and snuggle close so he doesn't get scared. The rain beats against the house like it hates us. I synchronize my breathing to his, and it lulls me back to sleep until the first streams of daylight appear.

I pick up Harry, and we survey the damage from last night's storm. The mess out front could be worse, and once the winter snow comes, no one will see the layer of branches and leaves covering the grass. The air in the room is a bit funky, so I leave the window open and take Harry to get changed.

"This is going to be a momentous day, bro," I tell him while putting on his onesie and fake denim pants. "What happens today may once and for all settle our fate. Are you ready to run away with me if my plan fails?" I ask him with a smile, knowing that option might be impossible, dangerous, and would certainly land me in major trouble. Still, it might have to be my last resort.

Harry doesn't smile back at me. His expression is as serious as he can get, as if he suddenly has keen radar and understands his situation might be precarious.

"No adoption for you," I promise him, and seal it with a kiss on the top of his head. Those wide innocent eyes of his slay me every time.

While I feed Harry from cute little jars of mush, Dad calls again. Twice in two days is unusual. Maybe he regrets his comments about my new haircut. But I'm happy he did, because after last night's Googling session, there's an important piece of information only Dad can provide. My approach to asking these questions needs to be subtle.

"Hey, Clarry, just wanted to see how you're doing as an eighteen-year-old. Feel any different?"

"Actually, I love being eighteen, the age of majority. It does make a difference," I reply, and draw on yesterday's leftover sugar to sweeten my tone before I plunge into my questions. "How's Bella?" I ask with words dripping in syrup, setting the mood.

"Adorable. She's so much fun and a lot of work. How are Harry and your mom doing? Isn't it fun to have a baby brother? And if you need more baby time with a baby girl, come here and play with Bella."

I'm already drowning in baby time, but he has no clue. I ask my first question. "Dad, do you remember when I was a baby?"

"Of course. You were adorable too."

"But was I a good, I mean, a mellow baby or one of those criers?"

"You were pretty calm. After all, you had nothing to complain about." He laughs and continues, "You were well fed, outside in the sun on every warm day. Mom cuddled you all the time and had the patience to sing you the same song until you knew all the words and could sing it with her—or try to. You were, and still are, a bona fide genius."

"So, Mom wasn't all stressed out having her first baby."

"She loved motherhood and was a pro, as if she had trained for that role all her life."

I keep my tone light so Dad doesn't suspect my motives. "Did you guys have a nanny, or did Grandma help a lot when I was born?" I need the full picture of Mom as a new mother.

"Grandma came for visits, but not too many, and we didn't have any babysitters. Your mom went back to work when you were two and in day care. She never complained about being tired or wanting more help. Why all the questions?"

"No special reason. I came across some old photos and was just wondering." I applaud my lying abilities, which lately have been incredible.

"You were the best baby, Clarry. Are you perhaps a bit jealous of the attention Harry and little Bella are getting?"

What a ludicrous question. My inner editor, whom I thought I permanently fired but won't seem to leave, steps in to warn me off a testy response. Why would Dad think anyone would be jealous of a baby who knows nothing, often reeks of something repulsive, and can't take care of himself?

"Um...no, not jealous. Happy you have Bella, really."

"Is there a chance you'll come here for Thanksgiving?" Dad asks.

"Oh, I'm not sure." *Think quick, Claire, you can't leave Newton now. There's no way to be certain Harry would be here when you got back.*

"I meant to tell you, the seniors are planning a big event that weekend after the Newton-Brookline football game," I say and again offer up praise for my sharp and swift lying ability to hatch a plausible excuse.

"Senior year is the best. Well, check your calendar and find another time to come. I'll send you a ticket."

"I will," I lie.

"Bellissima is calling for me. Got to go. Bye." He calls her "Bellissima." Maybe I am jealous of all these babies, but I got the information I needed from him.

The mom who took care of me isn't the same person as Harry's mom.

CHAPTER 19

When the toaster rings, I take out my Pop-Tart, and Harry drools with envy as I bite off a hunk. I suppose the strawberry filling is way more appealing than his jar of bland beige applesauce.

"Too bad, kiddo. No Pop-Tart until you get more teeth." Perhaps I should learn the Heimlich maneuver and CPR before he eats real people food. Do parents do that sort of thing?

I print out excerpts from the law to bring to the meeting today, even though I'm sure Mr. Sunday doesn't need my legal research. I just want to look competent. I shove the adoption form my uncle sent into the folder with the other papers.

While Harry's napping, I do some snooping in Mom's room, hunting for financial information about the house. Just maybe I'll discover some information about Harry's father tucked away. It feels indecent to paw through her things, but under the circumstances, I have no choice.

It isn't until I get to the bottom dresser drawer that I hit pay dirt. There are five file folders, all labeled with a different color Sharpie. In one there's a stack of bills, including one from Citizens Bank for the mortgage. I'm surprised at how easy it is to understand. We still owe almost $100,000 on the house and pay close to $1,100 a month to the bank. What the bill doesn't show is how much the house is worth, but now I have a starting point. Maybe Chad could ask his father to help me with this real estate stuff, but that's on the back burner until Dr. Goldstone green-lights my idea of selling the house and moving to a cheaper place.

Behind the mortgage paper are credit card bills from three different places. We owe money on all of them. Dad would throw a fit if he saw them, but what else can we do with no money coming in? We have to live. There's nothing here about my college account, so I assume the whole thing is gone by now.

I hear Harry getting whack-a-doodle in his crib, so I close the drawer and get him. We both could use some air to clear our heads, so we head outside for a walk. I pick up the pace to get my blood circulating because I've become so sluggish lately from lack of exercise. If we had money, I might invest in a jogging stroller.

When I look at those sweet eyes and pudgy cheeks, I know I'm completely attached to Harry, as if he's my own baby. Going to court is a risk, and I might lose but I'll never forgive myself if I don't try everything in my power to keep Harry with us.

In my head, I recite the Robert Frost poem Mrs. G. made us memorize last year about the man in the woods reaching a road that diverges into two paths. He has a dilemma about which path to take, but he knows his decision will make all the difference in his life. I should ask Mom which path she wants to take and then pray we're going the same way, because if the two of us diverge, it *will* make all the difference.

When Harry and I get home, the red Mustang is already out front. Chad's listening to music and seems mellow, not churning with anxiety like me. Chad asks if we can go to his house for dinner after the meeting with Mads's father. I agree. I know I owe him big time. But now, I have to change my clothes and Harry's too so we make a good impression, especially with his father. I have a hunch he's the hard-to-please type, and I might need his real estate expertise.

I dress Harry in his green gremlins one-piece and warn him not to spit up on it. I go through three different outfits, unsure what's right for this occasion. In the old days, I'd probably ask Mom or Mads, but it might be too soon to get Mads involved in picking clothes to wear to meet Chad's family. The only person I can consistently rely on is me.

I decide on my blue-and-white checkered mid-thigh dress, black flats, and no makeup. Better to be conservative, I think. After all, this isn't a party.

When we leave, I stop at my car door, but Chad keeps walking to his Mustang, carrying Harry.

"Car seat, remember?" I call.

He opens the car door and pulls the front seat forward. "Feast your eyes on this. This was my sister's, and it's almost new, according to my mom."

It's the gold standard of car seats, way better than what I bought for Harry. Chad grins and puts Harry in, saying, "Harry, my man, you're about to ride in a wicked awesome car today."

As soon as Mads opens the door, she reaches for Harry, but he swivels his head owl-like, pleading with me not to hand him off.

"Wait till he gets more used to being here," I say and hope Mads doesn't take offense at Harry's dumb move.

Mrs. Sunday comes up behind Mads and says, "He's adorable, Claire. How old is he now?" She takes him, but this time Harry seems okay with it. That baby is so unpredictable. We follow her inside.

"He's five months."

"I miss having a little one around," Mrs. Sunday says, "but I couldn't imagine going back to those days of diapers and waking at all hours of the night. Kudos to your mom. She must be a dynamo. I should call her for coffee."

"She's in the hospital."

"What happened?"

"They don't know exactly yet. She's been taking some pills, and they weren't good for her. Her doctor promised to update me tomorrow."

"I'm so sorry to hear that. If you need anything at all, Claire, you can always call me." Mrs. Sunday flutters her eyes at Harry, which hypnotizes him. "You don't have to be on your own. Do you want to stay here with us until your mom gets home?"

"No, thank you. Harry has so much stuff at home. It's kind of unbelievable what a baby needs. I've been helping with Harry since he was born. I'm okay, but thanks. If I need something, I'll ask." But I won't do that, because if I can't take care of Harry myself, how would I explain to a judge I'm a responsible adult who can become his legal guardian?

"Chad, I'm surprised to see you here." Mads's mother says, sliding into her vice principal's voice.

Chad looks her straight in the eye, ever confident, and says, "Claire asked me to come." Lots of kids shake when they face her, even when they aren't guilty of anything.

"My husband is waiting for you in the study. Harry and I will be in the family room making mischief. I'll get you if he fusses."

"Thanks," I reply and hand her Harry's bag with all the tools to keep him happy, I hope.

Mr. Sunday stands when we enter. I introduce Chad and almost giggle when they're side by side, dressed like twins in khaki pants and light blue button-down shirts. Chad even wore regular lace-up shoes and instead of his usual Nikes. They shake hands like they've concluded a business deal.

Chad sits next to me on the sofa for two and Mads takes the adjacent plush burgundy velvet chair. Whenever Mads and I hung out in this room, I used to love to run my hands over that fabric. It always had a calming effect on me. Her father's wooden chair is designed for serious work and not comfort. His stares at my folder with lots of papers sticking out. I brought my research. *Claire, always the high achiever.*

Mr. Sunday positions a yellow legal pad on his lap, which reminds me of the note-taking Dr. Goldstone. I have known Mads's dad since forever, but today he's different, treating me like a client. This is all very professional.

He begins. "Claire, why don't you tell me what's going on and how you think I can help?"

I fall into class project mode and present my thesis first before bringing in all my research to back it up.

"My mom can't take care of Harry full-time right now. She's in the hospital. I'm not sure yet what's wrong with her. I do everything for Harry, but I have no legal authority for him. If I wanted to add Mads to the approved pickup list at his day care, I can't. If there's a medical emergency and my mom isn't available, they won't listen to me, even though I'm Harry's closest relative. I want to become Harry's temporary legal guardian."

Mr. Sunday sits upright as if a puppet master yanked his head strings, and he stops writing. His jaw drops, and the lines in his forehead deepen into valleys. I guess he wasn't expecting that.

"I have researched this idea, and it seems possible if my mother agrees—and I think she will." I pull out one of my papers and start reading. "Chapter 190B, Article V, Section 5-209 of the Massachusetts laws says that a guardian of a ward has the powers and responsibilities of a parent regarding the ward's support, care, education, health and welfare." I put the paper down and add, "I'm the best person for that job."

Mads pokes my knee. "Tell him about your uncle."

"My uncle, my mother's brother, is trying to persuade her to give up Harry for adoption. I'm not sure if he plans to keep Harry for himself or pass him off to another family. He's not a nice man. He claims it would be better for my mother and me, and if we do what he says, he'll lend us money, which we very much need."

"Money. You mean he wants to buy the baby?" Mr. Sunday asks.

"No, not like that. Money for my college and for supporting my mother until she can work again. But when you put it like that, it does sort of feel like bribery. As I said, he's not a nice man. I don't want Harry to be with him." I present a more mature Claire to Mr. Sunday and refrain from using any colorful vocabulary to describe the bastard.

"And what does your mother think about this?" he asks.

Ha! Right off, he zeros in on the central question, the one I've never had the courage to ask, because I'm scared of Mom's honest answer. What if she really wants to give Harry up for adoption, and I'm standing in her way?

"She's under a lot of pressure," I reply, not explaining that some of that pressure is coming from me. "For now, things aren't going well for her. She hasn't worked for months. We're living on savings." I put the papers back into my folder and push my non-existent hair off my forehead. Old nervous habit.

Mr. Sunday writes more, stops for a second, and then flips to a new page and continues. Mads, Chad, and I glance at each other with blank faces, waiting to hear what he'll say.

Finally, he locks his eyes squarely on me. "Claire, do you have any idea what guardianship entails?"

"I do."

"You will have to place Harry's needs above yours. You will be totally responsible for a helpless baby."

"I understand."

"If your mother doesn't agree to sign the papers, it would mean a court fight against her, and you probably wouldn't win. The biological mother has all the rights unless she's deemed unfit. You don't want to become your mother's adversary even though you're only trying to help her and your brother."

"She'll agree."

"Are you sure?"

"I am," I say confidently. I know have the upper hand with her and can always play the guilt card and remind her about taking all my money. This is my leverage to get her to sign. Mr. Sunday might find those tactics too devious, so I keep them to myself.

"Why would she agree to this?" He's cross-examining me. I've seen how this plays out on *Law & Order* many times when a witness is on the stand. It can be brutal, but I suppose he has to probe my motives.

"She'll agree because, unlike the adoption my uncle wants to happen, this guardianship would be temporary until she's well and can do the mothering."

"But what if that never happens, Claire? Have you considered what that would mean to your life?"

"This was a complicated decision for me, but there's no other way to make sure the three of us stay together. I'm the only one standing between Harry and adoption."

"If your mother agrees, the courts would probably be favorable to a first-degree family member taking the child rather than having them go into the system, but..."

And there it is. The big BUT. For a minute, I thought he was on board with this guardianship deal.

"But what?" I ask in a monotone to mask my inner hysteria. It's important Mr. Sunday sees me as calm and capable and not the six-year-old who bellowed when her ice cream fell out of the cone.

"Do you know who Harry's father is?"

"No. No one is listed on his birth certificate." I'm not sharing Becky's suspicions that Mom may know the guy's name. It would only muddy things, and Becky might've misinterpreted Mom's words. It's bad enough dealing with my uncle. I sure as hell don't want whoever is Mr. Blank Line making a play for Harry too.

"Oh," he says.

Yikes! Did I give him the impression my mother was sleeping around and has no clue who might be the father? I have to fix that immediately.

"I didn't mean it like that. It's not like she dated after the divorce and can't be sure which man is the father. This was a one-time thing," I say, but of course, I can't really be certain of that. "It just happened. She says she doesn't know how to contact him."

"Okay. If you're sure the father can't be identified and is out of the picture, it will help, but it might be a good idea to do a DNA test on Harry, so the court knows you're willing to find the father if possible."

"I can do that," I say. I don't want to find Harry's bio-dad, but I have to show I'm willing to do anything.

Mr. Sunday continues, "Good. It's easy to do the test. Another option might be to consider applying to be Harry's caregiver instead of guardian and then your mother won't have to relinquish any of her rights. And you could get a health care POA."

"A what?"

"Sorry, legal-speak. POA is power of attorney. You'd be the one with the responsibility for all medical decisions for Harry. It's like a financial POA where you control someone else's finances. Is that something you also might need to do?"

"No. I don't want to take control of the financial stuff, but if I have to, I guess I will. Would 'caregiver status' be better than guardianship in this situation?"

"I'll talk to a colleague at the Probate Court and discuss the options available for you. You're aware their primary focus is what's in a child's best interests. That will be the basis for any decision, although judges often prefer to give custody or guardianship to a couple, especially a couple who can prove they have the financial ability to care for the child. You said your uncle has money but didn't mention if he's married and has children of his own."

"He is married, but no kids."

"That might help his case. Being married is a point in his favor, plus you're so young. I don't want you to fight him in court. That can get nasty. You are a legal adult, aren't you, Claire?"

"I turned eighteen on Saturday. And, Mr. Sunday, I will go to work. I can finish high school at night or during the summer. This won't be a problem."

"And what about college?" he asks, sounding more like a friend's dad than a lawyer.

"I'll be taking a gap year to work."

Mr. Sunday's face relaxes, and even his heavy eyebrows let go and fall. "I'll prepare the paperwork and do my best to convince the court to grant this. In the meantime, you need your mother's consent, and then she'll have to sign some documents in front of witnesses and a notary. Can you handle that?"

"A notary?"

"That's a person who puts a seal on the document to attest she signed without coercion. It makes it all official."

"Got it. Mr. Sunday, thank you so much. I, uh..." I'm not sure how to tell him, but if I'm a real adult, I have to approach things maturely. "I wish I could pay you—"

He stands and hugs me. "I would never charge my daughter's best friend. Introduce me to the little person who's at the center of all this commotion."

We find Harry enjoying a jar of baby mush and listening to Mrs. Sunday babble nonstop while he eats. He's enthralled by her rendition of Goldilocks and the Three Bears.

"Linda, you're great with babies. Brings back memories." Mr. Sunday smiles at his wife.

By the time we leave, my brain is as pureed as Harry's baby food.

On the drive to Chad's house, his silence is agonizing. Does he think my plan is stupid? I want to crawl inside his head and roam around in his thoughts, all of them.

When I can't hold it in another minute, I blurt out, "Can you please say something? Not knowing what you're thinking is driving me bananas."

"What you're doing for your brother is amazing. You deserve a gold medal for the best sister in the all-around competition."

His compliment embarrasses me. I never thought about the guardianship in that way. I'm humbled and self-conscious. "This is something I have to do," I say.

"I'll help you." A picture flashes before my eyes of Chad running into a dark alley to change into his superhero outfit.

"There's nothing you can do."

"I may have some ideas of my own."

"Like what?"

As we drive through two white pillars onto a magnificent red brick driveway, he says, "You did your research before sharing. I will too. I learn from the best."

"Intriguing."

CHAPTER
20

Tall pine trees create a wall along one side of the driveway shielding everything behind them. As the driveway circles around, an enormous mansion comes into view. This would be a perfect movie setting, easy to visualize a steady stream of chauffeur-driven limos dropping off Hollywood types and other rich people for a party.

Four marble columns holding up huge potted plants stand guard at the entrance. Mom's house looks like a bungalow in comparison. Chad opens the door, depriving me of an opportunity to bang the round handle hanging from the snout of a brass lion's head on the door.

A girl, probably nine or ten is waiting inside and smiles at me. I'm not sure which sister this is, so I only say, "Hi."

She immediately falls to her knees to get closer to the baby. "Can I touch him?" she asks, as if she never saw a real baby this close.

"Of course," I reply. Chad puts Harry's seat on the floor, and she starts to play with Harry's feet while practicing her baby talk. The little dude is in heaven. That boy is convinced he's a big-time celebrity, and the whole world is his fan club.

My eyes are drawn to the kaleidoscope of colored glass in the center of the ceiling, which extends two floors in height. The architect must've been in love with English palaces when he designed this place.

Another girl shows up, and I crouch to the same level with them and Harry. The smallest one is adorable, with her hair in two neat bunches on the top of her head and a sparkly silver headband. She has the same exquisite gold-speckled brown eyes Chad has. They are as much alike as Harry and me.

The other sister is older and wearing large red-framed glasses, a black dress, and cute red leather shoes.

"I love your glasses," I say to her with a broad smile.

"Thanks. Are you Chad's friend from his new school?"

"Yes. I'm Claire, and this is Harry."

"Is he your baby?"

"My brother," I reply, as another girl bops into the massive hall. She's taller and must be the oldest, Angela. Chad talks about her all the time. She joins us on the floor. The youngest of the three girls holds the baby's hand and studies his tiny fingers. Angela makes faces at Harry, who acknowledges her efforts appreciatively. He's devouring the attention, and the girls are delighted with his charming response.

Chad pats the head of the little one and says, "This hyper ball of fire is my sister Maya, and the middle one is Michaela."

"Angela, do you want to hold him?" I ask the other sister.

Her eyes glow as if I offered her a bucket of money. I unhook the harness and lift Harry out, pleased he's in a good mood. Way to go, bro. I pretend his cooperation is intentional to help me out, but I know it's just luck with a fickle baby.

I pass the blobby ball of baby fat to her. She cradles him. Chad hangs back as a silent observer and then leaves. His sisters pepper me with questions about babies like I'm some great authority. Can Harry crawl? When will he learn to talk? How come he has no teeth on the top? Mostly, I make up the answers because without my pals Google and YouTube I know nothing about babies. Mom certainly never taught me much. I learned the hard way about things like babies pooping in the bath. More than once, I had to scoop him out of some pretty filthy water.

Angela, on the other hand, wants to talk about Newton North and asks me if freshmen really have to eat in a separate section of the cafeteria.

"That's a rumor," I reply. "People like to scare the ninth-graders, but mostly it's all harmless. I can fill you in on the deets so you know how to navigate the big bad high school."

Chad returns and says, "Okay, the homeowners, AKA, my parents, are ready."

I strap Harry back into his seat, and Chad carries him. I follow, and Maya takes my hand. So sweet. As we enter the dining room, or should I say dining hall, sweat glides down my sides even though I used an extra layer of anti-perspirant to handle this occasion.

A massive, dark wooden table dominates the room. It's set with red-and-gold embroidered placemats, white dishes with a royal blue border, and lots of silverware. I'm going to have to dive into my memory palace of sixth-grade homemaking, or I'll embarrass myself and use the wrong fork. My family doesn't prepare anything like this even for holidays. I'm curious if this display is for me, or if they eat formally all the time. My first take is that family dinners here might be stressful.

After the introductions, Chad's mother shows me where to sit. He definitely gets his height and glowing smile from her, but her skin is darker and more like Angela's than his. His mother is wearing a silky navy pantsuit that didn't come off the rack at Taylor Imports. I put Harry on the floor between me and Chad so he's in easy reach in case he needs an emergency bottle.

A maid or a waitress, not sure what to call her, serves the first course, which is a type of tomato soup with croutons swimming on the top. Very posh. None of my friends have people waiting on them at home. Chad's sisters don't have to leave their seats to bring in food or take dishes away. This is like being in a five-star restaurant.

Chad's father emits a chuckle and says, "Well, Chad, I'm happy that baby looks nothing like you."

Simultaneously, Chad and I redden. Wow, that's rude, or he has a disturbing sense of humor.

Chad's father is chunkier than Chad, and he's definitely not as handsome. He did give Chad the glitter in his eyes, but his face isn't kind. His smile seems menacing, as if he's lying in wait to pounce on someone.

"Mr. Williams, he isn't my baby. He's my brother," I say to clarify the situation.

Did Chad's dad wink at him as if he didn't believe me? Quick with the judgments, aren't you, Mr. Williams? Like so many others, he's thinking I'm a teenager who got into trouble and is trying to pass off her kid as her sibling. I glance at Chad's mother, hoping she'll say something, because I'm sure Chad told her the truth, but she says nothing. Either she's afraid of contradicting her husband, or she has her own suspicions about Harry and me.

I have to confront this head-on. "My mother is in the hospital, so Harry has to come with me everywhere."

"You have to admit, he could be your twin, Claire. He could be your son," Chad's father says, driving home his incorrect assumptions. It's becoming quite clear why Chad wouldn't want to work with that man.

His father says, "I'm sure your parents are thrilled with their new addition."

I let that remark pass. I don't want to tell him my parents are divorced, and Harry has no father. That's a surefire way to bring on a slew of unfair judgments on my family.

Happily, the subject of Harry's parentage ends as the main course is served. I consider the small, whole chicken placed in front of me, and Chad's mother tells me it's squab, whatever that is. It seems a bit repulsive to eat, plus I have no idea how you're supposed to tackle it. I observe how the others handle this poor baby chicken.

When Mr. Williams breaks off a leg, the cracking sound is jarring. I'm not doing that. I cut off a tiny piece of this unfortunate dead creature and use my mother's recent trick of pushing the food around on her plate to pretend she's eating. In the meantime, I scarf down the safe mashed potatoes and veggies instead.

"Dad, Claire knows Newton North High School as well as you know the price of real estate, and she's in the top five percent of the senior class," Chad says, eyeing my squab. As much as I'd like to put it on his plate, I'm pretty sure his father will consider that too familiar, and this family may be too proper to share food.

Chad pushes his case. "She can give Angela all kinds of advice about that school."

His father's eyes narrow, and he stops eating. "You don't get a say in this, mister. She's going to a refined boarding school where they'll teach her how to succeed in the world. You blew your chance at a pedigree diploma. Why would you wish that on her?"

Chad told me his father wants to send her away so she can mingle with the wealthy, play tennis, and learn manners, which probably means curtsy lessons in case she meets royalty. Ha. Ha. She's a smart girl. Who would want to be part of that fake life?

Chad says, "Boarding school is a terrible idea, and she doesn't want to go."

Way to go, Chad. Now that I've met his father, I'd say pushing back like that requires some courage.

His father holds his knife and fork upright on the table and glares at Chad, as if he's going to slice right through him. Chad doesn't flinch.

"Mom, tell Dad you want Angela here."

His mother remains quiet. There's no question who's in command in this family, and it isn't her.

Mr. Williams says, "She should stay away from those loser boys at the high school. They're not fine enough for her. We don't need a Newton North lowlife sniffing around here."

"I'm not a loser Newton North boy," Chad says, not backing down. But seriously, any guy who wants to date Angela and tangle with her dad would be nuts. She should come with a warning label.

The more I listen to Mr. Williams, the more he reminds me of my uncle. They're two control freaks who believe having gobs of money gives them the right to bark out commands to everybody. I love that Chad goes to the mat for his sister. It will be many more years before I know if Harry will be that kind of stand-up brother.

I pick up Harry from his seat and hold him on my lap as a distraction. I sure as hell don't want to get into the middle of this family business, but Mr. Williams won't let me do that. He asks, "Miss... I don't know your last name. Oh well, never mind, I'm positive you've seen drugs and bums in your school, and I'm sure you agree my daughter deserves better."

It's amazing how some people think private schools are immune from some of the problems public schools face. Those schools have been burnt by stories of buyers and sellers swarming their campuses, and I don't mean doing transactions for the latest designer jeans. Drugs are not limited to public schools. That's ridiculous and ignorant, but I will temper my words.

"Mr. Williams, there are some bad dudes at Newton North and Newton South, but they're also at the fancy private schools. Those schools aren't all pure and innocent."

"It's a numbers game, like in business. What's the ratio? What's the percentage? And which environment can be controlled? There's a lot to scrutinize when you're a parent."

He's right about the weight of being a parent, which I'm learning each day, but his mind is closed to any argument that might prove him wrong. The rest of dinner proves less combative, and once the main dishes have been cleared away, the focus falls on Chad's excited younger sisters, who are eager to dig into their chocolate mousse topped with whipped cream. Wish I could slip Harry a spoonful, but I read somewhere no chocolate for babies for a while. Poor guy.

When I say goodnight to all of them, I have no sense if Chad's parents like me or not. I was friendly, but this isn't an easy house.

In the car, I say, "Did that go well? I really can't tell."

"Yes. It did. Trust me. Didn't my dad ask you to come out on the boat?"

"But without Harry."

"Only because he doesn't want the responsibility of a baby there."

"Are you sure that's the only reason?"

"Yeah, I'm sure. He has a rigid idea about what his family should do, and he's convinced he always right, and the rest of us are fools. It's a struggle to remember his intentions are good even when he's being unreasonable."

"I can understand why you wouldn't want to work with him."

"But it's not so easy. He is my father."

Chad carries Harry into my house but leaves right away. Maybe he doesn't want to give his father an excuse for some snarky comments about how much time passed until he got home.

An hour later, I receive a text from Chad.

> Hope you're okay.

> Do you think your dad would ever help me with real estate stuff?

> Tell me what you want to know, and I'll get the answers. I'm calling you now.

The phone screen lights up. I pick up, and we continue the conversation.

"Actually, there's no hurry asking him," I say. "My mom's doctor wants me to put off moving until she's better. I'm relieved. The thought of leaving Newton makes me seriously nauseous."

"And I don't want you to move. My sisters are in love with Harry, and Michaela says you're way nicer than my last girlfriend."

"Only one girlfriend? Are you playing me? I demand to hear all about her. And tell Michaela I'm not your girlfriend."

Chad grins and says, "Yeah, I know you're not. She saw and assumed."

"People are always assuming things about me."

"Michaela hated the kids from my old school. She thought they were all obnoxious. And you never told me about your real boyfriends. I don't mean Harry."

I roll my eyes and lay my best smirk on him. He laughs. I'll keep that part of my history under wraps for now.

"Angela posted a selfie with Harry on 'gram. Her handle is @sweetangela. Wish my grandma had been there tonight. You have to meet her."

My mouth expands into an involuntary yawn. Chad probably had an intimate view of my tonsils.

"Got to crash," I say.

"See you in horrible Newton North High School tomorrow," he replies with his own smirky face.

"Are you one of those bad boys of Newton North?" I joke.

"Not copping to anything, Jackson."

CHAPTER
21

Monday mornings used to be the dividing line between the weekend's fun and the re-entry to serious life. That's when scoring A's and wowing a teacher with a brilliant essay were the driving forces in me.

Now, school is the break from meaningless household duties and watching my brother. When the delightful Amelia greets Harry at the day care with great enthusiasm, I'm grateful for the precious hours of freedom she gives me.

This morning, after the Harry handover, I tell Mrs. Sample that Mom's in the hospital for a couple of days and that it's nothing serious just in case she decides she has to call her. I don't offer any details or mention possible mental health issues. Fortunately, Mrs. Sample doesn't pry and instead hugs me. I briefly rest my head on her warm, spongy body and hope I'm not overstepping boundaries. Harry's a lucky duck that he can get her hugs anytime he wants. Maybe that's worth $20,000 after all.

I step through Newton North's main door and the whole dance night replays in my mind. So much has happened since then. I wonder what today would've been like if Chad hadn't helped fix things between Mads and me.

As soon as I cross the threshold into my homeroom, Alvene pushes me into a far corner. "That's one heck of a hacked-off hairdo, Claire."

"Yeah, right."

She raises her hand to touch my hair, which I allow, even though she hates it when people want to play with her box braids. Sometimes she ties them back in a sort of ponytail, but I love it when they hang loose and she swings them around.

"This haircut was a birthday present to myself," I explain.

"So, this was no mistake. You asked for this style?"

"Yup."

"Hot damn! You've got guts, doll."

I catch Nando staring at me from a distance before he waltzes over. He also makes a motion to touch my hair, but I step back. For him, I set boundaries.

"Consent, Fernando. You need consent to touch," I scold him. He drops his hand.

"My hair is longer than yours, Jackson," he says, running his fingers through his wavy locks.

"Hell, Nando, everyone's hair is longer than mine." I smile, and the final homeroom bell rings. We take our seats.

Mrs. Gillespie goes through her morning announcements, gazing across the classroom at me. I'm the shiny new object at school. A body piercing would've spared me all the attention my eighteenth birthday haircut is instigating.

Between first and second period, I bump into Mads.

"Chad isn't answering my texts. Did you see him?" I ask.

"He's not here. Must've blown off school today."

I wonder if he had a thing with his dad. I try calling him while I dodge oncoming hallway traffic. The call goes to voicemail, leaving me with the same unease I felt on Saturday when I didn't hear from him all day.

In Latin class, while my teacher discusses our translation assignments, my phone vibrates in my pants pocket with an incoming text. I assume it's Chad, and he knows I can't answer during class. People with smartwatches are lucky. They can glance at their wrist with no one knowing they're checking their phone.

The moment the bell rings, I zoom out of there and find an out-of-the-way spot between two rows of lockers. The text is from Dr. Goldstone, asking me to call whenever I can. I fly out of the building to find a private place under the bleachers.

"Dr. Goldstone, it's Claire Jackson."

"Hello, Claire. I saw your mother this morning. The hospital doctors and I agree a visit from you would be a good idea. Your mother is eager to see you."

"How is she? Did she..." I can't ask the question. Sometimes being in a protective bubble of ignorance is preferable. I can't believe she'd do something if it meant never seeing me again. My thoughts are rambling. It would gut me if she took all those pills on purpose.

"She's doing better. The overdose was unintentional. When she received her new medications from the psychiatrist, she misunderstood the directions and didn't realize she was supposed to discontinue all the old pills her internist had given her. Unfortunately, she took everything, and the side effects were considerable. But we feel quite confident she did not attempt suicide. That's good news."

"And you're sure?"

"Claire, I'm as sure as any doctor can be. Come visit her. You'll see for yourself she's improving."

"When should I come?"

"Today is fine. Afternoon is best. You can wait until school gets out. Check in at the front desk when you arrive and bring ID."

"Great. Thank you. Dr. Goldstone, can I bring Harry?"

"Not yet. Just you."

"Okay, and thanks again." I end the call before I go gushy with gratitude. I text Chad the news.

> Visiting my mom today!

I add a super-excited emoji face for emphasis.
Now he replies after dodging my texts all morning.

> Great. I'll drive you.

> You don't have to.

I don't ask why he's skipping school.

I HAVE to talk to you.

Putting a word in all caps isn't like him.

Meet me at 2. You can pick me up in front.

After everyone witnessed our dance together, there's no sense playing hide-and-seek around school. I don't have to meet him blocks away.

Are you sure?

I reply with a thumbs-up and then head inside straight to the caf, feeling like Dr. Goldstone knocked a one-hundred-pound weight off my shoulders. Whatever is wrong with Mom, I will deal with it. I just need to be sure she wants to be with me—and Harry too, I hope.

During lunch, I give Mads the low down. She beams as she listens to my good news, and I love her for that. I start telling her about my dinner at Chad's when Vivian stops by our table and sits. "Claire, let's tap into your mother's brain for the election. It's a big one this year, and we should start planning early. Would your mother help us put on a congressional debate where students get to ask the questions for a change? And she'll know about any changes in the voter registration laws since the last election."

"Sure, but not right now. She had to go away on a business tri—" I stop mid-sentence, disgusted by how easy I slip into lying. Lies can come back and bite you. And when you do finally tell the truth, people are still pissed you lied to them in the first place. It never works.

"Viv, my mom's in the hospital. She's okay but she can't work with us now. I can ask her friend Becky to help us. The two of them worked together in the League of Women Voters.

"Sure. Set it up. I hope your mom is better soon. Do you want to stay at my house for a few days, so you're not alone?"

"I can't. My brother—" I'm also no longer keeping the lid on Harry to protect my mother's rep. Truth time.

"Since when does an only child have a brother? How old is he?" she asks.

"He's five months old," I answer.

"Congrats. Call me if you need help. I got my baby-sitter's badge in Girl Scouts years ago."

"Thanks."

No snickers, raised eyebrows, or embarrassing questions. If she has an opinion about my brother or my mother, she's keeping it to herself. I'm making progress in the not-caring-what-other-people-think department.

⚓

CHAD'S WAITING for me at 2 p.m. in front of the school. I hop in and put the address for Newton Wellesley Hospital into his GPS. "Where were you today?"

"Had things to do," he answers cryptically.

"What kinds of things?"

"You'll find out soon."

"Does this have to do with me?"

"No grilling me. Were you sad I wasn't in school today?" he asks with a big grin.

"Not sad, curious, but I'm too jittery about visiting my mom in a psych department to think about anything else right now."

"I feel you," he says.

"Am I a weirdo because I'm trembling?"

"Not weird. You're entering the unknown, and that can make your teeth hurt. I'll wait for you here."

He parks the car. I've been to this hospital a few times. Once I twisted my thumb between the wrought-iron bars of a fence and needed a splint, and another time Dad had surgery for a broken arm after he fell ice skating with me. The ambulance ride with him was the worst part.

The hospital has a rotating door, and I marvel at how some people navigate those so smoothly, but I'm never confident about the timing, and the doors seem like a sadistic merry-go-round with a life of their own. My usual strategy is to wait until everyone is out and get in before someone else pushes on the doors, possibly crushing me.

My knees weaken as I make my way to the information desk. I'm third in line. The guy behind me gets too close, and I hate his hot breath on my neck. I'm sure he had an onion sandwich for lunch. I inch forward to put distance between us but step on the heels of the woman in front of me, who gives me the evil eye. I move back and endure the guy's smell until it's my turn at the desk.

"Patient's name?" the woman asks, keeping her fingers on the keyboard and her eyes on the screen.

"Melanie Jackson."

"ID please."

I hand her my license. She studies it, and then says, "Happy Birthday."

"What?"

"Your birthday was two days ago."

"Oh, yeah, I forgot for a second. Thanks."

She hands me a name tag to stick on my shirt, so I guess I've been officially approved.

"Back elevators." She points behind her. "Third floor. Follow the sign to Psychiatry and Mental Health."

Yikes! Could she say that any louder? Onion breath doesn't need to know that.

"Thanks." I leave before she adds anything else. What happened to hospital privacy?

On the third floor, I find myself in front of double doors with high windows preventing anyone from peeking inside. The doors are locked. Although my hospital experiences are limited, I'm pretty sure locked doors are unusual.

There's a buzzer and an intercom on the side. I press the button, and a woman answers, asking the same questions I answered downstairs. Again, I pass the test, and she says, "Someone will let you in and give you instructions."

I need instructions to see my mother? The locked doors make this place seem like a prison. Will I have to talk to her behind a glass window? Will touching be allowed? Do they search visitors for drugs? My shivering is now accompanied by a cold sweat.

One side of the double door opens, and a short woman in pale blue scrubs appears. "Your first time here?" she asks.

"Uh-huh."

"Follow me." She walks briskly while talking. "You can visit with Ms. Jackson in the lounge or her room, but the door must remain open at all times. No photos on the floor. If we see anyone taking pictures, we'll confiscate your cell phone, and it's a can of worms to get it out of the impound." She laughs as if that's the best joke ever. Not. "Your first visit is limited to forty minutes."

I nod my head to each of the rules as I scurry to keep pace with her.

"Room 450 is straight down this hall," she says. "Take a look in the lounge on your way in case she's there." Then the woman does a U-turn, leaving me on my own.

The lounge is a combination living room/game room with lots of sofas, a large-screen TV, and square tables where people are playing cards and board games while others have pulled chairs up close to follow the action. I guess in a place like this even a game of Scrabble is worth watching to break up the boredom.

No one is wearing those awful hospital gowns, making it difficult to distinguish between patients and visitors unless you spot someone's visitor's tag. The place is crowded, but no sign of Mom, so I go back into the hall to find her room.

A couple of people in recliner-type chairs line the hallway. As I pass, they pay me no attention. One has his eyes closed, and the other stares at the opposite wall as if the pale, putrid green paint is a Picasso masterpiece.

I pause at the threshold of Room 450, shake the tightness that has built up in my limbs, and step in. The room is like and unlike every hospital room I've seen in real life or on TV. It has two of everything: beds, TVs on the wall, chairs, and night tables, but only one bathroom. There's no medical equipment in sight. Come to think of it, I haven't seen any IV poles or patients hooked up to machines.

Mom's lying on the bed. I approach and say gently, "Mom, I'm here." She stirs and sits up with a brimming smile that I was afraid was lost for good. I wish I could glue that smile onto her face forever.

"Clarry, I must've dozed off waiting for you." She holds out her arms to draw me into a hug. I nod my RSVP to that welcome invitation and move in for her embrace, conscious not to squeeze in case her bones might crumble from too much pressure. I briefly touch my cheek to hers, which is clammy and damp, the telltale signs of a recent crying jag.

When I lower my arms and study her face, trying not to stare, I notice her swollen and red-rimmed eyes, confirming the crying. Perhaps letting out those emotions is part of the therapy. I want to believe her raw eyes are a positive sign.

"Your hair!" she exclaims. "When did you do it?"

"On my birthday."

"Eighteen and a new haircut to mark the occasion. You're definitely not a child anymore. It's cute."

"Ha. You'll have to tell Dad that. He was blown away when he saw me and seemed sure this haircut made me unfit for college interviews. He almost collapsed when we FaceTimed."

"Some people have a problem with change. No judgment from me. You look fantastic."

I get up to sit in a chair when Mom pats the spot next to her on the bed, so I sit there. I notice she isn't in those awful baggy sweats. She's wearing a button-down white blouse and black pants.

"Where did you get those clothes?" I ask.

"A social worker on the staff called Becky for me, and she dropped off some clothes but didn't visit. Only you, for now."

"Why didn't you ask me to bring clothes for you? I would've done that." My reply surprises me. Am I jealous she called her friend and not me? Before all that has gone down between us lately, it would never register with me that she called Becky instead of me. I was too busy with my own friends to get up in Mom's business. I never resented her relationship with Becky before. So why am I brooding about this? Perhaps my uncle is not the only one on a power trip in this family, although I believe with all my heart that *my* motives are righteous and correct.

"Do you know I can only stay for forty minutes?" I ask.

"Yes, but you'll come again."

"What's your roommate like?" I say, glancing at the other bed.

"I don't have a roommate. They thought having to interact with someone right away might create too much tension for me."

"Makes sense. You aren't here to make friends anyway," I reply. "What are they doing to you? How long do you have to stay? Do you feel any better? Are you taking a lot of pills?" My questions roll out, each one uttered prompts a new one.

Mom chuckles to herself. "Slow down, Clarry. One question at a time!" she says. "It's best for me to be here until I can come to terms with some things. I've been slack in the mothering department. Here they hand out the pills, so there's no chance of me screwing up like I did. I did not abuse my medication. I'd never do that."

I guess the doctors believe her, so I should too. Still, if I had kept track of her pills at home, she never would've gone to the hospital. Dr. Goldstone thinks it's good for her to be here. I hope they can help her get her feelings about the pregnancy sorted out.

"If it helps to be here, I'm all for it," I say, but now I'm getting anxious she hasn't mentioned Harry, as if she's Photoshopped him out of the family portrait. Should I bring him up, or is that a trigger for her?

"Maybe you can visit again soon," Mom says, sounding like she expects to be here for a while.

Still no mention of Harry and that's all I can think about. I'm ready to bring him up when a jarring voice from the hallway stops me.

I go to the doorway to find out what is going on. An unhappy or angry woman is standing with a nurse and gesturing ferociously. The nurse gently grasps the woman's elbow and guides her down the corridor. The woman goes with her but continues to complain about someone who didn't come to visit. She underscores how upset she is with a few foul words. I'd say the lady seems wired; could be from drugs or from a lack of them. As they disappear around the corner, her words vanish like vapor. The scene leaves me shaken.

I resume my seat, and Mom says in a trembling voice, "I'm sorry about that. They have a special room for people who need help to calm down."

"And you have to listen to that all day?"

"It doesn't happen often, but it destroys me you had to witness that."

I assume she'll add this woman's meltdown to her list of things to feel guilty about. But she's right: visiting your mother in this place isn't easy. My insides could also use a calming room.

"Some people's problems aren't easily controlled with meds," Mom explains. "Lucky for me, I'm not one of those. No screaming here." She points to herself and forces a smile to dispel the seriousness of what happened.

Stop procrastinating, Claire, I yell at myself. *You're slipping into your old habits of editing yourself. Just do it!*

"Don't you want to know how Harry is?"

"I'm sure you're taking good care of him. I have placed such heavy burdens on you. It's unfair to make Harry your problem."

But she never says what she wants, so I say, "*You* have to make the decision about Harry. But I want you to know I'm ready to take care of him for as long as I have to."

"He's small. He'd never remember us, and he could have a better family."

"I disagree totally, and I'm prepared to fight for him." I want to say that if he goes, I go too, but that's too threatening. She needs to fully want him—no ifs, no strings, no nothing. I struggle to keep my voice low, so I don't bring any staff in here to haul me off to any of their special rooms. "And I have a plan to make sure Harry never leaves us no matter what your jerk-for-a-brother does."

"Uncle Pat said—"

"I don't give a rat's ass what he said. You shouldn't talk to him. He messes with your head, and then you don't know the difference between his thoughts and yours. And I should be listed as your next of kin. Tell the hospital that!" I protest.

"Yes, of course, but you're considered a minor and—"

"I'm eighteen!" I announce, as if she doesn't know how old I am. "And Uncle Pat doesn't scare me. If he asks you to sign any papers, we'll lose Harry. I want to be his temporary legal guardian until you're well. The process is straightforward if you consent."

"Bu...but..." she sputters, and her eyes register shock like Mr. Sunday's did when I mentioned guardianship. That seems to take everyone by surprise.

"But nothing," I say. "Don't let Uncle Pat trick you into anything, even if he offers you a million dollars." I take her hands in mine and moderate my voice. "We can solve the Patrick problem together and protect Harry, if that's what you want in your heart."

"Why would you do that? You're applying to college and—"

"College can wait. I need the guardianship authority to make decisions for Harry when you can't, and it will stop your brother's push for adoption. I know it's a complicated choice for you, and it is for me too."

"I'm always on your side, Clarry."

"And Harry's side too."

"And Harry's side too," she agrees. "But what about money?"

"I'm working on that, but one thing at a time. First, put Uncle Pat on your no-call and no-visit list. I don't want him to talk you into something you'll regret for the rest of your life."

Once again, we're in role-reversal mode. I'm explaining to my mother how not to make an irrevocable decision that can't be undone. And if I don't want her succumbing to pressure, I can't use the guilt card about her taking my college money. I want her to want Harry. He deserves that, especially if he has to grow up without a father.

Mom cries. Was I too harsh? I put the box of tissues from the nightstand on her lap. She may need a bunch for the heavy flow.

"Bullies need to be dealt with," I say. "Mads's father is helping me, I mean us, with the forms, and he's doing this for no money. How great is that?"

The time on my phone shows I've only got another five minutes before the hospital wizards turn me into a visitor pumpkin.

"Mom, trust me on this." I stand.

"Clarry, I trust you. No more decisions without talking to you first."

"Got to go. I don't want to get on the hospital's disallowed visitors' list. I'll come again soon."

We hug. I tell her I love her because I do and because she needs to hear it.

I leave, grateful there's a time limit on this visit.

CHAPTER
22

As I walk outside the hospital, the pitying glances of people passing me suggest that I must've just heard devastating news. I struggle to keep my head upright, look straight ahead, and walk with purpose. I don't even remember going through the revolving door on my way out.

In some ways, Mom seemed better than I expected, but I really needed to hear her commit to Harry fully, and that just didn't happen. She's not there yet. Time will tell if the doctors and medications can pull my mother back before her problems consume her.

When I get into the car, Chad wisely asks no questions. I'm not ready to describe this experience. Once we're out of the parking lot, he asks in a gentle tone, "Do you want to go for coffee?"

"Let's pick up Harry," I reply, because holding the baby at this moment is essential for me to maintain my equilibrium.

Chad takes a left directly into the blinding sunset. We simultaneously lower the visors. I lift the cover of the mirror and see my ghostly white face. This ordeal has had the same effect that a vampire draining my blood would. I wonder if I frightened Chad when I first got back into the car.

At the day care, Chad asks, "I'll come in and help you."

"I don't want to do introductions today. Another time."

"Got it. I'll wait here."

While I get Harry into the car seat, Chad folds up the stroller and loads it into the trunk.

"Let's go to the park," I say.

"Which one?"

"Cold Spring. Harry and I spent days on end there this summer."

Sometimes I hated the solitude and many summer days I felt so lonely, but today I'm eager to return and hope to find some peace there.

Chad parks, and I buckle Harry into the stroller. I bet people might assume we're a couple on a walk with our baby. Who cares what they think? No more cowering under their judgments. I'm so done with that.

We head to the best spot for seclusion in a grove of dense oaks and maples, but the branches now are almost bare, and their leaves have created a carpet on the ground below.

At the huge oak that dominates the rest of the trees, we stop. I put the brakes on the stroller and drop to the ground, leaning against the rough bark. Chad sits beside me. I close my eyes, expecting to replay the hospital scene, but my mind produces a vision of Mom holding Harry and singing to him while I do homework at the dining room table. This is what the family painting should've been: all unicorns and happiness in bright colors, but instead we got an ugly abstract of gray and black splatter.

Chad digs at the dirt beside him with a twig. "Claire, I listened carefully to Madison's father, and I think we have to do everything we can to prevent your uncle from getting control of Harry. You could lose your petition for guardianship unless the judge is King Solomon, and he decides to cut the baby in half."

I gasp.

"Not literally. Didn't you read King Solomon's story from the Bible? My grandmother tells me Bible stories all the time. Anyway, the king threatened to slice a baby in half when two women claimed the kid was theirs. Solomon was joking, because he knew the actual mother wouldn't let him do that, and the fake mother would have no problem with it. But seriously, a court fight with your uncle would be mega risky. We have to have a solid strategy."

He says "we" as if this is his battle too.

Chad says, "I have a plan." His tone scares the bejeezus out of me. I imagine this is how a doctor might sound informing a patient of bad news.

"We have to be bold and proactive or your uncle will steamroll your guardianship request like you're just some pesky gnat."

I'm now barely breathing as I wait for what's coming.

"Promise me you'll keep an open mind," he says. "I have a monster of an idea, and it might make all the difference between success and failure with the judge."

This sounds ominous. When someone asks you to keep an open mind, they know what they're about to say won't go down as smoothly as soft-serve ice cream. I wait for the hammer to drop.

"It's a two-parter. The first thing is to call your uncle and demand he stay away from here."

What was I worrying about? I agree with that.

"I will," I say enthusiastically and take out my phone, fired up. I'll prove to everyone I'm no coward, despite what Dad used to think about me.

"Put him on speaker."

I tap the button on my phone for audio and say, "Uncle Pat."

"Claire, my favorite niece," he replies. His voice is coated with melted butter to give the impression he's all mellow, but I'm not a child so easily fooled.

"Bullcrap, your favorite niece. I want you to stay away from me and my family. You aren't allowed to see Mom. You're on her no-visit list, and she won't sign any papers you give her."

"Of course she will," he says. "And you know what? This is none of your business. Do you really think your mother wanted a baby at this stage of her life?"

"Maybe she did, and maybe she didn't, but Harry's here, and no one should refer to him as a mistake. I'm telling you: do not come to our house, and do not call."

He loses his pretense of sweetness, and with a mocking cackle, he says, "You can't tell me what to do. You're a child. I have to take care of my sister, and I'm looking out for you, too, believe it or not."

I steel myself. He'll learn I'm not my mother's mini me.

"I don't need you looking out for me or my mother. You never even say the baby's name. He has a name! It's Harry. Got that? Harry!"

"Best to let him go. I know you want to go to college. You're a brilliant student. It would be a shame if you gave up on your future. And I'll give you all the money you need."

His manipulation won't work on me. "I don't need your pity college money, and I sure as hell won't join forces with you against Harry."

"The fact is you have no money. What schools are you applying to?"

"Better than any you could ever get into, I promise." If I can find a career where lying is required, I'll be the perfect candidate. I should apply to the CIA.

Uncle Pat clears his throat, and I hear him sucking on a cigarette. "I'm coming to see your mom at the end of the week. Soon as my lawyer finishes up a few details. I'll make certain she does the right thing."

"What you think is the right thing, and what we're going to do are polar opposites. Don't waste your precious time and money. Stay in Florida. My mom and I are on the same page. We don't want you here. Stop badgering her."

"You can't do—" he says, as I press the red button, ending the call.

"You hung up on him," Chad says. "You go, girl." He raises his hand for a high-five, but I can't celebrate. Nothing is settled, my uncle is still a threat, and Harry is in danger.

"I'm going to edit his contact info."

"Don't delete it," Chad says. "You may need the number. We're not done with him."

"I'm not deleting him, just adding an avatar to his information. Now when his phone number shows up, a creature with horns and blood dripping from his fangs will appear." I finish and ask Chad, "What's the other part of your plan?"

Chad takes my hands in his, much I like did with my mother, except I get the impression he's holding on, so I don't bolt. "Madison's father said the court might have a more favorable attitude if a couple wants the child, especially couples with money. You need to make sure you have presented yourself as the most stellar candidate for guardianship. We should get married."

What did he say? My ears must be blocked, or else his words punctured my eardrum. My head jerks backward and bangs against the tree. Ouch! I rub the spot. What is he thinking? He's not thinking. He's lost his freaking mind. He's still hanging on to my hands.

"You promised to keep an open mind," he reminds me.

Now I'm thinking this is some kind of gotcha joke, but his lips are in a firm straight line and there's none of the usual gleam in his eyes.

"Married! Are you high or something?" That question is both logical and stupid. He isn't into drugs, but there has to be some explanation for this insanity.

I wait for him to respond with something like: "Ha. Ha. Got you that time." And then we'd laugh together, but that doesn't happen.

"We can be married soon," he says. "I have researched this all day. We have to do everything we can to ensure victory."

"Mr. Sunday will be shocked. Hell, Chad, everyone will be shocked. I'm shocked."

"We won't tell him until it's done, and nothing has to change between us." Chad has given this a lot of thought. "This isn't me sneaking around to get you to do something you don't want to. This is for Harry, and that's all. And one more thing."

I'm not sure I can take "one more thing." My breaths come and go in spurts, matching the rhythm of whatever invisible force is drumming on my chest. I'd better not hyperventilate like Mom did; there isn't a paper bag in sight.

"If you marry me, you can tell the judge you have enough money to support Harry. I have a trust fund."

This joke keeps getting funnier and funnier. I should play along until we get to the punch line. I take the bait. "You lucked out being born into a rich family."

"My father wasn't born rich. He struggled and used his brains to wheel and deal his way to the top. It's a great story, and if he's in the right mood, he'll go on and on about his early times and how he succeeded without college. That's why it surprises me he can't understand that I want the same opportunity to make it on my own. I inherited his drive to prove myself. I don't want to waltz into a ready-made business, where all the employees will assume I'm there because I share DNA with the boss. It will be one more tale about how the son advanced over everyone else."

"So, he gave you a trust fund to be nice to you?" I remove my hands from his and let them fall limply onto the ground beside me.

"I have Uncle Sam to thank for the dough," Chad replies.

"I guess when it comes to uncles, you got the nice one. Wish I had an Uncle Sam. I have an aunt on my father's side who sends me $100 for my birthdays and Christmas when she remembers."

"Not my Uncle Sam, *the* Uncle Sam," Chad laughs. "My dad put the money in my name to dodge some hefty taxes. I get an annual income from that. All legal. So yes, lucky me."

"Your dad will kill you if we get married."

"And your mom might kill you too. Two dead teenagers in the posh city of Newton. Scandal." His confidence can be unnerving. "But seriously, I've figured out a way to settle things with my father once and for all so we both get something of what we want. That will be my first professional negotiation. Excellent experience for my role in his business, right?"

"I can't let you give up on your dream and go work for him because of me. That's too much." Harry breaks up this serious conversation, getting antsy in the stroller. I take him out and sit back down with my knees propped up to support him so he can see me. Chad makes some silly faces for Harry, which works to reassure that baby he's still number one and everyone admires him.

"I have to give working in the business a shot. I owe him that. I'll offer to work part-time while I'm at college, and hc has to let me major in whatever I want."

"And your parents won't hate me if we get married? Not that I'm agreeing to this, but I want them to like me, even your father."

"I've told you; you've got to stop caring so much about other people's opinions. Trust your gut. You do you, Claire Jackson. This plan will coldcock your uncle once and for all." He lifts Harry's hand and high-fives him as if the two of them are in agreement.

No one in their right mind would offer to marry someone to help them out of a bad situation. Harry isn't Chad's problem, but Chad is no bubblehead. From our first encounter, I sensed he was different from the other guys—more mature, with finely developed principles, combined with strength and confidence.

"And when your mom is all better, we can get a divorce," Chad adds. "I won't hold you to anything."

And the weirdness increases. One minute, we're talking marriage, and the next divorce.

Chad reads my mind. "Promise you will consider this carefully."

Marriage, money, Mom. When did life get so damn complicated?

"I have to talk to Mads about this. I promised no more secrets between us."

"But ask her to keep this locked up tight until we're ready to tell her father. Once she's part of the inner circle, she has to be sworn to secrecy. And if you agree, it's urgent we do it this week."

"I understand."

CHAPTER
23

Back home, I call Mads, but at the last minute, I decide this wild plan is too strange to discuss over the phone, so instead I invite her to come over and spend the night.

While I wait for her, I try to immerse myself in mind-numbing chores to prevent my brain from thinking. This might be one of those times when having mashed bananas for brains would be most comforting.

When Mads arrives, I get shy about sharing Chad's marriage proposal. She knows there's something going on and pesters me, but I manage to hold her off by blabbering about my visit to the hospital and the nubs of two new teeth in Harry's mouth.

Fortunately, just as I'm running out of topics, she takes control of the convo, diving in about a new guy she met in the red-hot Natick Mall, which seems to be better than a dating website. She sounds happy, but is playing this more cautiously than she did with Chad.

It isn't until we're in my big bed, which we always share, and the lights are out that I get up my nerve to unveil the insane plan.

"I have something to tell you," I whisper, dipping my toe in the water.

"Lay it on me, babe."

"Mads, hold on to your... I don't know what you should hold on to. Brace yourself." I wade in further.

"OMG, Claire, you aren't usually a drama queen. Just tell me."

I go in all the way, and the water is over my head. I'm gasping for air as I say, "Chad wants to marry me."

Mads flips on the lights and sits straight up wide-eyed and mouth open. I detonated the marriage bomb.

"You cannot be serious. Marriage! What the hell, Claire. No, I don't believe you."

I stretch my neck as if trying to keep my head above the water and sit up too. "First, I haven't agreed yet, and second, this won't be the kind of marriage you're imagining. Nothing will change between Chad and me. Remember, your dad said that being a couple might give people a better chance of getting guardianship."

"And you trust that's all Chad wants from you? Do you love him?"

"Love never entered into this. The words boyfriend and girlfriend were never spoken. This will be like an arranged marriage, except in this case, it's a baby who's bringing us together and not our parents."

"This is beyond weird. It might be a trap. Aren't you suspicious about his motives?"

My face pinks up, because I know what she imagines. "He promised—"

"Duh. He's a boy. One thing controls their minds. This might be his way of tricking you into doing something you don't want to do. Remember when Chloe got suckered into believing that jackass Jono was in love with her? I repeat, 'Can you trust him?'"

"He's different from most guys. He's very protective of his sisters, and he stands up to bullies. If I agree, he says I won't owe him anything. We'd be doing this strictly for Harry."

"That's a helluva a lot to do for Harry. Did you forget that baby is your brother? Is he worth all this?"

"I didn't forget, but I want to keep my family together, and I feel sorry for a kid who won't know his father. He doesn't need any more difficulties in his life. I guess, yeah, he's worth it."

"I repeat, do you love Chad?"

"Love has nothing to do with this. Should I place a limit on what I'm willing to do to protect Harry? I don't want to have any regrets." I grab my fluffy toss pillow and hug it close to hide my shaking body.

The marriage idea may be idiotic but also the only way to

guarantee success in the legal battle ahead. This is one time I can't ask my parents for advice. Mads is the closest person in my life. I make up my mind that if she isn't down with this, I won't go through with the marriage. Chad and I have a special connection, but damn, marrying at eighteen was never on my radar and certainly not getting married to protect my half-brother.

"This wasn't a get-down-on-your-knees proposal," I tell her. "And who's got the right to say what a traditional marriage is, anyway? People used to meet their future husband or wife on the wedding day after someone was paid off with some goats and feather pillows."

Mads shuts the light, and we put our heads on the pillow. I hear her chuckle. "Whatever the two of you are, this isn't a business arrangement. You are blind, but what the heck, Claire Bear, I'll be your bridesmaid."

"Very funny," I say. "Absolutely no bridesmaids wearing dresses with floppy pink bows on the butt."

"Everyone will think you're pregnant," she adds.

"But when I don't produce a baby, and I won't, they'll realize they were wrong."

"So, you'll become Mrs. Williams."

"It's the twenty-first century, Mads. There will be no Mrs. Williams."

"Just teasing. My parents have friends who married young. Carole was only sixteen, and Pete was eighteen. They kept it a secret, and when Pete's parents found out, they went ballistic, but they're still married decades later and happy. Who's to say marrying young is a recipe for a breakup?"

"Also, Chad said that once I have the guardianship, we can get divorced."

"So, married and divorced before you finish high school? This is bold and brave or stupid and risky, but I guess you'll never forgive yourself if you don't do everything you can for little Harry."

In the dark, Mads says, "You'll always be my heart-sister."

"Thanks for not disowning me." We try to settle down but thinking about getting married doesn't let me sleep.

I whisper, not sure if Mads is awake. "I want you to come with us when we go to the justice of the peace."

"Absolutely. Wouldn't miss it, but I need a new outfit. Let's hit the mall tomorrow."

"Ha. Wish I could. Too much going on."

And that ends the talking. Chad is positive this is really important, and Mads seems to be leaning into it. Perhaps if I had more time to churn this wild plan in my mind, I'd never agree to it. But, then again, not having time will prevent me from overthinking this.

THE NEXT MORNING, as I change Harry, I fill him in on the news. "Buddy, someday you'll enjoy your arrival story and the details of how you single-handedly pretzeled your sister's life into a continuous game of Twister." He giggles as I talk. I lift him up and squeeze him close until our hearts touch.

Mads is awake now and in her usual early morning daze, barely speaking. She doesn't mention last night's conversation, and neither do I. The decision is in. No more voting on this matter. I text Chad to meet me at the side door.

When Mads and I arrive at school, Chad's leaning against the building with one leg bent so his foot rests on the brick wall, a sort of tough-guy stance.

Mads snickers. "I'm going in and leave you two lovebirds alone."

Chad puts his leg down and says, "Hey..."

"See you in the caf," she says and scurries off.

Chad and I walk toward our homerooms.

"I'm in," I say as casually as if I'm RSVPing for the next school basketball game.

"I'm jacked. And as a bonus, because you're legal, I saved a ton of money not having to buy you a fake ID. Lucky me."

"Very funny. Do I appear the type who would do something illegal, Williams? We're going before a judge. I can't take care of Harry from jail."

He gives me a sly smile. Is he putting me on?

"Okay, everything legal," he says. "Let's go for the license this afternoon because there's a three-day waiting period after that."

"Fine," I answer as we arrive at the door of his homeroom.

"Hey baby, I think I wanna marry you," he whisper-sings a line from an old song I recognize. He swivels his hips, rocks his arms to a beat inside his head, and he's gone.

As I climb the stairs to my homeroom, I recognize that this is all very exciting, or very dumb, or both.

Later in the morning, I get a text from Dr. Goldstone and go outside to my private spot during lunch period. I call him while I search my backpack for a forgotten energy bar. I find a peanut-chocolate-sea salt bar.

"Hello, Claire," he says. "I hope you and Harry are doing okay. I know you're eager to have your mom home, and I'm eager to get her there. She's doing better in her treatment, and her therapists have agreed to move her to a facility with an excellent program and that's less hospital-like. She'll still have intensive therapy there but in a more pleasant environment."

"Where?"

"It's in Westwood, about twenty minutes from Newton."

"Can you give me the address?" I ask, taking out paper and a pen from my backpack.

"I'll text it to you," he says. "But, once again, she could use a day or two to settle in there. The good news is you can bring Harry with you."

"Should I do that?"

"Most definitely. Your mom is in a different place than she was the last time you saw her."

"Dr. Goldstone, can I, as her next-of-kin, put my uncle on her do-not-contact list and make sure she doesn't sign any papers he sends her?"

"Sorry, Claire, but that isn't a next-of-kin decision. Your mother is fully able to decide these things for herself. She hasn't lost any rights. As a matter of fact, she'll have a lot more freedom in this new place."

This isn't the answer I want. Fast-tracking the guardianship is vital.

Dr. Goldstone says, "The therapy is helping your mother work through her guilt."

Again, I tell him she doesn't have to feel guilty about me and Harry. We forgive her.

Dr. Goldstone replies, "Her guilt isn't only about the two of you."

"Oh," I say, baffled someone else is occupying space in her conscience, but he says nothing more and leaves me guessing the identity of the other injured party.

After we hang up, he sends contact information for West Village Lodge and that he'll text me when I can visit. A lodge sounds more like a ski resort in the White Mountains than a halfway house for people dealing with their issues. I hate not seeing her for a while, but at least she's making progress.

At three, I head for the parking lot to meet Chad and begin the marriage process. In the car, Chad informs me we can go to any city or town hall in Massachusetts for the license and, not wanting to run into anyone we know, we opt for neighboring Brookline.

When he parks and I get out, a shiver rises from my feet as if I'm barefoot on an icy sidewalk. I always thought "cold feet" was just a silly expression, but I wish I had worn a pair of woolly socks.

I ask, "If my mom's getting better, perhaps we should postpone this?"

Chad reminds me that until I have legal authority, Harry's not safe from my uncle; but that thought never leaves my mind. Chad takes my hand and intertwines his fingers through mine. I try to redirect his warmth into my feet.

The Brookline Town Hall is nothing like Newton's official, old-style red brick building. This could be any random office building. The town clerk's office is on the first floor. It's pretty empty, but it seems to take forever for someone to come to the counter and ask what we want.

While we wait, I lower my eyes, ashamed at the state of me on the day I'm getting a marriage license. My sneakers are caked with mud the stroller wheels spit back on me this morning on the way to Sunny Acres, and the front of my skirt has a blotch that I hadn't noticed before. Harry must've left one of his donations.

A lady slowly walks over, and Chad does all the talking, calm and in control as always. We show her our identification and fill out the form that must be signed under the pains and penalty of perjury, making it a crime if we lie.

Chad pays the license fee, and the woman reminds us we have to wait three days before we can get married. I detect a slightly cynical tone, which probably means she suspects I'm preggers and in a rush. But perhaps I should chalk it up to my own sensitivity about this. I'd better get used to that.

When we're almost to the door, I stop and say, "I forgot something."

Chad shrugs his shoulders and raises both hands in the air like the questioning emoji, then follows me back into the clerk's office. This time, the woman gets up from her desk quickly likely curious about why we returned.

"Can I help you?" she asks, without any snark in her voice.

"Yes, you can. I want to register to vote!" I say as the proud daughter of the former president of the League of Women Voters. Can't wait to tell Mom. She'll be thrilled. We can go vote together in November and take Harry. It'll be a family outing.

Chad lowers his eyes and says, "Um, one for me, too." For the first time, he seems embarrassed. He should be. Obviously, he blew off registering when he turned eighteen. The woman hands each of us a form and returns to her desk.

When I get to the place where you mark the box for which party you want to belong to, I try to peek at Chad's form, but he hides it with his hand.

"Why is your choice of political party a secret? Are you afraid I'll be mad if you pick the wrong one?" I ask.

"It isn't a secret. You should guess to see how well you know me."

Chad and his guessing games. I tap my index finger against my chin and scrunch my eyes inward to mimic deep concentration.

"Hmm...sounds like a trick," I say, keeping the ball in the air. "Do I get a hint? You're not always up-front when hints are available. It's one of my rules that you have to tell about hints. That's not optional," recalling Chad's first guessing game with me.

"No hints this time."

I scan him for a clue, but really, it's an excuse to stare at him. I know the answer. "I've got it," I say. "You didn't sign up for any party."

"You do know me. No party owns me. I'm an independent man."

"By the way, Mr. Williams," I say, showing off, "the technical term for an independent voter in Massachusetts is 'unenrolled.' In some states, there are actual political parties called 'Independent' so it can get confusing."

"How the heck do you know that?"

"My mother knows everything about voting. She always said I was a League of Women Voters baby."

"Not sure what that is."

"The League is a nonpartisan organization that gives people all kinds of election and voting information. My mother volunteered for them for years, dragging me with her to the polls and candidates' debates."

We hand in our forms and leave. A marriage license and registered to vote all in one day. Very adult.

At Sunny Acres, Chad stays in the car. I spot Harry fixated on a much older baby girl who's already standing by holding onto a low table. When she flashes a ginormous smile at him full of adorable tiny, white teeth, he smiles back, unloading some of the Jackson charm and showing off his dimple, which is getting more obvious every day. I pick him up and whisper in his ear, "My brother, the stud muffin." He giggles at me.

While I strap him into the car seat, Chad finishes a phone call and informs me we have an appointment with a justice of the peace on Sunday at 10 a.m. So soon. I text Mads the day and time. A part of me hopes she'll complain it's too early on a Sunday morning, and then I'll use that as an excuse to hit the pause button, but she sends back a thumbs-up emoji, so we're on.

All of this marriage business makes my mouth and lips go dry. I fumble in the bag for my lip gloss and begin rubbing it over my lips repeatedly, which is definitely overkill.

⚓

AT HOME, once Harry is down for the night, Chad orders pizza. We're about to eat when my phone rings with an incoming FaceTime from Dad.

"Hey, Dad, can't talk long. I have a friend here, and our pizza just arrived."

"Is it Madison? I haven't seen her in forever. Let me say hi to her."

I lower the phone and mouth to Chad, "Do you want to meet my dad?" He nods yes. Perhaps I should I ask my father if he wants to meet his future son-in-law?

Lifting my phone back to my face, I say, "This is Chad," and Chad moves in closer to be in the frame. There isn't an inch of space between our faces and taser-like electricity passes between us.

"Hey, Mr. Jackson," Chad says.

"Hi, Chad, it's nice to meet you. I guess you're new in Newton. I know most of Claire's friends from school."

"I've lived here since I was born. I'm only new to Claire because I transferred to Newton North this year."

"Whereabouts in Newton do you live?" Dad asks.

"Prince Street in Waban," Chad replies, and Dad's eyebrows do an elevator lift. He knows it's one of the ritziest sections of the city.

"Waban is a lovely village," Dad says. "Clarry, you look exhausted. Are you okay?"

"I'm fine. Lots going on here. By the way, Mom was in the hospital for a few days, but she's out now." That's technically correct, but not really accurate.

Dad loses the smile. "What was the matter with her?"

"She was on some medication that was too strong for her, and they had to regulate the dosage. And the other news is, I'm applying to become Harry's temporary legal guardian in case Mom needs more of my help with him."

Dad's face reddens, and his expressive bushy eyebrows narrow to the center. Chad moves out of the picture when he sees my father's boiling. "Why the hell would you do that? What's the matter with your mother? How can she let you take on this responsibility? I want to talk to her."

I didn't expect such a negative reaction. I was hoping for some praise for being a stand-up sibling.

"Mom's having difficulty handling everything. She's getting better, and I have to do this because Uncle Pat insists the baby is only trouble for Mom and he's pressuring her to give him up for adoption. And no, you can't call her now. I'll tell you when you can." I leave out everything that has to do with our money problems.

"I can't believe your mom would agree to you having that responsibility."

"While she's recovering, and her brother is threatening to take over her life, it's important for me to do everything I can to keep this family together." As soon as those words are out of my mouth, I want to push them back inside. Dad might take that as a criticism since he couldn't—or didn't—keep the family together, but I stopped blaming anyone for the divorce a couple of years ago.

"Patrick was born without an iota of empathy," Dad says. "But exactly how does it help for you to be the kid's guardian?"

"If I'm in total charge of Harry, Uncle Pat won't be able to get anywhere near him. When Mom's back to herself, the guardianship will end. Madison's father is a lawyer. He's helping me and for no money. Mom's totally on board with this."

"This is lunacy, Claire. You shouldn't be saddled with the kid. You're a teenager. I can talk to Patrick." Dad is agitated, and I'm sorry I opened my big mouth.

"Please don't call Uncle Patrick. That might make everything worse. This is what I have to do. I'm sure it will be very temporary. I'll tell you when it's settled."

"Shall I come and be with you? I'll get a flight out tomorrow. You shouldn't be alone dealing with all of this."

"I'm totally fine, Dad. There's nothing for you to do here, and I'm busy with school and student government meetings. I'd hardly have time to see you, plus I've got Chad and Madison for support and Becky too." I hope that reassures him.

"I'm glad you're leaning on Becky, but I mean, you should have a parent with you to help."

And a roiling laugh begins in my belly, but I stifle it so Dad isn't offended, but he completely misses the point. I gently explain the facts of my life to him.

"Dad, that's so sweet to offer. I'll let you know if you should come, but I don't need a parent with me. It's like now I'm going to be the parent."

CHAPTER 24

For the rest of the week, I sleep in Mom's bed to feel close to her, but it isn't the same as when I was little. I'm not the girl with pigtails crawling in with her for comfort.

On the way to day care, I get a call from Dr. Goldstone.

"You and Harry can visit your mother this afternoon," he says. I could jump through the phone and kiss him.

"Great!"

"You'll see a big difference in her."

I'm psyched to bring Harry. Mom hasn't seen him in a long time, and I'm praying she missed him so much, she's ready to fight for him, but my euphoria might be completely misplaced.

What if she got used to being without him and might want her before-Harry life back? She has to make her own choice, and then I'll make mine. Mr. Sunday wants me to ask her about signing the guardianship papers. If she's cooperative about that, it will tell me everything.

Both Chad and Mads offer to come with me, but this visit is only for Harry and me. I pick up Harry early and have to admit, he looks particularly cute today and is in his usual good mood from living it up at Sunny Acres.

I almost miss the place even with the GPS. The entrance sign to West Village Lodge is small and discrete as if they don't want you to know the place exists. I follow the driveway around back to visitors' parking. I put Harry in the stroller and remind him there's a lot at stake for this visit. His baby eyes signal he has no clue what I'm telling him. It's the same blank gaze I got yesterday when I swabbed him for the DNA test like Mr. Sunday suggested. I felt bad for the little dude when I did it. All kids want to imagine that blaring trumpets heralded their arrival into the world. Harry got no fanfare when he appeared.

Maybe when he's older, I'll dream up an awesome version of his birth to thrill him because that's the excellent kind of sister I am. The DNA test is probably a good idea, and I have no right to deny Harry knowing his father if they can find the guy. Maybe he's a millionaire who can give Harry a cushy life. But it's a gamble.

The DNA kit contained a swab for the father which I tossed into the kitchen junk drawer, but I doubt I'll need it.

West Village Lodge is a large, old house that's nothing like a hospital. It has a huge wrap-around porch with a row of white, wooden rocking chairs. People are chatting in small groups, drinking coffee or tea and nibbling on cookies set out on a table nearby. An older man waves at us as we walk by, and a young woman gets within two inches of Harry's face.

"Yours?" she asks.

"Uh-huh. He's my brother."

"What's his name?"

"Harry."

"Harry, you're a cutie-pie. I want to hold him." She reaches for him, but I push the stroller away.

"Sorry, I'm in a rush. Maybe another time." I can't let everyone hold Harry. He isn't a basketball to be dribbled around.

The lobby has a wide staircase at the back that breaks off to the right and the left at the landing. I head over to the desk in a corner with a discreet sign that says, "Check in Here." A woman welcomes me warmly and after the usual enthusiastic ooo's and ah's about Harry, she asks for my ID and who I'm visiting today. I sign in, and she gets up and leads us to a room off the lobby which is nothing like a hospital room.

It's bright and cheery with floor-to-ceiling windows on one side with an amazing view of a lush garden. The yellow sunflower wallpaper adds to the feeling you're allowed to be happy in here.

The woman explains, "This house was originally a couple of

rooms and was owned by one of the signers of the Constitution. Through the years and generations, his family enlarged it. Twenty years ago, they donated it for this hospital. This room used to be the conservatory. It's a lovely place for a visit, much better than having to sit in someone's bedroom. Ms. Jackson will be here shortly."

"Thanks."

I set up Harry's play mat with a couple of toys and transfer him to the floor as Mom enters. I'm stunned. Her hair was cut, and she's even wearing lipstick. Wow! This is my real mother.

"Your hair," I say.

"They have a salon right on the premises. I had it cut and blow-dried. Much better, huh?"

"Wonderful." She pretends to fluff her hair, and I copy the movement for my missing hair. We both laugh.

She hugs me and smiles at Harry, who's straining toward her, probably to make sure he hasn't been forgotten. Mom sits on the sofa right in front of him. Once she's settled there, the kid goes back to his toys.

"Do you think he remembers me?" she asks and lowers herself onto the floor to be more on his level. I take that as an excellent sign.

"He's smiling at me," she says with delight and maybe a sense of pride. I let her have that and don't mention that Harry pretty much gives anyone who smiles at him his grin, which currently shows off two tiny white teeth on the bottom gum.

"Of course, he remembers you," I reply. "He's chill if you want to hold him, although be prepared: the butterball is heavier than the last time you held him. He's an eating machine. The only food he hates so far is peas, but who can blame him for that?"

Mom laughs again. This visit is exceeding expectations. Her mood is good, and her skin isn't gray anymore, and her eyes aren't red and wet. Those crying jags must be over. *Dr. Goldstone, you're a miracle worker.*

Mom observes Harry playing and doesn't lunge at him. Clearly, this isn't her first baby rodeo. She gives him time to get used to her again. I sit in a comfy, wide chair and let my muscles unwind as I slump into the plump cushions.

After a bit, she picks him up. He smiles in gratitude, and she presses her face into his and brings him onto the sofa.

"Did the doctor say when you're getting out of here?" I ask.

"Soon, I think. I'm much better. They've lowered the dosage on some of my medication. I'll still need therapy until I can pass my program."

"Your program?"

"Right, I know it sounds like I'm in AA or something, but it's part of the therapy. You have to pass certain steps toward recovery."

"What step are you on?"

"The one that requires you to make amends to anyone you have wronged."

Harry gets fidgety, so I take out a bottle to give her, but instead she hands him to me.

"I'm a little tense. Could you do it?" she asks. At least she seems to feel bad passing him off to me, and it's not like, "Hey, Claire, he's your job."

She's better, but not perfect.

I feed him and ask, "Mom, are you still on board with me becoming Harry's temporary guardian?"

"Yes," she responds.

"And are you sure you never want to give Harry away?"

"I am."

"You're in control, and no one, not even me, can pressure you to do something you don't want to."

"I understand. You should have whatever authority you need to help me. I promise not to let my brother take him. But, I think I did sign a—"

"Oh, no! You promised me."

"It was a while ago when I wasn't in a good place, and Patrick insisted I had to do it for you. I'm sorry. I'm not even sure what that document might've been."

"I can't believe you did that!" My voice rises with each word.

"Shush! No one shouts in here. Please, Clarry," she begs me.

No childish outbursts, Claire, you're an official adult. I center my breathing to cool my rage.

"I'm sorry," she says. "I was in a bad way, and I'll explain all that to my brother when I can."

I'll have to tell Mr. Sunday there may be some signed papers that could become a problem.

Harry finishes the bottle, and I hand him to Mom. She rubs his back, and he responds with a modest burp. Then she says, "Patrick left a message here. He said he's planning to be in Massachusetts soon. I'm scared for you and Harry."

"I can handle Patrick," I say with bravado, hoping that's true. Who knows if I'll melt when I come face to face with him on the battlefield? "Finish your therapy program," I tell her. "I'll protect Harry until you're home."

Every cell in my body wants to blurt out I'm getting married, and Uncle Pat's hostile takeover will be moot, but I can't risk that the news will set her recovery back. And I'm pretty sure it would.

A young guy pokes his head in the room. "How's everything going, Ms. Jackson?"

Mom replies, "Just fine, Matt. This is my daughter, Claire, and my son, Harry."

Woo hoo. She didn't introduce us as Clarry and Harry. She remembered.

"Another five minutes before it's time for your group. This is a reminder," Matt says. He's too young to be a doctor; probably more like an orderly or something.

"We should go anyway. Harry needs a bath."

Mom stands and hugs us both before we take off. She even leans over and kisses the top of Harry's head. This is not a mother who's going to give up her kid for adoption.

Harry rides out of there in his stroller, and I float.

CHAPTER
25

Two days later, the avatar of the Prince of Darkness pops up on my phone screen.

Uncle Pat has texted me.

> 5 p.m. Today. BE HOME.

His threatening tone is obvious. Although I knew this was coming, my body trembles. I text back, but unlike him, I decide to lower the temperature by not putting my words in yelling caps.

> I'll be there.

I sort of memorized Chad's schedule and hurry to wait outside his French classroom until he's dismissed. As soon as I spot him, I grab his arm and pull him away to show him my uncle's text.

"I'll be there," he says.

"But you'll miss practice."

"I'll talk to Coach. We have a big game this weekend, and he wants me on the field, so he might give me a pass to skip practice this time."

Chad never gets flustered and is the essence of coolness. I wonder if he was born that way or works on that. There is more to this boy than I know.

"How about giving me a transfusion of your courage? Let's hook up the needles." I try to smile, but dizzy feelings consume me. I might require a sugar fix before I pass out.

"No need for needles," Chad says. "Direct infusion." He leans over to kiss me directly on the lips. It happens so fast I don't have time to check my surroundings to see if anyone's there. I suppose it doesn't matter if someone sees us. We're pretty much always together these days. I run my tongue over my lips and taste the delicious moistness he left there, hoping it contains some magic to give me strength.

As the sensation dissipates, I realize Mads might be right that there's more to my connection with Chad than I'm willing to admit. But I can't dwell on that now. I've got to stay focused on the confrontation with my uncle that awaits.

I stop at Sunny Acres on the way home from school in case I can't make it there by the six o'clock deadline.

Once Harry and I are home, I stuff him with food, hoping it will hold him until the dreaded encounter is over. When it's almost five, I put him in his crib whether or not he likes it. It's the one place where he can't get into any trouble.

Then I go down to wait for Chad.

Once Chad comes and is inside the house, I immediately tell him how scared I am. He takes my hands in his and squeezes. It helps, but only until he lets go.

We take our positions. Chad stands by the front door, peering out of the peephole, and I station myself at the living room window, peeking through the blinds.

At precisely five o'clock, a big-ass black car parks in front of the house. Of course, a "great" man like Uncle Pat wouldn't rent some low-end ride. No, this is a vehicle designed to instill tremors in people. I dash for one more trip to the bathroom to avoid "pee pressure," which I learned can be an awful distraction after I lost an easy argument on the eighth-grade debate team because of a bathroom emergency.

My uncle takes his sweet time getting out of the car, and I suspect it's for dramatic effect to scare the crap out of us.

"Let's roll," Chad says, and we go outside and stand side by side near the end of the walkway. The dried-up leaves that crunch under our feet break the quiet on Ivanhoe Street.

I glance next door, and sure enough, Mrs. Pearl, known as the neighborhood sheriff, is perched by her window guarding our street. She'll have a front-row seat for this event.

The car door finally opens, and the tanned hulk lumbers toward us. He's dressed all in black, and his shoes are polished to an oily sheen for this occasion. It's an outfit for someone who wants to intimidate, probably his version of shock and awe.

I tilt my head toward Chad to gauge his reaction to seeing my uncle in person, but I get nothing. Chad's expression is as frozen as his body standing next to me.

My uncle has none of Mom's delicate features. His nose is wide, and his face is covered with potholes from years of teenage acne. According to my mom, he suffered a lot from that and popped his pimples on a continual basis, leaving the scars as proof. I used to feel sorry for him about that and prayed it wasn't an inherited trait. Now, I have no sympathy for him. Why should I? He doesn't care about us.

He stops a foot or so away from us and raises his aviator sunglasses, which are useless on a late fall afternoon in the northeast, to the top of his head. They're just part of his effect. His ocean-blue eyes are the only thing that tells anyone he and Mom have the same parents, but now he's using those beauties to glare at me. My crossed arms should convey my message not to leap forward and attempt an unsanctioned hug.

Sure enough, he doesn't read the situation and opens his arms, as if expecting me to run into them. When I was small, Mom would nudge me in the back and urge me forward to do my family duty, even though I thought he was creepy and had sweaty cheeks. This time no one pushes me and after a few awkward seconds, he catches on and lowers his flapping, empty arms.

"Hello, Claire, it's been too long," he says with his gruff, wheezy smoker's voice. "Let's go inside to talk."

"We'll talk here," I reply and keep my arms pressed against my chest. Chad is like a piece of granite next to me, but my knees are unsteady. I struggle not to visibly shake and show weakness.

Uncle Pat's eyebrows knit into a menacing unibrow, and his top lip tightens against his fangs. "This is a private family matter, Claire. I want to talk to you alone."

"Not happening," I say as he takes a step closer to us. I put my hand out in front of me to stop him like I'm directing oncoming traffic. He'll soon discover I'm *not* my mother's daughter in the way he thinks.

"Who is this guy?" he asks, narrowing his eyes into dragon-like slits while widening his stance into a fighting position.

"None of your business," I say. I glance at Chad, who's standing at attention. One might think he lost all ability to move. I hope he's breathing, at least.

"Claire, I'm going to take care of the baby from now on. Your mother can't do it, and you're a child."

"You will *not* do that!" I bare my clenched teeth and hiss out the words.

"Sometimes adoption is the best answer," he says. "Melly knows in her heart that's the best course."

"We'll fight you hard." My skin burns in anger, and I'm desperate to jump into a bathtub of ice.

"This is getting ridiculous, Claire. At least let me go inside to see my nephew. Stand aside."

Interesting. He could just try to go around us, but I suppose he prefers to order people around. The last thing I'll allow is for him to get near Harry. He may try a grab 'n' go, as if the baby's a lunch sandwich.

I raise my voice to get him to back off and leave before this gets any more intense, but you can't reason with a bully. I say, "I'm going to be Harry's legal guardian until my mother is better, and you will have nothing to do with him."

His lips form an offensive sneer, and my blood whirls in fury when he says, "No judge would let a child be a baby's guardian."

Mrs. Pearl must be getting quite an earful. I try to lower my voice and hope my uncle will follow suit. Meanwhile I wonder what Chad is thinking. I'm going to take his silence to mean I'm doing a great job on my own.

"I've been caring for Harry since he came home from the hospital. And I'm eighteen. Legally an adult, for your information."

"That kid needs a stable family."

"Ha, and you think that's you?" What nerve.

"It's not you or your mother, who can't cope with having a baby at this point in her life."

"The baby has a name, and I have an attorney. I just saw Mom, and she's doing great. We're ready to fight for Harry."

Uncle Pat's eyebrows flare. It's obvious this encounter isn't going as he planned. The bully isn't accustomed to being on the receiving end. I'm so proud of myself.

His voice mellows, either to match my tone or as a new tactic to throw me off guard.

"Listen, Claire, don't you want a better life for yourself? College, parties, all the teenage stuff. You can have that without the baby sucking up everybody's time and money. He's not your responsibility. I talked to your mother a month ago, and she wants to do the right thing for you. She was open to moving to Florida to be close to us."

Then he redirects his focus to Chad, and says, "Sonny, or whoever the hell you are, step aside. I want to talk to my niece in private in the house."

Calling Chad "Sonny" is so disrespectful. Chad doesn't flinch but looks at me, perhaps wondering if he should do something. I nod and smile slightly as if to reassure him I'm doing okay. I bet he's itching to get involved.

"No one is going with you anywhere, and for your information, we are engaged."

"You're engaged? Now that's funny. I see you've got about as much sense as your mother. Be sure to invite me to the wedding."

"My mother is a wonderful woman."

Uncle Pat's face reddens, and I lift my hand and point a finger at him. "You could've given your sister a loan without strings attached when she asked for it, but you didn't. My friend here is a far superior brother than you are. He could give you some lessons because you obviously skipped the class on how to be a decent person."

Chad assumes my mentioning him again is his cue to step in, and he does. "Harry belongs with Claire and her mother. Why don't you head back to sunny Florida? Claire will be the guardian, and you'll lose in court and probably get crossed off the Christmas card list too. Have a nice trip, Uncle Pat." He lifts his hand in a sarcastic goodbye wave.

"I eat guys like you for breakfast," Uncle Pat bellows and takes another step forward, as if attempting to bulldoze a path through us. When he's closer, he slams his palm into Chad's chest with amazing strength. For a second, Chad stumbles backward, but his athletic gracefulness kicks in, and he rights himself.

What just happened? I never expected this to get physical. My uncle must feel threatened I have someone by my side. But this is my fight, and I won't cower behind Chad. I have my self-respect, so from somewhere deep in my gut, I unleash my wrath. "Don't touch him again. Get the hell back."

My uncle pulls a piece of paper out of his pants pocket, which he waves over his head. "Your mother signed this so I can take authority for the baby. I plan to file it with the court. What happened to you, Claire? You never used to—"

"That's a bluff. Whatever you think you have there, she's not going through with that. My lawyer will fight you every step of the way, so you can just tear that paper up."

"She signed this when you were still a child. She understands this is the only solution. The baby—"

"Harry!" I shout at him.

"Calm down, Claire," he says. "And stand aside, I'm going in the house."

He's practically on top of Chad.

I say, "Harry isn't going with you. Not now. Not ever. We won't let you take him. Bye-ee," I mimic Chad's brush-off.

"Safe flight back to Florida," Chad adds.

"We? So your bodyguard here gets a say in this. I don't think so."

With that, his fist rams into Chad's stomach, and Chad goes down, doubled over and winded.

"Sorry, whoever the hell you are," Uncle Pat smirks. "My hand accidentally bumped into you because you refused to get out of the way. You're obstructing me from seeing my nephew."

Chad gets upright and in my peripheral vision, I see him begin to raise his hand and form it into a fist. I can't let him do that. It would bring a reign of terror on him. My uncle would like nothing better than to report him to the police.

My instincts kick in, and I rest my left hand on Chad's arm, pressing down on his knotted muscles. Chad slowly lowers his partially raised arm. In a simultaneous motion, my right hand flies up and sends my fist straight into my uncle's face.

Uncle Pat's legs sprawl out from under him, and something cracks when he hits the walkway. Blood cascades down his chin from his nose.

I've never hit anyone in my whole life, but he went after the one person who has been a constant in my battle for Harry, and I lost it. I never knew I had a violent streak, but I guess everyone has a breaking point, especially to protect those you love. I mean to protect your friends.

"Okay, we're done here," I say. I take Chad's hand.

My uncle is still on the ground. He winces as he tries to get up, but his oversized body weighs him down, unless he broke something that's preventing him from standing. I wait, hoping it's only the shock keeping him on the ground. And he wouldn't be the only one shocked. That punch was powerful, and its force sent vibrations through my body.

He says, "I'll be back for that baby, and next time I won't be alone. I'll bring a court order that allows me to take him. Your stubbornness is going to destroy you and your mother. The baby will be placed elsewhere, far from this dysfunctional mess. Sorry, but you can no longer strut around, pretending to be his mother."

"I'm not his mother, but I will protect him forever."

Finally, Patrick is back on his feet, gawking at me. "And I will report you for assault."

"You started this fight," I say.

"You won't get away with this. You have no idea what I can do to you."

The threats leave me shaken, and Chad and I go inside. I take up my position at the window to watch my uncle's actions. What I've done with that punch could ruin my chances of getting guardianship if the judge thinks I'm too reckless to take care of a baby. If the legal route closes to me, Harry and I may have to go into hiding from this brute.

I watch as Uncle Pat removes a tissue from his jacket pocket and wipes his purple and red nose. He starts up the walkway toward the house, but midway, he U-turns and heads back to his car. I exhale as he drives off, unaware I'd been holding my breath.

"Tough guy," Chad says.

"Yes, he is," I reply.

"That's not who I meant."

"That didn't go exactly as planned," I say, examining my wet, sticky fingers. The sight of my bruised and bloody knuckles grosses me out. I have to wash my uncle's drippings off my skin immediately. "Honestly, I'm not a dangerous person," I say, surprised at the need to voice that. It's as if I went to the dark side of the moon.

Chad stares at my hands. "Neither am I violent, despite what some people have said about me."

I go upstairs, fill the sink with warm water, and plunge my hands in. My instinct is to scrub off the signs of what happened, but the pain is unbearable, so I switch to a gentler approach. The water reddens, and it takes willpower not to heave at the sight. It's a disgusting mix of my uncle's blood and mine.

I take my hands out of the water, pat them dry, and notice that my knuckles are swelling. My uncle left me no choice. He had already pushed Chad and was getting more aggressive, taunting him. Was I supposed to wait to act until he hit Chad again? Actually, I'm proud that when faced with that choice, I showed courage. Someday, I'll share this fight story with Dad to prove to him how brave I've gotten. He'll be surprised. Damn, I'm still surprised.

While I apply a thick layer of antibacterial ointment and start to wrap my hand with gauze and tape, I call down to Chad to get Harry, who's been complaining after getting unceremoniously shipped off to the crib.

Chad stands at the bathroom door holding Harry. "That's hard to do one-handed. Here, hold Harry in your good hand, and I'll do that."

He gently wraps my hand, doing a much better job than I could've.

"What do you suppose your uncle might do because of that punch?" he says. "This could go a lot worse than me getting thrown out of a school. Would he press charges against a niece? If the judge finds out, this could deep-six the guardianship deal."

I say, "You're scaring me, but he started it." What Chad said is exactly what has been churning in my mind.

"I know," Chad replies. "I doubt that's the story he'll tell. Your uncle is one bad dude, but knocking down a bully was satisfying, wasn't it?"

"Oh yeah, sure, I guess."

The doorbell rings. My uncle is back to finish me off. I hand Harry to Chad and rush down to peer through the door's peephole and almost have a heart attack. He called the cops on me!

"It's the police," I tell Chad, who's right behind me.

"You have to open it."

"I know," but my brain froze and isn't speaking to my hand. I can't seem to raise it to the doorknob.

Chad lunges across me and opens the door.

The police officer introduces herself and explains they got a call about a disturbance at our house. She asks for our names, if we live here, and to show her some ID.

"Who called you?" I ask.

"I ask the questions, Ms." She takes out a notebook and a pen from her shirt pocket. "Any weapons in the house?"

Holy hell, she thinks we have a gun.

"No," I answer weakly. All my jubilation celebrating my bravery is replaced by overwhelming fear.

Chad takes out his wallet and hands her his license.

"And is that a no for you too, Mr. Williams? No guns or knives?"

"No," Chad replies, very subdued. I think he's extra nervous. I go into the kitchen to find my ID. When I get back, I hand it to her with my good hand and put the bandaged one behind my back. I'm sure the sight of that would generate lots of questions I don't want to answer.

She writes our names and addresses in her notebook. Uncle Pat must have called 911 as soon as he drove off. My knees are jelly.

She takes a photo or scans our licenses and sends it to someone. A few minutes pass and someone calls her on her walkie-talkie or radio thing. That person rattles off a bunch of numbers, probably police codes.

"Well, you both have clean records. So, we'll go from there. Claire, your neighbor reported a fight in front of your house."

Aha! So not my uncle. Good old Mrs. Pearl was spying on us from her usual perch. That's better, I think.

"She's so thoughtful," I say, attempting to defuse this situation quickly. "I love Mrs. Pearl, but I can see why she might've gotten the wrong impression. There was no fight. My uncle came to bring me an important document, and he dropped it. The two of us bent down to pick up the paper and clunked heads. It was pretty funny."

Claire, liar extraordinaire. You outdid yourself with that creative masterpiece.

The police officer makes more notes and asks, "Can I talk to your uncle?"

I smile. "He's fine. He went on his way. No problem."

"I need his name and contact information to verify this," she says.

I can't take a chance on her calling him. He'd probably do something to escalate this situation. I could be in handcuffs and headed to the police station if he talks to her. Option one is to give her a fake phone number for him, or just say I don't have his contact information. Lying to a police officer is on a whole other level, but I have no choice.

"Sorry, officer, I don't have his number, and my mother, his sister, is in the hospital. The next time I visit her, I'll get it for you."

This policewoman is the first person I've met who doesn't give Harry a second look. She probably thinks interacting with the baby would diminish her image.

"You're positive he was fine?" she asks.

"Oh, yes. I made sure of it before he got into his car and drove away."

"Okay, well, I guess I don't need to call him right now. Text me the number when you get it." She hands me her card and closes her notebook. As she steps out, she suggests I let Mrs. Pearl know I'm okay. I promise her I will.

Once she's gone, full-on panic sets in. That officer could've just as easily been coming to arrest me for assault. I've given my uncle leverage to use against me. He's probably snapping selfies of his face from every angle for evidence to blackmail Mom in exchange for not turning me in.

I have to get to Mom first and explain everything, so he doesn't convince her she has to give in to his demands. Hitting him might be the stupidest thing I've ever done.

"I'm more scared now," I say. Chad, for the first time since I know him has lost his super calm expression and raises his eyebrows in alarm.

Chad says, "You need to calm down. There's nothing we can do now. Let's go to my grandmother's house for dinner. Once you step inside her house, you'll be surrounded by an amazing peace."

It's sweet how he talks about his grandmother. I'm not sure I'm in any condition to meet her, but how can I refuse him?

"Let me change my clothes." I don't want to go there wearing any telltale evidence of the fight. I put on a clean top, splash my face with cool water, and spike the ends of my hair with a bit of gel. Even in the midst of chaos, I want to be presentable.

I pack up things for Harry and bring them downstairs. Chad gives me the once-over and says, "Very nice."

"And before we go to your grandmother's," I say, "Let's stop by my neighbor's house for a minute, so I can explain to her that nothing bad happened."

Chad adds, "Remember to keep that hand out of sight."

CHAPTER
27

Chad parks in front of Mrs. Pearl's house and waits in the car while Harry and I go speak with her. Bringing Harry will hopefully divert her attention from what happened. She opens the door before I ring the bell and scans me top to bottom. I hide my sore hand.

"Hi, Mrs. Pearl, so nice to see you. I heard you were worried about me, and I wanted to thank you for your concern. I'm fine. My uncle and I clunked heads when we both went to pick up a piece of paper that had fallen."

Mrs. Pearl pushes her glasses higher up on her nose. "It looked like trouble. I know trouble when I see it."

I'm waiting for her to fling a slew of questions when Harry starts his baby talk which distracts her.

"Look at how big this fella is getting," she says and reaches out to shake his little hand. "Too bad he didn't get your mother's gorgeous blue eyes." She chucks him under the chin, and he gives her one of his trademark open-mouthed smiles.

"And he has your dimple," Mrs. Pearl says. "My, my. He looks more like you than your mother. I'm sure that makes you happy."

"Yes, it does," I tell her and then finish by promising Harry and I will stop by again soon to see her. I guess it's smart to keep on the good side of your nosey neighbors.

Once I'm back in the car after reassuring Mrs. Pearl she didn't see what she saw, I call Mr. Sunday.

"How are things going with my case?" I ask him.

"Everything's in motion, and the documents for your mother to sign are ready. I'm going to bring them to her with a notary."

"When?"

"Early next week," he replies.

"My uncle claims my mother signed something a while ago, and he's going to file it in the court. I think it's about adopting Harry, but I'm not sure." I struggle against the urge to cry as if I'm six years old again, and add, "Um...also, my uncle might make some accusations against me."

"What kind of accusations?"

"We had an altercation, and I had to hit him."

"Had to?" Mr. Sunday sounds skeptical.

"He hit Chad," I explain. "My uncle didn't get hurt. He drove off with no problem. But he's the king of payback, so I'm afraid of what he might do."

"Claire, you're under a lot of pressure, but I wish you hadn't done that. I'll inquire if he's filed anything in court."

"Honestly, Mr. Sunday, it was split-second decision. There was no time to think. You have to believe me."

"I understand. Let's talk again in a couple of days. Are you okay now?"

"I'm all right. I'm going to Chad's grandmother's house for dinner." I should add, unless a cop stops us and drags me off to jail before I get there.

The call ends, and I say to Chad, "I've made everything worse, but I was afraid about what might happen if you had been the one to hit him."

"That was never going to happen."

"But you made a fist."

"From nervous energy. Believe me, punching your uncle would've put Harry on the fast track to Florida and me in deep shit. Actually, I was planning to let him pummel me, if that's what had to happen."

"Are you kidding me?" How could I have known that? And would I have stood there and watched Chad get beaten up? "But what about that kid at your old school and tripping a guy from Wellesley?"

"There's a huge difference. My father doesn't just lecture me about school or business. He has drummed into me how to react in dangerous situations. He wants to save me from stuff he had to go through."

"So, I guess it's me who might've bought Harry that ticket to Florida."

"We have to wait this out. Your uncle may have second thoughts about using that against you. Try to get it off your mind for a while. We're here."

Chad pulls up to a wooden house, sea green in color. Compared to the mansion he lives in, this could be his sisters' playhouse. The shutters are pastel blue, and lawn trolls guard rows of pink and purple pansies. Two bird feeders stand near a stately oak tree on the front lawn. No birds are using them now, but they must be busy and noisy in the early mornings. I wish Harry was old enough to appreciate this delightful place.

"What should I call your grandmother?" I ask, as I unbuckle my seat belt with my good hand and remind myself not to shake hands with Chad's grandmother.

"Gran," Chad responds.

"I can't call her that. I should call her Mrs. whatever her last name is."

"Trust me, call her Gran," Chad says again, completely unhelpful, leaving me no choice but to opt for the reliable no-name approach.

Baskets full of perfectly shaped pinecones are on either side of her front porch. Their simplicity and symmetry are proof that Mother Nature is a gifted artist. I like his grandmother already.

Chad presses the bell, and chimes ring out a beautiful melody of welcome, unlike the harsh buzz of most doorbells. That song fits with the tone of this captivating house. I hang back and let Chad, who's carrying Harry, lead the way.

A woman almost as tall as Chad opens the door and tilts her head to get a better glimpse of Harry, who's resting on Chad's shoulder.

He's too tired to give her his usual appreciative gaze in return for her gift of attention.

She's wearing a blue turban that shows a bit of gray hair in the front. The wrinkles on her dark skin are deep. She's the perfect picture of any grandmother. She personifies elegance in her long, flowing dress covered in multicolored flowers, as if she just stepped out of a garden. I can see the resemblance to Chad's mother.

Chad introduces me and Harry. I grasp the handles of Harry's baby bag with both hands, so she doesn't attempt to shake the injured one.

"Gran, Claire has to feed Harry before we eat. Okay?"

"You think I don't know about babies and eating? You can feed him in the sunroom." She swivels to the left and her dress swings with her movement.

His grandmother sits in a high-back chair covered in gold fabric with red threads running through it. It could be a throne. Chad sits on the sofa while I dig out a couple of jars of baby food and Harry's tiny spoon. It takes no time to feed this chowhound, and I'm crossing my fingers he keeps it all inside. We don't need to be cleaning up Chad's grandmother's beautiful house.

I hold the baby on my lap while he takes the bottle.

Chad's grandmother says, "Your brother looks exactly like you."

Why is everyone so obsessed about comparing us? Lots of siblings look alike, but I know I'm definitely overly sensitive about this because the next step is usually to assume I'm his mother.

"He's my half-brother," I tell her. "My mother's in the hospital, so I have to take him with me."

Her eyes travel from Harry to me again, and she grins slyly, "Oh, honey, that baby is a full loaf. He ain't half of anything."

"Gran, they have the same mother. He's a half-sibling like you and your sister Minnie."

"I can assure you I know the difference between a half and a full."

"My parents are divorced, and my dad got re-married recently and lives in Wisconsin," I explain.

"Some women want their secrets," his grandmother says, "and they're entitled to them. I don't want to crack that egg."

"Gran, let it be. Claire should know," Chad says.

"Whatever you say, darlin'." Chad's grandmother smiles and shakes her head from side to side ever so slightly, clearly not backing down from her opinion. Still, it's wonderful to have a grandmother who knows what she thinks, unlike mine, who struggles cognitively and probably can't even remember that Mom had a baby.

"You're a dutiful older sister like my Chaddie is the best brother. He has saved his sisters from their father's bougie ways more than once. Chaddie would make a great defense lawyer, don't you agree?"

Chaddie. That is beyond funny, he's no Chaddie. I can't resist and give him my finest mocking face as I say, "Chaddie could be whatever he wants to be, and I do think he'd make an excellent lawyer."

Chad, in turn, adopts a fake scowl, which he won't be able to hold. I'm right; a second later he breaks into a silly grin.

"I agree. It should be his decision," his grandmother says. "She's a smart girl," she tells Chad, who nods in agreement.

We go into the dining room, and the food smells delicious. I'm hungry and eat nonstop while listening to Chad and his grandmother reminisce about when he was little. It seems that even as a kid, he had a highly developed passion to protect all creatures. He once saved a spider from being crushed by his father, according to his doting grandmother.

Chad clears his throat and says, "I had to save him because I thought he was a relative of Spider-Man."

This makes me laugh, and boy, that feels wonderful for my soul. "Everything is delicious," I say, when I can pause long enough from stuffing my face. "I love the mac 'n' cheese. This is the best I ever had."

His grandmother responds, "It's the supreme comfort food and tastes like everything good in this world," his gran says.

I take another bite, attempting to fill every empty space in me with more of that goodness.

Talking to Chad's grandmother gives me a twinge of jealousy because I can't do the same with my grandmother. When my life reboots and resembles normal, I want Mom and me to take Harry to New York to meet Grandma. I'll tell Harry how loving she was and how she'd be over-the-moon with him. To her, I was perfect, and everyone should have at least one admirer like that to sustain them in times of self-doubt.

As we're leaving, Chad's grandmother grabs both my hands and squeezes. My eyes water from the pain. She drops her gaze and loosens her grip. Her eyes lift again to meet mine, and she says, "Oh, my dear, something bad happened. I hope you won that fight. I'm sure my Chad helped you. There's no one better."

"Thanks, Gran." He kisses her cheek, and then she wraps her arms around me. I fall into that hug, stealing a bit of Chad's grandmother for myself. She has the same sweet aroma of lilacs my grandmother had before the nursing home, where they replaced her grandmotherly scent with a sharp, unpleasant institutional soap.

I don't want to break off the hug, and I just hope I don't cry at Chad's grandmother's kindness. We stay in that pose for a while.

Chad was right. Being at his grandmother's is like immersion into a warm, delicious-smelling bubble bath. Her serenity is contagious.

Before she closes her front door, she says, "You two are passing special glances with each other like you're carrying a big secret."

OMG, nothing escapes this woman. It's as if my skull is transparent, and she knows our marriage plan.

Chad says, "It's complicated, and I can't tell now, Gran."

She claps her hands. "Ooo, I love stories that are full of secrets; Claire's mother loves her special secrets too."

CHAPTER
28

My hand is still wicked sore the next day. I have concocted an explanation about wrecking my knuckles while raking leaves to explain the bandage. The only person I'm really concerned about is Ms. Hernandez. Turns out this isn't a good day to have an appointment with her. She'll have enough to cope with when she hears my new college plan. I suspect she'll be majorly disappointed, but I'm not the same Claire I was the last time we met.

At lunch, Alvene angsts about college stuff, complaining how she won't know anyone next year and begging everyone at the table to all apply to the same place.

"That's not how you pick a school, Al," Mads says. "Maybe I can't get in where you do, or we can't afford the same school. It's a personal choice. Like Claire here is probably going to an Ivy League school, and I sure as hell couldn't get my toe in there."

"But Claire said she's taking a gap year," Alvene says.

"And when were you going to tell me that?" Mads huffs.

"Right after I tell Ms. Hernandez."

"Yeah, so spill now," Mads says.

"Later." I get up to go to my appointment.

Mads must think this has something to do with Chad, but I didn't share my decision with him either, so there's no chance anyone can talk me out of it.

Alvene turns to me and asks, "You seem different, Claire, and not just because of the haircut."

"Are you failing your classes? Gonna quit school, bebé?" Nando taunts.

"Very funny, man," Chad says.

"For your information, Fernando," I say, "I have to take care of my baby brother, and my mother has been in the hospital." I consider this another stop on my truth tour after I told Vivian about Harry.

"Baby brother? Since when?" Alvene says.

Nando puts down his fork and fist-bumps me. "Congrats, Jackson."

Then his eyebrows raise into question marks and his lips twitch. "Jeez, when did your mom get remarried? You do keep secrets."

"Hey, guys," Chad says. "Stop grilling her. Did the cafeteria cooks add truth serum to the soggy pasta?"

I appreciate Chad running interference for me, but I'm tired of lugging secrets around. Once a secret is told, it floats in zero gravity: weightless and without power.

"My mother didn't remarry."

"Huh?" Alvene says as she applies red lipstick, which looks awesome with her brown skin.

"She had a baby five months ago," I explain. "And before you ask, there's no father; I mean, no known father."

For once in his life, Nando doesn't make one of his stupid, immature comments.

Charlie says, "I've got a ton of brothers and sisters, so if you need baby advice, I'm your man."

Sweet. And for the first time ever, I hug Charlie.

"We can have a play date," he says. "I'm a baby whisperer. I'll bring Jenny. Her real name is Genji. She's almost a year old."

"Sounds great. Sorry guys, an appointment with Ms. Hernandez awaits me. Gotta dip."

It's freeing not to have to keep Harry hidden any longer. Now I can take him to football games, and it won't matter who sees him. And if their minds go into the gutter about Mom, who cares? I have nothing to fear anymore from their judgments and assumptions.

I park myself on the hard bench outside the office. Poor Ms. Hernandez. She loves to brag that a high percentage of "her kids" get into the Ivy League. She was sure I'd be one of them. She opens the door and invites me in. Her eyes have lots of lines around them, and they sag at the end as if they are too tired to stay open. Fall is her busy season with seniors bugging her all the time.

"Hello, Claire, love the new look. Let's get started." I guess she doesn't agree with Dad that college admissions people might lose it about my haircut. If they do, I certainly wouldn't want to be in that school.

As I take a seat, I say, "Ms. Hernandez, I've changed my original college plans. My mother had a baby about five months ago and hasn't been able to care for him. She needs my help, and babies take a ton of time."

"Yes, they do. I've had three." She smiles.

"Money is tight now because my mother isn't working, and babies are very expensive."

"Yes, I know that, too."

"I don't want to take on debt that will bury me, and I'm not sure if I'll be able to go to school full-time anyway. Also, I'm planning to stay close to my family. I've decided to apply to UMass Boston."

"That's fine. A great safety school for you. What other local schools will you apply to? Tufts? Harvard?"

I hope I don't cave if she gets upset. "Ms. Hernandez. I plan to apply only to UMass. I think I can get in."

"Of course you can get in. They rarely receive an application from someone in the top 5 percent of their class who has above-average test scores. But you have plenty of other options. You could get grants and reduce the amount you have to borrow."

I knew that was coming. It's her job, but I'm holding firm and staying in control of my life. "I don't want Ivy League, and I might have a better chance of qualifying for merit scholarships without that competition."

"Yes, that's true, but are you sure?"

"Absolutely. I can have a stellar career if I graduate from UMass. And that school can propel me into a good grad school if that's what I decide to do."

Ms. Hernandez types on her computer, and her printer spits out a slew of papers. She stands and gives me a bunch of application forms for scholarships and grants. "In addition to being a superb student, you're to be commended for taking on responsibilities for your family and for financing your college career. I get many students in here who have their heads in the clouds when it comes to where to go to school and how to pay for it. Ivy League isn't the be-all and end-all, and it appears you've got things figured out. I'm impressed."

"Thank you. That's so nice of you. I can really use the kind words." I stand.

"Are you okay at home? Do you need help? There are resources available for the baby if he or she is too much for your mother," she says as we head toward the door.

"Thank you. My mother's in the hospital for a few days, but she'll be home soon. She's talking to people about her situation. I'm only the temporary stand-in. My brother is adorable."

"Will you promise to get in touch with me if you need any help?"

"I will." I give her the same answer I've given Dr. Goldstone and Mads's mother. I'm not letting anyone in who will take over the decision-making for my family.

Outside her office, I bump into Rob again. I guess he and I are on the same Hernandez schedule.

"Hey, Rob, I'm going to apply to UMass Boston. You should too. It'll be fun to see a familiar face on campus."

"I'll ask Ms. Hernandez if she thinks I could get accepted there."

I hope Rob does go there. It'd be nice to hang with him.

Heading to my next class, Mom calls, and I sneak off to answer it.

"Hey, I didn't know you had your phone."

"There are fewer restrictions here than in the hospital. Will you come for a visit this Saturday around seven? It's important," Mom says.

Maybe she's getting out. Wow, that would be great. "Should I bring a suitcase?" I ask.

"What for?"

"To pack your things."

"Not yet, sweetheart. Hopefully soon. Your father will be here."

"What the heck! Why is he coming now?"

"I asked him to."

"Why would you involve him? This isn't his problem."

What are the two of them up to? The only thing I can think of is it's a power play to get me to back off my plans for the guardianship.

"Your dad cares about you, and he still cares about me. Divorce doesn't always mean anger and hateful feelings. If we could've had a do-over, we might've handled things differently, but now he has Susie and Bella, so that can't happen. Life often plays out in ways you can't predict."

This is already strange before she adds, "And you should bring your friend."

"Mads?"

"No, I was thinking about that nice boy I met. You like him, don't you? I mean in a special way."

She met Chad briefly once while she was in her fuzzy state. I never said anything about liking him. Maybe the new medication gives her mind-reading powers. It reminds me of Chad's grandmother.

And I don't like that kind of exposure.

CHAPTER
29

What was already going to be a momentous weekend with the formal I do's on Sunday has been overtaken by Mom's weird request for a family meeting, including Chad, on Saturday. Although the day after whatever you call this event, Chad will be family in the legal sense, but Mom didn't know that when she suggested I bring him.

Chad is so Chad. When I ask if he'll come to this family thing, he's fine with it, leaving me as the only one who's annoyed. Now I have this "thing" to deal with on top of everything else I've got going on. Unfair doesn't begin to describe how I feel.

If my parents put up roadblocks about me and the guardianship, I may ask Chad if he thinks Harry and I can stay with his grandmother until I sort things out. That place would be heaven, like living in a decompression chamber.

The week drags, but eventually, Saturday does arrive. Chad comes right from football practice, so it's no surprise he's all sweaty and covered in mud when I open the door. He takes off his cleats and leaves them outside, which isn't necessary since I haven't cleaned in forever and extra dirt would blend right in.

Maybe I'll start the clean up tomorrow after our fake wedding while Chad's at his game. I should have plenty of time to vacuum and scrub toilets on my wedding day to get the house in better shape before Mom gets home.

"Did the guys practice their tackling on you today?" I say to him.

"Coach was rough on us because of the big game tomorrow. He didn't let up for a second. We had to run laps, and I must've had a hundred passes thrown to me. I'm a mess."

"Are you sure you still have the strength for my bizarre family thing tonight?"

"Yeah."

"I'll get you a towel, and you can shower. Do you want something to eat or drink first?"

"Yeah, anything. I'm starved, but don't get close to me. You'll be repulsed."

We go into the kitchen, and he decides on Cheerios and OJ. Once he finishes, I hand him a bath towel, noticing it's the last clean one. It's so pathetic how far behind I am on the laundry.

The shower's still going as I pass the bathroom and bring Harry into his room to change him. Chad walks in on us with the towel wrapped around him, low on his waist. My breath gets stuck in the back of my throat as my eyes follow glistening drops of water running down his chest. The vision of those drops makes me light-headed. I keep one hand on Harry to prevent him from rolling off the changing table, but my gaze is locked on Chad. His face reddens. *OMG, Claire, you are so embarrassing.*

"Um...where did I leave my bag?" he asks, averting his eyes.

"In. The. Kitchen."

"Oh yeah, right. I forgot." He goes down to get his bag and stops by Harry's room again to say, "Got it." On his way back to the bathroom, I'm undone as I glimpse the outline of that beautifully proportioned butt under the towel. I recall the first time that sight blew up my brain when I met him standing in line at Rosita's in the mall.

When he next emerges, he's dressed, and I sigh, wishing I could get a repeat of that earlier sight.

"Hey, little dude, want me to carry you?" he asks. Without waiting for Harry's okay, he picks him up. They go downstairs, and I make a beeline for the bathroom to splash water on my overheated face before I join them.

Chad is sprawled on the floor with his long legs off to the side, showing Harry how to put the ball on top of that spiral thingy and watch it spin to the bottom. Harry can't get the ball in the just-right spot without Chad's guiding hand, but he's mesmerized by the fast action and clattering noise as the ball heads for the bottom. I notice that he can almost sit up by himself. New skills, buddy. We'll have to show that off to Mom.

While Chad's on duty with Harry, I sneak away to change my clothes. By the time I'm ready, it's dusk, and Harry never peeped the whole time. Chad is an awesome babysitter. When I get to the living room, no one's there, and I find Chad eating a burrito at the kitchen table.

"I ordered UberEATS. Got a burrito for you too."

"Are you kidding? My guts are a jumping rope and my stomach is yelling at me not to send down any food that would disturb their game. Where's Harry?"

"I sold him to a gang," Chad says with a grin.

"Stop. I'm serious."

"Oh wait, we went for a walk, and I left him in the park."

"Chad!" I race around the house in my best Flash imitation, searching for the baby.

Chad follows me. "Relax, Claire, I thought you were joking, so I was too. Harry's in his best place."

I take the stairs two at a time, and Harry's in his crib, munching on his pacifier, clean, and dressed in his pajamas with all the trucks.

"Time to go, bro," I say as I pick him up.

"I'm sorry," I say to Chad, ashamed. "It's the pressure, I guess. I couldn't joke about Harry not being okay, but in my heart I knew he'd be safe with you. You did everything without me."

"The dude had a bath too, and his butt is cleaner than a—"

I kiss Chad on the cheek. "We've got to go. Mom called this family soiree for seven o'clock. Harry is about to meet his step-, no, I mean his ex-fath—" I pause. "Really, my dad is nothing to him."

In the car, I mutter, "Parents."

"Parents are a riddle," he says. "I'm convinced you just have to find the key to unlock the secret of how to deal with them. By agreeing to work with my dad, he thinks he won and won't bug me about studying anthropology at college. We're both getting what we want. And I was so masterful in the negotiations that I rolled in a commitment for Angela to go to Newton North as long as she does well there. The only thing I didn't tell him yet is that I'm getting married. But I will. I've softened him up."

"So, if you work for him, you have to stay in Boston."

"Yup. BU. I sent in my early decision application."

"That's great! You'll get in for sure."

"College is a crapshoot. You never know."

"I also made my choice for college. I'm applying to UMass Boston."

"I'm happy you're doing what you want, Claire. That's one of *my* most important rules," he declares in a teasing voice.

At West Village Lodge, we sign in at the desk and show our IDs. The lady recognizes me and says Mom's in the conservatory. As we get closer to the room, ominous horror-movie music plays in my head.

The sight of both my parents sitting side by side on the sofa, almost with their knees touching, startles me. My attention is drawn to a big bunch of roses tied with a ribbon next to Mom. Both Mom's and Dad's eyes are red-rimmed, and their cheeks glisten with tears, the telltale signs of a crying duet. Everything about this is suspicious.

Dad jumps to his feet and draws me into a giant hug. Then he steps back to look at me and reaches for my hand. I try to pull them away, but he doesn't let me.

Not waiting for any questions about my still colorful, healing knuckles, I say, "I punched Patrick and bloodied his face."

"Yes, your mother told me," Dad says.

"How did you know?" I ask turning to her.

"Patrick called," she replies.

"Oh. Well, in my defense—"

Mom stops me. "You don't need a defense. My brother claims he'll press charges, but I think it's a bluff."

"Big trouble for me if he does that. No guardianship," I answer meekly. Me, Claire Jackson, super student, and super sister might end up with a police record.

"I should've been stronger with him. I'm sorry." Mom slides right into her familiar round of apologies.

"Did you ice that? It looks painful," Dad says.

"I'm all right, and I had no other choice after he hit Chad."

"He did? He didn't mention that," Mom says. "Typical. He's not your problem anymore. Dad's going to handle him."

"Are you going to hit him too?" I laugh.

"No," Dad replies with a straight face.

I guess joking about this is inappropriate. The old Claire would've said "thank you" and been relieved to let the parents handle things, but old Claire is gone.

"I stood up to him. As far as I'm concerned, he and his plans are history. And Dad, I don't need you to run interference for me or for Harry. I can protect him."

"Claire, Claire, if I didn't fall apart, this wouldn't have played out the way it did," Mom says, slipping into her usual begging-for-forgiveness routine.

"You did what you thought was right," Mom adds. "You've been the rock in this family. I'm glad you didn't let Patrick in the house to snatch Harry."

"You're remarkable, Clarry," Dad interjects. Why is he here tonight in this place?

I glance at Chad, who's behind me holding the baby carrier, which seems to have become his permanent job. I step slightly to the left to make room for him to stand beside me.

"Dad, do you remember Chad from the FaceTime call?"

Dad sticks out his hand. Chad shifts the baby carrier to his left hand to shake properly. Dad says, "I'm happy to meet you in person. I've heard a lot about you."

That can't be true. Who would have told him anything? When Mom met him she was drooping like a flag on a breezeless day and barely held it together for a few minutes. Maybe her brother spewed some trash on Chad when he was giving her his blow-by-blow description of our encounter. I still can't believe I decked someone.

Mom asks if it's all right for Harry to play on the floor so we can all see him.

"Sure," I say and shudder as once again she feels she must defer to me on anything involving Harry. It's awkward to the nth degree.

Chad puts the carrier down, and I take the baby out and put him on his back on the play mat. He gets lost in the colorful small animals hanging on the arch above his head and ignores everyone. He'll be fine until something sets him off, and then he'll wail for no damn reason. This facility is so quiet; an outburst from Harry might get us thrown out of here.

Dad retakes his seat next to Mom. Chad sits in a chair facing them, and I plop myself on the floor near Harry. Dad can't take his eyes off the baby.

I know from student government meetings that the person who calls the meeting is the one who sets the agenda, so in this case, I'm expecting Mom to get this party rolling. She'd better do it fast because the atmosphere is heavy, like we're waiting for a funeral to start.

Dad nods to Mom, and she acknowledges his signal. I can't breathe. But then it's Dad who kicks this off and not Mom, which surprises me because this isn't his meeting. I must've read this all wrong.

"Claire and Chad, you are both very special. You have demonstrated a great unselfishness and commitment to keeping this baby safe." He flew all the way to Massachusetts to tell me he's proud of me after first rejecting my guardianship plan.

"I wouldn't call me unselfish at all," Chad answers. "Maybe it's selfish to push myself into other people's problems. But Claire's on a different plane. She's laser-focused on what's best for Harry."

"I agree," Dad replies.

"Mr. Jackson, I don't tolerate bullies, and when Claire had to face her own bully, I wanted to help. One way to make sure she gets the guardianship is for us to get married. We already have our marriage license. And I have some financial resources."

Hell's bells! He actually said that! I had no idea that was coming. Did he plan that in advance, or was that just instinct? The fireworks should be going off any second.

"Married? Melanie, did you know this?" Dad asks.

"No, but I understand why Claire would do that. That's a bold way to fight anyone who's threatening her baby brother. She's strong where I'm weak. What anguish I've caused everyone."

Everyone? It's only me. You caused anguish for me, not everyone. She should acknowledge that if she wants to make amends to me.

"Enough about my battle with Patrick. Why are we all here?" I ask, trying to get to the bottom of this mystery meeting.

"I fell into a deep depression after Harry was born." Mom states the obvious, but perhaps owning up to her problems is part of her therapy. "And as hard as I tried, I couldn't claw my way out. I closed off everyone because I was embarrassed that I couldn't take care of my own baby and even that I had a baby at this time. I didn't realize how much help I needed until I went into the hospital."

Dad holds Mom's hand and gazes at her full of compassion. This scene is whacked. What are they doing? They're divorced. Dad should not be holding her hand. He has a new wife.

Mom's jittery and gets up to stand in front of the large windows, rubbing her hands together in rapid movements, as if she wants to remove a layer of skin. She's fragile and whatever is happening may reverse all her good progress. Something bad is going down here.

My flight response has kicked in and I say, "Chad I forgot to pack enough diapers and food. We have to go."

"No," Dad says. "You can't go until..."

Until what? Until I have a heart attack from the stress of all this weirdness?

"Mel, tell her already," Dad instructs.

I brace myself.

CHAPTER
30

"This is difficult, very difficult," Mom says, and the constant motion of her hands draws my eyes away from her face. She's teetering on the edge of a cliff. With nervous energy, she paces the length of this room before Dad reaches for her hand and steers her back onto the couch. Then her hands fall limply in her lap, as if they're exhausted from all their activity.

"From one decision, I've created a domino train of bad effects that became unstoppable. And each choice I made caused a worse complication. I couldn't figure out how to save myself or anyone else, especially Harry. I have to make amends and beg forgiveness."

I don't think having an unplanned baby requires forgiveness, so I must be missing something. For now, I choose to remain silent and let this play out. At least Harry's taking this calmly. He fell asleep. I'd love to shrink myself and curl up with him on his mat.

Mom grabs a tissue from the table near her, but instead of using it to wipe her eyes, she crumples it into a ball and passes it from hand to hand. She's so nervous. Her voice gets whispery, requiring me to lean in closer to hear her.

"Months ago, your father and I happened to be in D.C. at the same time. He was at a conference, and I was meeting with a client. Fate put us in the same hotel. We ran into each other in the elevator and decided to have dinner together. It was nice. Mostly, we reminisced about our good times with our amazing and brilliant daughter, even telling stories from when we first met during our senior year in college.

"We hadn't done anything like that since the divorce, and although it was never said, perhaps we were thinking we might've made a mistake. For us, it all felt familiar and natural. After all, we'd been married for over fourteen years. We have history. We have a foundation. We know each other quite well."

Her voice gets stronger as she continues. "And yes, it happened. But the pregnancy was a complete shock. I was so sure I could never have more children. We had tried to provide a sibling for you, and I assumed the window on presenting you with a brother or sister had closed for good, but I was wrong."

"What are you saying?" I ask, "I don't under—" I sputter, choking on my own saliva.

"Let me finish, Clarry, or I'll lose what courage I have."

Her mouth is moving, but instead of her words, my ears fill with the smashing of cymbals. Dad's eyes stay on Mom, as if he's trying to send her a telepathic message, encouraging her to continue. Harry's baby snores grow louder and add to the noise in my head. I strain to focus as Mom continues her confession.

"Months passed after the D.C. trip," Mom says, now clasping her hands together as if they might fall off if she doesn't hold on to them. "And Andrew, I mean, your father, and I didn't communicate. I had no idea I was pregnant. I was sad most of the time, and my stomach was unsettled with waves of nausea slamming into me at odd hours, and I assumed these were signs of early menopause. My work started to suffer, so finally, I went to the doctor."

Dad switches his gaze from Mom to Harry, who's starting to get squirmy.

"The doctor examined me and ordered some blood tests. A week later, she called and told me I was pregnant and to schedule a follow-up appointment with her."

"This is unreal!" I sort of screamed.

"I thought that couldn't happen at my age, even with serious medical intervention. As I was trying to come to grips with the situation, your dad called to tell me he was getting married to a woman he had met at work who had a baby girl. He went on and on about how happy he was to find this lovely woman who needed him, and he was excited to help her with her daughter."

The picture is becoming sharper in my mind. I feel tricked, used, and enraged that Mom didn't trust me enough to tell me. I stepped up to do my share, more than my share when she was struggling after Harry was born, even when I, at first, resented Harry's presence in my life. What she did wasn't fair, isn't fair. There were other choices she could've made like telling everyone the truth.

Hot fury rises in my throat and exits with my words. "You lied! All this time you let me believe you had no idea who the father is. You knew it was Dad and never said. He should be raging mad too. Why aren't you angry at her?"

I don't wait for him to answer because I couldn't stop my rant if I tried. I stand right in front of Mom, pointing at her and say, "You let Harry have a blank on his birth certificate. He and I don't forgive you. And stop crying. You don't get to cry. I'm not feeling sorry for you anymore."

I turn to Chad but can't read his expression. "C'mon, Chad," I say, "We're getting out of here."

I grab Harry. "You take the stuff," I tell Chad as I head for the door.

Chad follows me into the hall but without Harry's bag and play mat.

"The seat, the mat," I remind him. "I want to go home."

"You can't do that, Claire. You have to hear everything. You just need a minute."

He takes the baby from me and goes back into the room, and I hear him asking my parents, "Can you watch him?" When he returns, he embraces me while I sob onto his chest. I don't want pity and force myself to stop crying as I look up into his eyes full of tenderness.

"I'm all right. Quite an announcement, huh?"

His response is to put two fingers under my chin and lift my face as he lowers his. He kisses my lips, and I respond eagerly, wanting to explore every part of his mouth. He gently bites my lower lip, and I do the same to him. We stay wound together for a while. His hold on me is tight, and his body is pressed against mine. His touch overwhelms me and quiets my anger. His lips part, and I allow mine to follow as if he has instructed them how to behave.

I'm not sure how long we stand like that or if anyone walks past while we embrace. We are in our own bubble, oblivious to any passing glances.

We disengage, but I'm not certain who let go first. What should I say to him? "Chad, you can't marry someone from such a crazy family," or "Your grandmother is wicked smart," or perhaps, "I love you"?

I've denied the possibility that I love him. At first, it was because of Mads and then I had no bandwidth for a relationship. The marriage-without-commitment plan did nothing to help me understand what was happening between us. I agreed to do it to save my family and didn't allow myself to think about any other meaning in that decision. And now, Chad might decide he doesn't want to go through with it, and I'm not sure how I feel.

"Are you ready to go back inside?" Chad says, breaking the passion of the moment. "Your parents need you to be okay with them."

I sniffle in the excess moisture in my nose and reply, "I know."

Harry is fully awake, and Mom has him on her lap while he chugs away at his bottle, making his customary slurping noises. He doesn't even notice me when I stand in front of him. He's enraptured by Mom, and it's embarrassing that makes me jealous like I'm second best when she's around.

"I should get everyone some water," Chad says. "You guys must be dehydrated." And he's gone. My guess is the water is an excuse to escape and leave us to sort out this family mess. If I was in his place, I'd disappear too.

Mom stares at Harry and says, "Everything is my fault. If I had told Dad right away, Uncle Pat never would've gotten involved. I wouldn't have had to ask him for a loan and allow him to make demands in exchange for the money. I didn't want to disrupt your father's new life and have Susie hate me, but now she'll have to know the truth."

"Susie will not hate you," Dad says. "She'll be grateful you stepped back so we could be together."

"So, in a hot minute, Dad, you find out Harry's your son, and you're not angry at Mom. How can you be laid back about something like this? Harry might've grown up believing his father's name is Blank. Why aren't you furious about what she did?"

Before Dad responds, Mom says, "If I'd told him I was pregnant when he was getting married, I would've become the horrid ex-wife rising from the ashes of our marriage to curse their union. I want him to be happy even though I shed buckets of tears until I convinced myself I was doing the right thing in not complicating his life."

"And you didn't figure it out? Dad, you weren't curious when you heard she was having a baby?"

"Because Harry arrived early, I couldn't reconcile the timing. Susie and I talked about it, and she thought your mother would've told me if the baby was mine, and if I questioned her about it, I'd be intruding into her personal life. I didn't have a right to ask if she'd been with anyone else.

"I called to congratulate her after he was born. She was like, 'I can't believe this happened.' She seemed very tired, and she never spoke about the baby's father, and neither did you. You never shared that there was no father on the birth certificate. No one told me anything. Was I supposed to question your mother about the men in her life?"

My anger is hard to stifle, and I struggle to control my tone. "Don't put any of this on *me*-that I didn't tell you something. And why am I the only one who's fuming? This betrayal is way worse than her taking my money without permission. How do you keep a secret like this and just say that you're sorry? Aren't there consequences?"

Dad and Mom stare at me with the same nervous eyes that watched me when I was four-years-old and scrambling to the top of the jungle gym, and they worried I might fall and smash my head.

"Why are you both staring at me? I did nothing wrong here. Harry and I are innocent parties to your deception and lies," I tell them. "Dad isn't all blameless here. He did half of the baby making. Maybe he should join you for a stint at West Village to take the program and make amends. They might give you a two-for-one special."

Mom says, "As the days passed and I didn't tell your father, I became more despondent, and the guilt was devouring me. I was confused and weak. You ask about consequences. Those are the consequences. I hated myself. I knew I should be happy with the baby, but I couldn't let myself be in the moment. I withdrew from everything and everyone. The more you stepped in, the more I allowed myself to sink in deep despair. It was like diving into a lake with weights attached."

"So, you could wallow in your misery, and I had to pick up the pieces," I snipe. "Harry, don't you agree she's mother of the year?" No answer from him, and why would he care? He has everything he needs.

"Enough, Claire," Dad says, stepping in. "It's difficult for all of us, but we're going to get past this. The choices we make are often convoluted and steeped in so many emotions. How can I be angry when I see this beautiful little boy? My boy. He's a blessing. And I promise to follow your example and do the right thing to protect him always."

"And I want Harry to know all you did for him when I wasn't well," Mom says, trying to soothe my raw, jagged feelings.

Dad stands and puts his arm around me, which sets off another torrent of my own tears. He grabs a handful of tissues and hands them to me.

Through the crying, I croak out, "And that's it. Off we go into the sunset, all happy. I gave up my whole summer. I might get replaced on student government for missing so many meetings, and I didn't get to go to the senior supper because I had to have Harry ready before I left. I got emergency calls at the mall. I did the laundry, I cleaned him, I fed him. I bought him his first baby food. I took him to the doctor and had to listen to those ear-piercing screams when he got his shots. And now you want me to say 'Isn't this all great?' One big happy family."

Chad comes back carrying four bottles of water, leaves them on the side table, and sits down. No one touches them.

"Clarry," Dad says, "Mom told me everything privately before you and Chad arrived, and my reaction was also tears. It isn't easy for me to understand how your mother persuaded herself she had to keep this secret; but I'm not mad, not at all. This baby is only joy. Your mother has given me a precious gift."

"But her secret—your precious gift—upended my life."

"You have every right to be upset and angry," Dad says. "We owe you so much. We're going to try to make it up to you."

Mom chimes in. "My mind wasn't functioning correctly. It will take work and time for me to regain your trust and earn your forgiveness, and perhaps I can never be forgiven for what I did to you."

Harry burps, not once but twice and exceptionally loud. He dissolves into giggles at his fine accomplishment, and Chad laughs with him, saying, "Way to go, buddy."

And Harry's contribution to the moment functions as a pressure valve, releasing the thick air in the room. My baby brother has some slick moves.

"There's more. I must get it all out," Mom says. "According to Dr. Goldstone, my guilt manifested into depression as the pregnancy wore on, and by the time of the birth, I was in a whole other realm of sadness with no lifeline to grab on to. I made everything worse when I used Claire's college money to pay for the day care. When my brother insisted there was no way I could handle this, I thought he might be right. It wasn't until I went to the hospital and got better medication and intensive therapy that I was able to see things more clearly."

"Harry and I have to go." I can't listen to another word. My brain is lurching from one side of my skull to the other, producing a massive headache. There should be an entry about me in medical books to explain how parents can give their children a migraine just by talking.

Mom passes the plump baby to Dad, who presses him against his chest while kissing his head nonstop. I'm having an out-of-body experience as if I'm flying overhead, ghostlike, observing this moment rather than being a participant in this brand-new fantasy movie.

Chad is packing up Harry's things.

CHAPTER
31

My parents hug and smother the baby between them, but he's too tired to enjoy any of that and cries. In another circumstance, I'd rush in to save him, but perhaps my work as number one caregiver is over.

Dad says, "Honey, I'm going to stay for a while and talk to your mother."

"Can you two be trusted together?" I ask like a smart-ass. "Should I hang around to chaperone?" No need to spare their feelings. This whole mess is on them. After all, often they're only thinking of themselves anyway. Thanks to Chad's constant reminders, I'm learning not to care what others think when I make a decision. "Remember, Harry doesn't need to be a big brother," I add.

As I revel in my cleverness, Chad stifles a laugh, and Mom and Dad, on the other hand, go slack-jawed, taken aback by my biting wit, but they deserve it. They'll learn I have freed myself from my inner editor.

"Are you planning to stay at the house, Dad?"

"Of course he's staying there," Mom answers for him. After all these months of dithering about Harry and her brother and life in general, she's finally able to make a decision about something, but it took a lot to get her to this point.

Chad, Harry, and I leave. Once we're settled into the car. A rather loud sigh comes out of me, dragging all the strength from my body with it. It'll be a miracle if I can stand on my legs when I get out.

"Whew, that was a lot," Chad says.

"I never imagined anything like that. It's beyond comprehension."

"You'll need time to process this. I don't know how to help."

"I don't know if anyone can help me. This is a story you might read in a book and admire the author's creative mind as he composes scenes that leave you stunned and rattled."

When we get home, I get Harry out of the car seat. The kid weighs a ton, especially when he's completely passed out. He goes straight into the crib, and then I join Chad at the kitchen table.

"We should cancel the wedding tomorrow," he says.

"I guess this changes everything."

"Maybe not everything," he says, and his eyes are sunken and sad. "But Harry is safe from your uncle, and that's the most important outcome. I should go now. I don't want to be here when your dad comes. You two need alone time."

Chad is so rational. He stands and clasps me to him. "This is a lot, Claire, and I wish I could help you more."

"Be sure to tell your grandmother she was right."

"I will, but I don't have to," he grins. "She knows she's always right."

"I love her."

"Me too. I'll call the justice of the peace and explain."

"I should do that. This isn't your mess," I say.

"I'd like to think of it as *our* mess."

Why does this boy want to be with me when he could have anyone? It's a wonder, but I'm so grateful for him in my life. My hand rises to pat his cheek. It's somewhat of an awkward gesture, but I had the urge to touch his face. I run my fingers over that patch of hair under his lip, and then I kiss him hard. He responds and takes both my hands in his so they are by my side, and he presses his body in close. I will him not to move, but alas, I don't get my wish. He breaks away.

"I've got to go now."

"Good luck at the game tomorrow."

He favors me with an exquisite eye roll. "Amen to that. You and Harry should come to cheer the guys."

"I would, but with my father here..."

"I understand."

When he's gone, I slump into the chair, but there are no more tears. The reservoirs of liquid are dry, and I can't cry on fumes. I have to tell Mads the wedding is off. She was so amped up to be part of our big secret.

"I've been waiting for your call, babe," she says. "How's your dad? Did you find out why your mom asked him to come?"

"I did, and the reason will rock you. For me, it was like being run over by an eighteen-wheeler."

"Claire, stop playing with me. What the hell happened?"

"First, Chad told them we're getting married to protect Harry."

"No shit! Did they faint?"

"They seemed shocked, but in another way it hardly registered because there was something even bigger happening."

"Claire, do you realize almost every time you call, there's been another major catastrophe in your life, or you have some new, weird news? Your life's a roller coaster, and I'm getting a stomachache on the ride."

"Do you want off?"

"Of course not; we're heart-sisters, remember? Spill already before my head blows off."

"It's not easy to say this. It's surprising and embarrassing and impossible to understand. My dad is Harry's bio dad too. I don't have time to explain everything now because my dad will be here soon."

"Stop fooling around and tell me what *really* happened."

"Do you think I could joke about something like that? It's true. Anyway, there's no wedding tomorrow. Meet me at Cold Spring Park at noon, and I'll give you all the details. Promise."

"You'd better. Okay. Tomorrow. Noon."

Having to talk about what my parents got up to in some hotel room in Washington, D.C. is disturbing. I don't want to share a visual of that. No one talks about their parents and sex. Never happens. It's like the strictest rule.

When Dad comes in a short time later, I'm still on the kitchen chair without energy.

"Claire, before we talk, may I see Harry?"

And so life continues its twisty journey, presenting me with the unexpected and the unwanted at every turn like when Harry's father asks for permission to see his baby. Dad follows me upstairs and enters Harry's room to stare at the curled-up baby ball. I wait in the doorway as a silent observer. When he steps out, he's dabbing at his eyes.

Back in the kitchen, he starts opening and closing cabinets.

"I could use a drink," he says. "This has been quite the day. We used to keep wine in the cabinet over the stove."

"No alcohol here. Mom stopped buying wine when she found out she was pregnant, and I'm not legal, so we're a dry house now."

He takes a can of soda out of the refrigerator. In a matter of seconds, he empties it as if he arrived from trekking in the desert. Good thing that wasn't a glass of booze.

"Claire, I hope you'll be able to forgive your mother. She was in a bad way, and at first the medication didn't help. She needed intensive therapy in a controlled setting. We are all fallible, including me. I've made some problematic choices, and I don't fully understand sometimes why I did what I did, because people and life are not simple. I have learned that consequences can be enduring. But your mother and I never wanted to hurt you or anyone else."

"She screwed up and made questionable decisions, if you ask me," I say. "I was sure her problems were hormonal and would pass, and when they didn't, I should've taken action immediately. So maybe I'm also at fault for some decisions I made. I guess we both could use a do-over."

"You did nothing wrong. I'm sorry for everything you went through alone. I should've been here to help you, but I had no idea. You never said anything about the situation you were in."

"Funny how I never told you because I thought Mom's problems and Harry had nothing to do with you."

The doorbell interrupts us, which startles me. It's too late for anyone to come by. I open the door to greet the delivery man from China Blossom. Dad steps from behind me and gives the guy a tip and take the bags.

Dad exclaims, "I called in an order on my way here. I'm starved! Haven't eaten anything since the mini pretzels on the plane. Nothing like a new son to rev up your appetite!"

While Dad opens the containers, I get the dishes and napkins. He bought all my favorites: the Peking ravioli, moo shu beef, and garlic string beans. Sitting here and eating together is like not a day has passed since he left.

I pour hoisin sauce on the moo shu, wrap it in a pancake, and eat with the same eagerness Harry shows when he's devouring his mushy sweet potatoes and squash.

"Harry took a DNA test," I tell Dad, as I stop a blob of sauce from leaving my chin and landing on my shirt.

"Why?" Dad fumbles with his chopsticks like always. It's fun to have this reminder of years ago when the three of us sat at this table. I speculate about putting on the timer to see how long he'll try to power through until he admits defeat and gets a fork.

"Mr. Sunday thought it would show the judge a good faith effort that we're trying to locate the baby's father. The paternity kit has a swab for an adult too. Do you want to do the other test? I didn't throw it out."

"Absolutely not!" Dad says, as if I asked him to drink poison.

"But then you'll know—"

"Clarry, I trust your mom. She's sure, and that's good enough for me. She would've told me if there was even a chance someone else could be the baby's father. Harry is mine."

"She lies for months, and you believe her completely. What if she's lying now, and that's part of her illness?"

Dad laughs. "I have not one doubt this baby is mine. He has the beginnings of the Jackson dimple. But if it's important to you, I'll do the DNA test. You can swab me."

"Yes, it's important to me." I have to be certain, and a maybe-dimple isn't solid proof of anything. Lots of people have dimples. Dad may want this so badly, he's ready to accept everything Mom says. I'm not there.

I get the kit from the drawer and lay it on the table.

"Clarry, your mother thinks she'll be home soon, and hopefully you won't have to take care of Harry as much, but it may be slow going for a while. First thing I'm going to do is to put back some of your college money so you can pursue your dreams. I'll take out another mortgage."

"Another mortgage?" I ask, horrified. "You, of all people, are willing to take on more debt? You have changed."

"Since when do you know about mortgages?"

Now I'm showing off. "I assume you're talking about getting a home equity loan. Those can be a problem unless you get a fixed rate." Chad gave me a lesson on variable and fixed rates on loans.

I'm on a roll and enjoying lecturing him. "Variable rates sound good, but when interest rates skyrocket, your payments will balloon." When Chad used the word balloon, I giggled and pictured our house ascending tied to a bunch of helium balloons. He insisted it's a legit word and explained what ballooning interest rates meant.

Dad raises one eyebrow as his chin drops. I'm loving his bewilderment and proceed to continue to dazzle him.

"You shouldn't gamble with your house. It isn't a piggy bank." That piggy bank comment isn't from Chad. I read that in an article titled *You and Your Mortgage.*

Dad's speechless, as if an alien accountant has assumed control of his daughter. He's definitely getting a front-row seat to the new me.

I go back to eating as if nothing unusual was said, grabbing a ravioli and dipping it in soy sauce, curious about what his reaction will be to my amazing financial knowledge.

"Mortgages and interest rates? Is this part of a class project?"

"No." I lay out my research about selling the house and moving into an apartment and living off the equity we'd be left with. I don't take all the credit and mention that Chad knows a lot about all this because his father is in real estate.

"You are impressive, Claire, and your commitment to the family is extraordinary. I want to help with college, but it'll take time for me to save enough unless I tap into my retirement or my house."

"Keep your money for Harry. He's a spending machine."

Dad laughs. "But I want to take care of both of you. You and Harry," he says nobly.

"Thanks for the offer, but I don't need the money. My college plans changed."

I clear the table, and he asks, "Assuming I could get some money together for next year, why wouldn't you need it?"

"I'm applying to UMass Boston. It's close enough that I can live at home and commute if I have to. The in-state tuition is low, and I'll work part time. This is solely my decision. I haven't told Mom yet, and I'm not asking for anyone's approval."

Dad stares at me blankly. Clearly, he's confused. I guess he deserves more explanation. "I'm not the same person I was. I've learned a lot about myself and to trust my own instincts which are pretty damn good. And one thing is for certain—I'm no coward." I wave my injured hand in the air as proof of my bravery.

In the past, if I sounded off like that, Dad would haul out another of his favorites and call me a "big shot" for speaking above my age level. Now his expression is one of awe or pride or a combo of both. I detect new respect.

"Uh, Claire, I'm sorry for the nicknames. I had no idea how bad my teasing got. I thought I was being funny, and when you didn't complain, I assumed you thought it was funny too."

"Complaining was useless and exposed me as being too thin-skinned, remember? It was a lose-lose situation for me."

"I apologize. Susie cautioned me not to tease Bella because she thinks sometimes teasing is borderline cruel."

That's an apology I wasn't expecting and kudos to Susie for speaking up.

"It's past history," I say, feeling generous. "Glad you will spare Harry and Bella from your not-so-clever attempts at humor. I love you, Dad." I hug him. "I'm happy Harry has you for a father. He couldn't do better."

His eyes are wet, and he uses his napkin to wipe his soggy cheeks. Poor Dad. The tears come easily today.

Dad loads the dishwasher and takes out the garbage. I forgot he used to live here and knows his way around. I follow him into the den, and he pulls out the sofa bed.

"Don't you want to stay in Mom's room?" I ask.

"Uh no, that's not a good idea," he says. "Help me get the sheets and pillows."

We go upstairs and load our arms with the stuff he needs, and again, Dad stops by Harry's room to peek in. Maybe he wants to make sure the baby is real. Wait until Harry howls at 6 a.m., then the whole world knows he's real.

While we're making up the bed, Dad says, "We should speak to Madison's father about all the legal issues. Having the temporary guardianship is probably still a good idea until we're sure Mom can cope with Harry. That is, if you're willing to do that. Also, I have to get my name on the birth certificate, and I don't know how that's done or how long it will take. The main thing is that for now, I'll be too far away to be helpful if there's an emergency."

"For now?"

"I have to talk to Susie, but I'd love to move here and be a regular part of Harry's life and not a once-a-month, drop-in father. Of course, that means finding a job, and I'm not sure Susie will be open to uprooting herself from Wisconsin. It's going to take a while to work out the logistics. Harry and I need you until Mom's back to herself."

"Okay. The court is sending a case worker this week or next to talk to us and see the house. By us, I mean Chad and me. I thought we'd be married by then."

"Is this marriage something you want, or is it only for Harry? I don't think you have to do that anymore. You won't have to fight off

Patrick for Harry. He'll be out of the picture once I talk to him. I promise you that."

"But he could still report me for hitting him. He was furious."

"Let's wait and see on that until after I speak to him. But you didn't answer my question. If not for Harry, would you and Chad get married now?" He asks as if the only question is when. I have to set Dad straight, so I say, "We never talked about marriage in that way. We were only ever doing this for Harry."

"So maybe you should wait on the marriage plan until we talk to Jerry Sunday about the legal issues and make sure you can get the temporary guardianship."

"Again, that will be our decision, Dad. Not you and me. 'Our' means Chad and me. No offense. But you should know the two of us already decided not to get married tomorrow. We need some time to see how everything plays out. The marriage license isn't expiring anytime soon."

Dad says nothing more about my possible marriage. He understands this isn't his decision. Once the bed for him is made, we say goodnight. In my room, I text Mr. Sunday to arrange a meeting with Dad and me. Then I call Chad, but we don't rehash the events of today. Although I do mention I might submit my family's unconventional story to one of those magazines that publishes stranger-than-fiction tales.

"I'm still getting used to the new normal," I tell him. "I need time."

Again, I wish him good luck for the game, and he promises to call right after.

I stretch out on my bed and will every nerve in my body to relax, but they aren't cooperating. I'm wired.

My grandmother's old saying, "Life turns on a dime," makes perfect sense. A thin coin spins precariously and can fall heads or tails, mimicking the unpredictability we face and can't prepare for. Life zigzags wildly, and you have to be strong to hold on no matter which course it takes.

A few hours ago, Harry was my half-brother, my uncle was threatening to take him and charge me with assault, and this evening would've been spent picking out my wedding day outfit. I toss in bed until the sheets are a jumble, unable to settle down. I finally subdue my nerves and push everything out of my head, except the vision of that powerful, delicious kiss at West Village Lodge.

CHAPTER
32

My eyes open to a quiet Sunday morning. 10:17! I haven't slept this late since forever. My glee is short-lived when I remember there are sudden and bad things that can happen to babies. The kid's a colossal pain sometimes, but he's pretty helpless and my brother. Why didn't he cry like always? I bolt out of bed and sprint to his room. The crib is empty.

I fly downstairs. In the living room, Dad's chattering nonstop to Harry, who's hanging onto his every word as if each one is a gem. I had forgotten Dad was even in the house.

"Hey," I say and fall onto the sofa, already drained from a rush of adrenaline. "Why didn't you wake me?"

Dad's eyes twinkle, and his face relaxes into a broad smile. "I was up early and as soon as he made a peep; I got him so you could sleep. Hope that's okay. I don't want to overstep."

Overstep? That's so funny. Boy, the dynamics in my family have been stood on their head. When it comes to Harry, my parents defer to me as I guess they should.

"Thanks. I needed the extra sleep. I'm meeting Mads in the park later, and I can take Harry with me."

"Great. I have to call Susie, and it might be a long conversation. Also, I'll stop by to see Mom again before I leave tomorrow."

"Tomorrow?" I ask, but I'm not sure what I expected. His life is elsewhere.

"I'm in the middle of a project at work, but I'll come back soon, very soon. And we'll do the meeting with Madison's father by Zoom."

I eat breakfast, shower, and dress taking my time, knowing Dad's with Harry. When I finish, I check the temperature outside and bring an extra blanket for the little dude because the fall sun is bright, but the air is chilly. I put on his hat with the cute rabbit ears, knowing Mads will go gaga over it.

We meet up with Mads in our usual spot near the life course trail, which is an easy mile and a half walk if you don't stop at the exercise stations.

"He's adorable. I could squeeze that bunny rabbit forever," Mads babbles excitedly when she sees us. I let her push the stroller.

"I was completely undone yesterday when I found out my dad and Harry's are one and the same," I say.

"Holy Daddy! So obviously, your mother knew all along. Why was she keeping it a secret? Thrill me, Claire Bear, and don't leave out a thing about how this went down."

"Do you want a lecture on the body parts involved? Shall I include diagrams?"

"Very funny. But you need a refresher sex ed class if you think you can make a baby when people live hundreds of miles apart, say like in Massachusetts and Wisconsin."

"They were in Washington, D.C., at the same time for work stuff, and they met up by accident. It wasn't planned, but they had dinner together, and I guess they couldn't help themselves. Believe me, I didn't ask for graphic details."

Referring to my parents' night in the hotel brings the heat to my face, and I probably have tomato cheeks. Mads and I talk about sex all the time, and we share our most intimate thoughts, but discussing parents having sex is taboo. I sure as hell never want to hear any stories about noises coming from Mr. and Mrs. Sunday's bedroom.

"So, is there a chance your mom and dad will get back together?"

"He has a wife." Although imagining the four of us as an intact family is pretty amazing, it would be unfair for Susie to pay the price for this.

"Well, never say never, babe. Harry has a dad. Are you going through with the marriage?"

"Probably not, but I'm not sure. My dad still wants me to apply for temporary guardianship or caregiver status until my mom is all better and he can get his name on Harry's birth certificate."

"Boo-hoo. I got a great dress for the wedding and came up with an intricate plan to sneak out early all dressed up without alerting my mom's exceptional vice principal's antennae that something's up."

"It might happen. Chad and I were totally prepared to go ahead," I reply.

Mads asks, "What did Chad say about the wedding postponement? Wait, don't tell me, he was bummed. He wants to marry you for real, and I think he's using Harry as an excuse."

"We never talked about our relationship. We haven't defined it."

"Oh babe, you need your eyes checked and while you're at it, your brain too. You're getting stupid."

"Okay, I admit it. There's something special between us. I think."

"You think? Your mouth sounds unsure, but your face is telling a different story."

I've pushed those feelings so far back, it's hard to drag them to the forefront and admit what Mads can see.

As we near the end of the path, she says, "OMG, wouldn't want to be you with all the drama."

"I guess coming clean was the best thing my mother could do to rid herself of the guilt she's been lugging around. And Harry isn't going anywhere—ever."

Mads walks me home, and I'm grateful when she changes the subject to the new love of her life, who she ranks an eight out of ten which is still handsome territory, but not Chad-gorgeous. He's from New York City and is a freshman at Boston College. She has herself a college man. We make plans for the four of us to hang out.

⚓

On Monday morning, Dad comes with me to Sunny Acres. I introduce him to Mrs. Sample as my and Harry's father but don't ask for him to be on Harry's approved list because I know I can't do that. And in any case, Dad will be in Wisconsin.

They shake hands, and Mrs. Sample says, "Claire, have your mother call me and we'll put your father on the list. We don't have anything on file about Harry's father."

"I understand," Dad says. Dad hands Harry to Amelia but not before he bestows a dozen kisses on the attention-grabber's cheeks. I notice how much older Dad appears than the other fathers dropping off their kids. His hair is almost all gray and his smile brings out deep wrinkles around his eyes.

He walks with me to school and when we're almost there, Dad says, "I'm going to miss him." In two days, they've bonded. It took me months to adjust to Harry and figure out how I felt about him.

"And I'll miss you, too, of course," Dad adds.

Glad he includes me. I may soon be relieved of baby responsibilities, but I'll have to get used to sharing my parents with Harry. It'll be different for sure.

We stop and hug before I cross the street. "Claire, you're strong and capable. I never saw it in you, and I'm sorry."

"You didn't see it because I never had to show that side of me before."

"Patrick and I talked yesterday when I was visiting Mom. He won't press charges, and he'll stay away until you or I allow him back into the family circle."

"How did you get him to agree to drop his threats?"

Dad replies, "His plan to take Harry is over. He insists he only wants what's best for your mother. I asked him to give us space to figure things out."

"Sounds so easy."

"Well, perhaps my asking might have sounded more like a warning," he says with a sly grin. "Can't let my daughter be the only fighter in this family."

"Ha! So, I won't be a felon?"

"If you were, I'd be in an adjacent cell because I'd pound him into the ground to protect my family, just like you did. I'll see you later tonight on our Zoom call with Madison's father."

"Have a good flight. Love you, Dad."

He kisses me and says, "I love you, Clarry."

Chad's waiting with some football guys near the door and breaks away from them when I approach. We head behind the building to a secluded spot past the bleachers.

"You're a star. A new Gronkowski," I declare, mentioning the name of the only professional football player I know who catches passes and was a star on the Patriots team years ago. Chad had left me a one-word text after the game yesterday: Victory.

"Two touchdown passes," he says. "I can't believe it. I was on fire."

"We should celebrate."

"Cake?" he asks.

"Def cake. Let's go in before we're marked late."

"Chill, Jackson. They don't put the number of your late days on your college information."

"Yeah, but I never want to disappoint Mrs. Gillespie. She's the bes—"

A call from Dr. Goldstone interrupts. Now I really will be late.

"Hello, Claire. I know you and your father visited with your mother over the weekend. She had a break-through and was ready to face her truth and accept it. This a major step, and I'm sure you will see that. The therapists at West Village Lodge and I think she's ready to come home."

"Is this for real, Dr. Goldstone?"

"Yes, for real, Claire. She's in a much better place. She has already contacted some clients and is making plans to ramp up her website design business again."

"When can I pick her up?"

"Tomorrow around three."

"Thank you for everything," I say.

"She will continue with her therapy when she's home. Call anytime if you need me. Bye, Claire."

Now I must have a cake tomorrow. Harry and I are getting our mother back!

I grab Chad's hands, and he lets me swing him around in a happy dance. Then I sing, "Tomorrow, tomorrow! I love ya', tomorrow! You're always a day away."

I'm dizzy spinning like a silly ten-year-old, but it's been so long since I've felt this much joy.

"It's all great," he says, but he drops the smile, and his eyebrows knit to the center.

"Aren't you happy for me?"

"I am, of course," he says the words, but those sad eyes send the opposite message. "But everything will be different for us. We've kind of been on our own. We were going to get married."

"Hang on to the license. You never know," I say, surprised my comment puts the sparkle back in those gorgeous, dark brown eyes.

I look around and make sure we're alone, drop to one knee, and take his hand in mine. Gazing up at this handsome man, who's willing to move the world to help me, I smile.

"Chad Williams, will you be my boyfriend?"

MENTAL HEALTH SUPPORT AND RESOURCES

The 988 Suicide & Crisis Lifeline (formerly known as the National Suicide Prevention Lifeline) offers 24/7 call, text and chat access to trained crisis counselors who can help people experiencing suicidal, substance use, and/or mental health crisis, or any other kind of emotional distress. People can also dial 988 if they are worried about a loved one who may need crisis support.

https://www.samhsa.gov

https://findtreatment.gov

ACKNOWLEDGMENTS

I appreciate everyone at Immortal Works who made *Complicated Choices* possible. My road to becoming a published author started when Staci Olsen, Acquisitions Editor and Production Manager, liked a Twitter pitch for my first book and brought me into the Immortal Works family. Holli Anderson, Editor-in-Chief, believed in my books from the beginning. Their faith in my writing means the world to me. In addition to their publishing and editing expertise, both of these women are talented authors. Their books should definitely be on your to-be-read list.

Every writer needs editors and proofreaders. Through Immortal Works, I've been fortunate to work with Audrey Hammer and Katie Lewis on this book. Also, a special thank you to Creative Manager, Ashley Literski, for an amazing cover design for *Complicated Choices*.

In addition to my Immortal Works editors, Rawles Lumumba, a professional editor, provided a sensitivity and diversity reading for an early draft. Jessica Bayliss, an author and psychologist, reviewed the manuscript concerning the mental health issues.

My Inked Voices critique partners offered stellar input on the book and always make me a better writer. I couldn't have done this without them. Thank you to Steve Arnold, Emilee Beyer, Kristine Carter, Heidi Casper, Kim Holster, Patricia Nesbitt, and Norma Wilow, as well as beta readers Jane Barron and Jerry Warmuskerken.

My friends are extraordinary cheerleaders and their support means so much to me. Thank you to Nancy Carapezza, Karen Kavet, Betsy Rigby, Diane Sredl, Lisa Stringfellow, Ina Tamir, Alvene

Williams, Linda and Jerry Benezra, Becky and Andy Ceperley, Annette Needle and Peter Meyersohn, and Carole Wagner Vallianos and Pete Vallianos.

Like a special dessert, I save the very, very best for last: my family. I'm forever grateful to my husband, Philip, my rock and partner in all things; my daughters, Brenda Malkiel, Pam Levanos, and Devora Reiss, who have all of my heart; David Malkiel, Mark Chapin, and Benjamin Reiss, who are so dear to me; and my grandchildren who bring me joy and pride beyond compare.

Thank you to all for joining me on this writing journey.

ABOUT THE AUTHOR

In addition to *Complicated Choices*, Risa Nyman is the author of two award-winning middle grade books, *Swallowed by a Secret* and *Spooked by a Suspicion*. Her contemporary novels deal with family issues, life changes, friendship, and loss.

Risa was born and lived most of her life in Greater Boston, and she has an authentic Boston accent to prove her heritage. No coincidence that all of her books are set in Massachusetts.

Her deep dive into creative writing began when she retired after decades working for the League of Women Voters, a nonpartisan organization that focuses on voter registration, getting out the vote, candidates' debates, and fair voting procedures. Risa served as president of the League of Women Voters of Massachusetts and the Director of the Diversity Implementation Task Force of the League of Women Voters of the United States.

Since Risa's first online writing class, writing has become a passion and a defining part of her life. When not writing, you might find Risa reading, exercising, or doing therapeutic ironing (yes, there is such a thing.)

Check out her website at https://www.risanyman.com and follow her on Facebook, Instagram, and Twitter.

This has been an
Immortal Production